D1002165

DISCARDED

THE NET OF STEEL

Also by Fiona Buckley

The Ursula Blanchard mysteries

* available from Severn House

THE NET OF STEEL

Fiona Buckley

**SEVERN
HOUSE**

ENTERED

MAY 0 4 2023

Grafton Public Library
Grafton, MA

First world edition published in Great Britain and the USA in 2023
by Severn House, an imprint of Canongate Books Ltd,
14 High Street, Edinburgh EH1 1TE.

Trade paperback edition first published in Great Britain and the USA in 2023
by Severn House, an imprint of Canongate Books Ltd.

severnhouse.com

Copyright © Fiona Buckley, 2023

All rights reserved including the right of reproduction in whole or in part in any
form. The right of Fiona Buckley to be identified as the author of this work has
been asserted in accordance with the Copyright, Designs & Patents Act 1988.

British Library Cataloguing-in-Publication Data
A CIP catalogue record for this title is available from the British Library.

ISBN-13: 978-1-4483-1059-3 (cased)
ISBN-13: 978-1-4483-1066-1 (e-book)

This is a work of fiction. Names, characters, places and incidents are either the
product of the author's imagination or are used fictitiously. Except where actual
historical events and characters are being described for the storyline of this novel,
all situations in this publication are fictitious and any resemblance to actual
persons, living or dead, business establishments, events or locales is purely
coincidental.

All Severn House titles are printed on acid-free paper.

Typeset by Palimpsest Book Production Ltd.,
Falkirk, Stirlingshire, Scotland.
Printed and bound in Great Britain by
TJ Books, Padstow, Cornwall.

For Anne and Alan, the best of friends
My thanks to you both

ONE

A Wall of Mist

My childhood home, Faldene House, stands halfway up the side of a valley, looking across it to the northern edge of the Sussex downs. Its village lies in the valley below and the fields – both of the home farm and those rented by villagers – are spread all around, draped over the hillsides like bedspreads. The downs protect Faldene from the sea mists that can creep over the south coast even in summer, but all the same, the house is high enough for low cloud to encompass it, now and then. On that sad morning in April 1590, it had done so. Waking that day, I looked out of the casement window into an impenetrable greyness and thought how closely it resembled the furnishing of my own mind.

I thought back over the preceding three days. They had begun with a funeral and today there would be another. Two such events in such a short time were enough to depress anyone. But the heavy downheartedness I felt, like a dragging mass in the depths of my stomach, seemed for some reason greater than it should have been. After all . . .

It wasn't as if I had ever loved my uncle Herbert, and I certainly hadn't loved Sir Francis Walsingham, nor had either of them loved me.

I had once caused Uncle Herbert to be imprisoned in the Tower of London; briefly, but still the Tower, that place of terror. As for Walsingham, he had found me useful at times but he had never approved of me, while I on my side had found him hard and intimidating. And yet, when I returned from his funeral at St Paul's Cathedral in London on the seventh of April, and went to my room in Whitehall Palace, I found myself crying bitterly, while my maid and long-time friend, Frances Brockley – though from habit I called her by her maiden name of Dale – tried in vain to comfort me.

And when, an hour after my return from St Paul's, a letter in Aunt Tabitha's shaky and aged hand was brought to me, bringing the news that my uncle Herbert Faldene, after much suffering with the joint evil, had died in his sleep, I knew that what had happened was probably best for Uncle Herbert, but nevertheless, I wept again, miserably, for yet another hour.

I couldn't understand myself. I had been reared by my uncle Herbert and his wife Tabitha, as a duty, when my mother, Uncle Herbert's sister, who had been at court as a lady-in-waiting to Queen Anne Boleyn, sought shelter with them, having been sent home in disgrace, heavy with a child whose father she would not name. They took her in and when her child – me – was born, they took me on too, though not with enthusiasm and most likely because my good-hearted grandfather was still alive then and insisted.

I was truly grateful (even without their constant reminders) for having a roof above my head, food and clothes and an education. Again, my grandfather had been responsible for seeing that I was allowed to share my cousins' tutor. After a time, Uncle Herbert had seen that, because of my education, I could be useful to him, and when I was older he used me as a secretary. But as a child I was roughly treated, often beaten, though my cousins were not, and my mother was treated coldly too. She died when I was sixteen and the four years until I was twenty were bleak and lonely – until my cousin Mary was betrothed to a young man called Gerald Blanchard.

When Gerald came to visit Faldene House and we met for the first time, we looked at each other and – how can one explain these things? – I fell instantly in love with him and he with me. One happy night, I got out of my bedchamber window, slid down the roof over the single-storey dairy, slithered and scrambled down some ivy and into Gerald's arms. We ran away together and were married.

We left the outrage behind us, an outrage that never entirely died, even after Mary had married somebody else and was well pleased with her new match. Meanwhile, Gerald and I were happy. Our daughter Meg was born. Then the smallpox killed Gerald, and I found that he had left me with very little money. My state would have been desperate, except that Gerald had had influential contacts. Through one of these, I found myself, as my mother had been before, lady-in-waiting to a queen.

Queen Elizabeth this time. I had a stipend then, just enough to support me and pay a nurse to care for Meg, in a little rented cottage.

But the stipend still wasn't quite sufficient. A queen's attendant needs to maintain certain standards of dress, and such things as silk and velvet and brocade, and jewellery good enough to make at least a pretence of being valuable, come costly. For the sake of a few extra earnings, I undertook a secret mission for the queen's favourite, Robert Dudley. It paid well. I found myself undertaking other such missions. And that is how I became one of Her Majesty's secret agents. Over the years, I carried out many missions, some of them dangerous. It was also how I came to poison family relationships still further by getting my uncle arrested and imprisoned, and how I came to know Walsingham.

Walsingham, always a stern and intimidating figure, dressed in black and rarely given to smiling, did not approve of women being used as agents. On the other hand, he often found it highly convenient to use me in that way. I seemed to have a gift for such tasks. On occasion, he sent me into danger and then worried about me, a state of affairs that I think annoyed him more than ever. Over the years, we came to respect each other, but I never thought that I would even come to like him, let alone love him, until he died and I found myself in tears.

My relationship with my uncle and aunt improved in the end. A considerable time after my uncle had been freed, and the whole episode had to some degree sunk into the past, a dreadful situation arose in the family and, in sheer desperation, they asked me to use my unwomanly gifts to help them. I did my best for them. After that, things between us were better, though never actually warm.

In time, I grew weary of secret missions, but I remained vulnerable to them for, as the years went on, the truth about my father finally emerged. I was the daughter of King Henry the Eighth, the result of a little adventure in the time when his love for Queen Anne was dying. He never knew of my existence. But after I had learned the truth of my paternity, and knew that I was the half-sister of Elizabeth, I also knew that if I should be asked to carry out any more missions, I could not refuse. The order might come from Walsingham, or perhaps Sir William Cecil, otherwise Lord Burghley, Secretary of State and later the Lord Treasurer. But in truth it would be for her.

And now . . . I was in my mid-fifties. My hair was still dark and my hazel eyes still clear, but my midriff had thickened and lengthy rides sometimes tired me. I had had three husbands. I was Mistress Ursula Stannard now, a well-found widow, with two houses and a third that I rented out (God forbid that I should ever set eyes on Evergreens again; I would send representatives in future). My daughter Meg was long married with four living children, and my son Harry was an upstanding eighteen years old and betrothed.

Eleanor Blake was the beautiful elder daughter of the couple who had lately bought Cobbold House, not many miles from my principal home, Hawkswood, in Surrey. Eleanor was not only good to look at but likeable too; I enjoyed her company and looked forward to having her as a daughter-in-law when she married Harry and came to live at Hawkswood. Eleanor walked with grace and she had glossy brown hair, gentle blue eyes and good skin. She had actually had smallpox but it hadn't marked her, beyond a couple of tiny indentations close to her hairline. Her expression was normally serious but when she smiled, and she smiled often, her face lit up as though a lamp had been kindled within her. She also thoroughly understood how a house like Hawkswood should be run, and when I heard her talking to Harry, I realized that she understood him as well. It ought to be a most successful marriage.

I did not only have Hawkswood to look after, however. Twice a year I spent a few weeks attending on the queen. She liked to have my company sometimes, because we were half-sisters and we had found that we had a rapport. I knew – though she never said it – that although she was constantly surrounded by people, she was nevertheless often lonely. The head of state, the one with the ultimate responsibility for the wellbeing of the realm, lives in a lonely world. I did what I could to give her some kind of companionship. I had just finished such an attendance, but had stayed on for Walsingham's funeral. After that, when I sat in my bedchamber at Whitehall with Dale and my son Harry, I felt a great desire to go home to Hawkswood as soon as possible. Aunt Tabitha's letter came as a most unwelcome shock for, as soon as I read it, I realized that I couldn't go straight home. I must first go to Faldene to attend another burial.

'*Must* we go straight from here?' Harry asked me. I had sent for him to join me at Walsingham's obsequies. I wished him to become familiar with such events. He was Elizabeth's nephew and must one day take his place in society. At this moment, I knew he was longing to go home as much as I was. He hadn't seen Eleanor since the day before yesterday.

'I think we must,' I told him. 'The funeral is only two days away. There's no time to spare. It's a good forty miles. We ought to set out at once but today has been too much. I thought the service would never end.'

I still felt exhausted from sitting through the interminable speeches and prayers. It was right for the service to be lengthy; Walsingham had earned his prayers and ceremonies. But I was oh so glad that it was over.

'We'll leave first thing tomorrow morning,' I said. I turned to Dale. 'It's too far for you to ride, Dale. You can travel inside our baggage carriage and we'll tether Blue Gentle behind.'

We left early the next day: me, Harry, my manservant Roger Brockley, who was Dale's husband, and, inside the little carriage where our baggage was stowed, Dale sat squeezed among the boxes and the enormous hampers. Packing the kind of gowns required for court wear was a work of art. The huge skirts and the embroidered kirtles and the great puffed and slashed sleeves must not be crushed, nor must any harm come to the bone farthingales or the elaborate ruffs. Even tirewomen like Dale had smart gowns for court wear, and the carriage was there because one really couldn't arrive at court with one's belongings in a cart.

Simon Alder, one of my grooms, had come as driver, and I rode, as did Harry and Brockley. Brockley was not only my manservant, he was also my trusted friend, and at times had been my companion in times of danger. Once, long ago, Brockley had come close to becoming my lover. It hadn't happened and never would, but a bond had been created then that never broke.

It still held, even now, when he was sixty and I was not much younger. He had changed very little over the years. He still had his high forehead with its scatter of pale gold freckles, his steady grey-blue eyes and his upright seat on a horse. His brown hair had thinned and was fading into grey; that was the only alteration.

The forty-mile journey could have been managed in a day, if we hadn't had the carriage, and if the roads had been better. As it was, we had to spend a night in an inn, and only reached Faldene in the afternoon of the second day. Though it was a house of mourning, everything seemed to be as usual, which was what I had expected. Uncle Herbert had well-trained servants. Any who didn't keep up his standards were unceremoniously dismissed. At the gatehouse, we were greeted promptly by the gatekeeper, John Hadley, who sent his sixteen-year-old son Tom running ahead to announce our arrival. We rode on up the track to the house, where grooms met us and took our horses as we dismounted. Our carriage horse was unharnessed and led away to the stables with the others, Simon going with them. Busy hands took the luggage out of the carriage, ran the carriage into an outhouse and bore our belongings indoors. The butler, a new one since the last time I had been here, came to welcome us, saying that his name was Field.

Field was unexpectedly young, no more than thirty, I thought, and looked somehow uncertain of himself. A little later, Aunt Tabitha told me that Field had only been in his post for two months. His predecessor had died suddenly and, 'We just took what we could get. Field isn't as experienced as we'd like, but I think he'll soon shape up,' Aunt Tabitha said.

Considering what a stickler Uncle Herbert was, Field would

have known that he had to shape up rapidly. He would be nervous of making mistakes. The poor man certainly couldn't have expected to be plunged into this sort of crisis while he was still raw. We followed him inside and into the great hall. The day was dull, and although the hall was lavishly lit with what looked like scores of candles, it was a big room with a few windows and the candlelight itself created pools of shadow. It was never a cheerful place.

And there was Aunt Tabitha, thin and trembly, frail as I had never before seen her, emerging from a dim corner, glad to see us, glad to have our company, even though other people were with her. The Faldene vicar had come up from the village and Uncle Herbert's valet, an anxious-looking man called Bowyer, who had been his most careful helper when the joint evil made it hard for my uncle to walk, was there too, looking bereft. He would have to find new employment when all this was over.

The roof of the hall was partly very high up, and partly took the form of a lower ceiling, supported by massive beams. Above this was a gallery from which bedchambers led off. They were the bedchambers used by my uncle and aunt and their personal attendants. The small one at the left-hand end had once been mine, and it was from that window that I had once crept at midnight, to meet Gerald and marriage and a whole new life.

In spite of the candles, the projecting ceiling cast quite a deep shadow. The hearth was below it, deep in shadow, even though a fire was burning. I was still exchanging greetings with Aunt Tabitha and the vicar when I noticed that another guest was present. He was beside the hearth and, once my attention had been drawn to him, I realized that he was busily conducting a low-voiced but finger-wagging conversation with a worried-looking woman whom I recognized as Aunt Tabitha's housekeeper.

I went on replying to the vicar's words of welcome, but part of my mind now attuned itself to this other conversation, and absorbed the fact that the man by the hearth was laying down the law about the accommodation for the three servants he had brought with him. Apparently, they hadn't been expected. However, just then, the housekeeper went, or rather scuttled, away, and Aunt Tabitha called the man over to us, addressing him as Francis. I looked at him with interest, wondering who he was. Then he said, 'Mistress Ursula Stannard! How are you? We haven't met in years and I hardly recognized you. I am your cousin, Francis. Surely you know me.'

Oh, of course, the son of the house. The only one now, since his brother Edward had died long ago, and tragically. We shook hands and exchanged the proper remarks about the sadness of the occasion and how much poor Uncle Herbert had suffered, how he had hated the pain and being crippled, and what a shock his sudden death had been for my aunt. Bowyer was hovering and Francis called to him and said he thought he could help him to a new position. Bowyer looked grateful.

Inevitably Aunt Tabitha, in a hushed voice, asked if I wished to see my uncle. I knew I was supposed to say yes, so I agreed. Harry and I then took part in a ceremonious, candlelit procession led by Aunt Tabitha and the vicar, into the room where my uncle lay. Two women from the village had attended to him, and he lay under a sheet, stretched out, straighter in death than the joint evil had ever let him be in life, his hands crossed on his breast.

'Near to eighty, he was,' Aunt Tabitha whispered to me and Harry as we stood beside him in the candlelight. 'And I am not that much younger. It'll be me to go before long, mark my words. And don't you go saying silly things like *Aunt Tabitha, don't talk like that, you've probably got years ahead.* Because I haven't, and I won't put up with nonsense.'

How typical of Aunt Tabitha. Frail she might be, but some things were the same. Once, she had turned to me, come to fetch me, when she and Uncle Herbert were in trouble, and I had done what I could for them, but afterwards, somehow, Aunt Tabitha had reverted to being much as she was before. Always, with me, my aunt seemed to be on the edge of anger, cross with me about things I hadn't yet done and probably hadn't even thought of doing. I held my tongue.

I looked for the last time on my uncle's face, pale and still, looking oddly younger, now that death had smoothed away the lines of pain and resentment that I so well remembered. Then we withdrew, and Aunt Tabitha said that I and my companions must want to see our quarters. There were several bedchambers in what was still called the new wing, though it had been built before I was born. Here, we were shown a small room for Harry, a capacious bedchamber for me, and a smaller bedchamber beside it for the attendant or attendants of whoever might occupy the larger room. The Brockleys would sleep there. Aunt Tabitha was very conscious of differences in social status. She had expressed surprise that Harry had no attendant. We knew that if he had, he would have been given a larger bedchamber.

'As if I can't do up my own doublets,' Harry muttered to me under cover of the clatter while a couple of Aunt Tabitha's menservants were bringing luggage in.

We had had dinner on the road, but supper was served early and the ride had made us ready for it. After that, tired from the long ride and too much emotion, I went to bed early. Dale came to help me wash in warm water and get into my night rail. Then there was the comfort of a feather bed and the blessing of deep sleep. A desperate weariness had overtaken me, more, I think, of the mind than the body. I knew that in normal circumstances I could still undertake a forty mile journey quite easily, even if I had to do it in one day, let alone two. What had so drained me was my unexpected grief over Walsingham, and the strain of his long funeral service, and then immediately – after all that – the sudden news of Uncle Herbert's passing.

My sleep did help. I awoke feeling better, but the grey mist outside cast my spirits down again. I was heavy-hearted as Dale helped me to put on the black gown that I had worn for Walsingham's funeral. She settled my ruff neatly, tidied my hair into a black silk net and put a hood, covered in black silk and set with pale moonstones, on my head. Today, Uncle Herbert would be buried in the churchyard down in the valley. Two funerals so close together, and a thick grey fog, aren't what anyone wants in April, with springtime on the doorstep.

I felt as though that wall of mist was hiding something from me, as though changes, dangers, mysterious forces, awaited me behind it.

The mist smelt cold. I shivered, and closed the casement.

TWO

The Laws of Hospitality

The mist was thinning by the time the funeral procession set out, but its remnants still hung round us, damp and depressing. We made our way down the track to the churchyard, with the bier, respectfully hidden under a pall of black velvet, borne on a cart drawn by a black horse. I wondered where either the velvet or the horse had come from, for I knew that my uncle's stables didn't contain any black horses, and a velvet cloth of that size was highly expensive.

Later on, it was Francis who told me that the black horse had been hired from a gentleman in Little Dene, the big village in the valley beyond the hill to the south.

'He keeps black horses and white horses, breeds them and sells them and hires them out for funerals and weddings,' Francis said. 'As for that velvet, it was bought years ago when my grandfather died. It's been kept ever since for this sort of occasion. My father told me that it was to be used for him. He'd been very unwell for some time, but he found the strength to write to me, instructing me to lift the organization of his funeral off the shoulders of my mother and giving details of his wishes. He was a great one,' said my cousin dryly, 'for giving orders, even from the grave.'

Now, as I walked beside Francis, following the bier, I said, 'I notice that your sisters are not here. Have you written to them?'

'Oh yes, but Mary and her husband live in Yorkshire, and Honoria and her family are in Norwich. They're a long way off. They sent appropriate messages.'

The truth was, I thought, that even the real children of Faldene House hadn't had all that much affection from their parents, and perhaps felt little grief now. I did not pursue the matter.

It was an ordinary Anglican funeral, presided over by Dr Greene, the current vicar of Faldene's church. My uncle and aunt had been secret Catholics, and for a time had had a Catholic chaplain in their house, but there was no sign of one now. Aunt Tabitha was not present, but had remained at the house, though she had company in the form of her personal maid, Agnes, a statuesque woman, not much younger than my aunt was herself, but obviously very attached to her mistress. Aunt Tabitha's attitude to Agnes was gentle and smiling and completely unlike the stern Aunt Tabitha with whom I had grown up.

There was a big crowd in the church and at the graveside, for most of the village had turned out. I doubt if my uncle had ever been a popular man, but he was their landlord, and by all accounts a reasonably fair, if not an amiable man, and so they came dutifully to say farewell.

Afterwards, nearly everyone, including the vicar, followed the empty cart, in which the precious velvet now lay neatly folded, back to the house for the funeral viands.

Aunt Tabitha might be frail, but she had an ample supply of servants and had only to issue instructions. In the big hall, two tables had been set out, one for the villagers, the other for the family and the vicar. Both tables were provided with cheese, butter and honey, but otherwise, the villagers had rye bread, tureens of pottage, serving dishes piled with hot sausages and small cold meat pies. To drink they had jugs of small ale. The family had white manchet bread, cold roast chicken, hot mutton pies, platters of salad, and wine.

Harry made himself useful, passing dishes to and fro. Aunt Tabitha didn't want to eat, but he coaxed her into accepting a few slices of the chicken and poured wine for her before moving on to help Francis to a slice of mutton pie. I was pleased with him.

As so often happens when a funeral is over, the atmosphere lightened. In an anxious fashion, Field was busy, making sure that everyone knew where to sit and urging the maids to be brisk. The talk became cheerful. I found myself seated beside Francis. He had brought three servants but no wife, for he had been widowed the previous year. Francis had for

years been part of an ambassador's suite and had lived in
Norway, but he was now retired and settled in Oxfordshire.
His children were all grown and married and we exchanged
news of our offspring, enjoying each other's company,
at last.

I say *at last*, for in the memories of my childhood, my elder
cousin Francis had been something of a bully (judging by
his conversation with the housekeeper, this hadn't changed
overmuch), and in adult life had not been encouraged to be
friendly with me. I had once overheard my uncle Herbert, in
conversation with Francis, describe me as *that cuckoo in my
nest, though she may be useful as a secretary. I don't intend
to concern myself with finding a husband for her.*

Oh, well, I found a husband without his assistance, only
one year later.

Now all that was over and gone. I was Mistress Stannard,
the lady of Hawkswood House, half-sister and aide to Queen
Elizabeth herself, with no need any longer to be timid in the
presence of my lawfully born cousins. And therefore I was
free to make friends with them or not, as I pleased. I now
found that Mistress Ursula Stannard, who was most unlikely
to be impressed by any attempts to bully her, was able to meet
Francis as an equal and even to like him. He in turn was
clearly getting on very well with my son, who had now taken
a seat opposite us.

I had failed to recognize Francis at first because it was so
long since I had last seen him, and now I was surprised to
notice how like me he was in appearance. His dark hair was
greying at the temples, but he had my hazel eyes and his nose
and mouth were also like mine.

My mother, oddly enough, had had some resemblance to
Queen Anne Boleyn – indeed, that may have been why King
Henry had wanted to make love to her. At any rate, the result
was that, like Queen Elizabeth, I had a slightly pointed chin
and some delicacy of bone structure, although it wasn't
actually due to our blood relationship. Francis did not share
these features. His jawline was square. Nevertheless, there was
still a considerable resemblance between us, and I found
him as comfortable to talk to as a brother might have been. I

found that I was glad to have news of him and his children. After all, they were my cousins too.

After the meal, Francis asked me whether I intended to leave for home on the morrow and, when I said yes, he asked me to stay a little longer. 'It's a matter of business – of your uncle's will, in fact.'

'Uncle Herbert's will? That's one thing I never thought would concern me, not after I stole your sister's betrothed, and then, there was that episode when I got your father arrested . . .'

'All long ago and overlaid by many other things,' said Francis calmly. 'Will you stay?'

'Of course, if it's necessary.'

'I can assure you that it is,' my cousin said.

The day wore on. The villagers took their leave and so did Dr Greene. He was a pleasant middle-aged man, calm of manner, very kindly as he condoled with Aunt Tabitha on her bereavement. A supper was planned for those of us still in the house. No one quite knew what to do to pass the time until then. Aunt Tabitha now seemed to be at a loss. To call for music or play cards seemed heartless. It was quite a pleasant distraction when young Tom came up to the house and rang the bell to say that there was a benighted stranger at the gatehouse, asking for help.

Field brought the news into the hall. 'It seems that the gentleman, who is travelling alone, is bound for Little Dene but has lost his way. He saw the lights of our house from a distance and meant only to ask directions here, but now his mare has cast a shoe and gone lame. He begs directions and a bed for the night and hopes there is a smith somewhere nearby.'

Aunt Tabitha exclaimed, 'Oh, not now! How can we take a guest in on this day of all days?'

But Francis demurred. 'There are such things as the laws of hospitality,' he said, taking command. 'Field, tell Tom to bring him in. Mother, I'm sure we can find a bed for him – there are still empty rooms in the new wing. I still keep calling it that,' he added, addressing me. 'Everyone does, though it was built so long ago now. It's only new compared to the rest of the house. Did you know that the rest was built in the last century and was raised on the site of one even older than that?'

'Yes, I did know,' I said. 'And I agree about being hospitable. Surely we can help this gentleman, Aunt.'

'Oh, very well,' said Aunt Tabitha wearily. I thought that, for once, she was handing over the reins of authority with relief. 'Field – where is he? – Field, find a groom for the mare. She can have a stall in our stables and tell the man that yes, there's a smith in the village. And order the maids to prepare a room for Master Trent. We are shortly to have supper and he can join us. He is probably famished.'

All this was done and the stranger was brought indoors, exuding polite concern at having arrived on a funeral day, and also, because it had now begun to rain, looking rather bedraggled. Uncle Herbert's valet, seemingly glad to have someone to look after, took the fellow's wet hat and riding cloak from him, steered him to a chair and removed his boots. Francis conferred briefly with the stranger and now introduced him.

'This is Master Nicholas Trent. He is in the employment of a Devonshire gentleman, Sir Ambrose Walsh, and has been sent with a message to a relative of Sir Ambrose, living in Little Dene. He hoped to be there this evening.'

'I saw your candlelight, just as night was coming on, and I thought: there are people there who will know how to get to Little Dene. I even wondered if this *was* Little Dene. But it seems that I have missed my way completely. And now to find that the master of the house has this day been buried . . .!' Embarrassment flowed from Master Trent. It was nearly as visible as chimney smoke.

'This is Faldene House, as I assume Field told you,' said Francis. 'You are welcome to have a bed here tonight. You can hardly get further now.'

'I am more grateful than I can say,' said Master Trent.

Divested of hat and cloak, we could see that the newcomer was a well-built young man with a tanned face, dark, curly hair worn a little long, dark brows and a short, dark beard, with light eyes that came as a startling contrast.

'In the morning,' Francis was telling him, 'one of the grooms will show you the way down to the village, where you will

find an excellent smith, and they'll put you on the track for
Little Dene. You're not so far astray; it's over the hill on the
other side of the valley.'

And so, unrecognizably, utterly unsuspected, it began. It
was like a vortex, dragging people in from its periphery,
changing lives, capturing and consuming innocent people. All
I knew at the time was that I had a curious, niggling feeling
that I had met Master Trent somewhere before, though – for
the life of me – I couldn't remember where.

THREE

Red Sky in the Morning

No one was late to bed that night. Agnes, who had been hovering anxiously around my aunt all evening, led her mistress away as soon as supper, a simple matter of cheese, manchet bread, chicken soup and ale, was over. Master Trent then said that he would seek his bedchamber as he would like to be away as early as he could on the morrow. Field assured him that the grooms were always up betimes, and promised that one of them would be ready to lead him and his lame mare down to the village and the smith as early in the morning as Master Trent wished. Trent then bade us all goodnight and, before long, the rest of us drifted away to bed as well.

It had been a difficult day and I didn't expect to sleep well, but surprised myself by plunging at once into unconsciousness. I didn't stir until I woke at dawn. I got up to look out of the window and was relieved to see that there was no mist this time, though the sky was overcast, breaking into barred lines of cloud in the east, with red streaks between. Tradition said that such a red sky meant bad weather to come; shepherds should look to their sheep. I hoped that, for Master Trent's sake, tradition was wrong. He would have to travel to Little Dene today and it was quite a long ride.

Because it was still so early, I didn't want to call for Dale at once and decided to read for a while. Dale, however, had heard me moving about. She dressed herself quickly and came to me without being summoned. She helped me into the black gown, brushed my hair, confined it once again in the black silk net and carefully arranged the silk-covered hood on my head.

'Not a grey hair yet, ma'am,' she said. 'For all the troubles you've known.'

'All the troubles *we've* known,' I said dryly. Dale's own hair, originally brown, had many a grey hair in it, and I had probably been responsible for putting them there. 'I hope that trouble is over for us,' I said. 'I foresee a quiet life now, at last. I don't think the queen will send me off on any more alarming missions. Philip of Spain may well have ideas about launching another Armada, but we have competent spies keeping watch on him without my help, thank God. I'll wear a necklace this morning, I think, Dale. My pearl rope would be best.'

'The one with the real sea pearls, like those your royal sister wears?' Dale asked.

'Yes, that one. I wonder if it's too soon for breakfast?'

Brockley joined us and, in what was still an early light, we went through the door to the old wing and descended the polished oakwood staircase that led down into the hall. I had expected to find it still empty, but Field was there, watching over the maids who were setting the table with bread and butter, dishes of sliced meat and jugs of small ale. He had pulled out the benches that ran along both sides of the table, so that the first-comers at least would find it easy to seat themselves. It was rather a wasted effort, because Harry appeared only a few moments later and undid some of Field's good work by choosing a seat on one of the benches and pulling it back to its normal position for his own convenience.

'I woke up hungry,' he explained. Dale said indulgently that all boys of his age had voracious appetites. We all sat down and began helping ourselves. Presently, Francis appeared, followed by Master Trent, who looked surprised to find that he wasn't the first.

'I must be on my way as soon as I can,' he said, joining us at the table and cutting a slice from a loaf. 'But I ought to thank my kind hostess. It was so good of her to give me a bed last night, after she had had such a dreadful day. I am so very sorry for my intrusion. Where is she?'

'Sleeping late, I imagine,' said Francis. 'No doubt she needs rest; yesterday must indeed have been hard for her. She and my father had been married for not much less than sixty years.

She was just eighteen when she was married to him, and he was only a little older. They had all their lives before them . . . it's hard to understand how time can go on and on and change young folk into old ones. Each day is much like the one before; one can't see the changes, and yet, they happen.'

From Harry's solemn face, I could see that he was thinking over all this, trying to imagine himself sixty years on. He was probably trying to visualize himself and Eleanor as an elderly couple and finding it difficult. He was still only eighteen and she was seventeen. Just a young couple. But soon they would be a young married couple, then parents, and then, all of a sudden, they'd be middle-aged . . . it was very difficult indeed to imagine these things and, by the look of him, Harry was finding it impossible.

'I have often myself wondered at the secretive way that time brings its changes about,' I said, 'and I'm sure that some time or other I have made exactly the same remark as you did just now, Francis. We think alike in many ways, it seems.'

'Why not?' said Francis, smiling. 'Are we not cousins? I should think . . .'

He stopped short and then shot to his feet. 'Good God, whatever's that?'

A moment ago, we had been talking in quiet voices because all around us the house was quiet. But now, suddenly, somewhere on the floor above us, someone had started to scream. We all stood up, looking at each other in alarm. On the gallery above, a door slammed and there were running feet. Francis stepped over the bench and started towards the staircase, and Agnes, distraught, emitting jerky screams, her cap askew and her eyes distended, ran headlong down it and threw herself at him. He caught hold of her and shook her, which stopped the screams and produced words instead. 'It's the mistress, oh, my God, it's my lady! It's Mistress Tabitha . . .!'

Francis shook her again. She gasped and fell silent. Francis demanded, 'What is it, Agnes? What's this to-do?'

Agnes gulped and wailed, 'She's dead!'

There was a horrified silence. I said, 'She can't be!' Dale moved to Brockley's side, as if seeking protection. It was

Francis who said, quite calmly, 'We had better come and see. Show us, Agnes.'

Still sobbing, Agnes led us back up the stairs to the gallery and we all followed her, even Nicholas Trent. All the bedchamber doors were shut, but Agnes ran to one of them and threw it open.

The first thing to hit me was the smell. It brought me to a horrified halt in the doorway. I had to put a hand over my nose before I could force myself to go inside. Only to recoil again, appalled at the sight of what had happened during the night. My aunt's last hours had been dreadful.

Agnes, through her tears, said, 'I went to wake her! She likes to rise early; if she oversleeps she expects me to rouse her. She's always been so particular about that . . .'

I knew that. In my youth, I had been thrashed for sleeping past the daybreak hour decreed by my uncle and aunt.

'But when I opened the door . . .' sobbed Agnes.

Words failed her. She clung to a bedpost and pointed. Francis himself, white and shaken, was leaning against a wall as though he feared he might fall. Dale had stepped backwards on to the gallery, and she too had a hand over her nose. Brockley had stepped into the room but then stopped short and was standing like a frozen statue, his mouth twisted in shock and disgust. Trent was simply silent, withdrawn to the rear, as though he wished he could vanish.

Unlike Uncle Herbert, Aunt Tabitha hadn't died in her sleep. She had died in some kind of convulsion. She was hanging half out of the bed, and she had been violently sick on to the floor below. A small table that had stood beside her bed had been thrown over. The bedcovers were twisted, as though she had wrenched at them in a frenzy, and she had emptied her bowels into them.

'*Sweet Christ!*' Francis said at last.

He regained command of himself and came forward to look at everything more closely. He found a drinking glass on the floor beside the fallen table and picked it up to show us. The glass hadn't broken and, by some freak of chance, it had landed half propped against a table leg. There was a little liquid still in it. He sniffed at it and stiffened.

'This is foul stuff. How did my mother come to have such a thing at her bedside? She must have drunk this and died. But why did she drink it? She can hardly have believed that anything so nasty was *fit* to drink. This is – it must be – it's poison!'

Brockley went to him, took the glass from him and also sniffed. Because he was my manservant, and I had had an unconventionally adventurous life, there were many unexpected things that he knew. 'It's hemlock,' he said, with certainty. He looked round at us with as much authority as though he were the master of the house. 'This means an inquest.'

Harry had followed us upstairs. I turned to tell him to go back to the hall and then realized that he had seen. He shouldn't have. I was shocked to realize that I had forgotten to protect him. But when I signed to him to go, he shook his head and stood firm. Other members of the household had now appeared, and it was Field, the inexperienced butler, who ran back downstairs and collapsed into a chair in tears, while Bowyer, as though he had once more found a new patient to care for, patted his shoulder and murmured platitudes. Agnes was now exclaiming that oh, no, such a thing was unthinkable, and Brockley was steadily repeating himself and holding Francis's eyes while he spoke. And in spite of Agnes's wails, Francis was agreeing with him.

There was a good deal of talk – as I recollect, it felt like aeons of talk – before anything was actually done about calling in the village constable. Agnes, now seated in a chair in the hall, had much to say, if none too coherently.

'I begged her, after the master got so ill – that was a week before he died, God rest his soul, and she moved into another room so that Bowyer could take care of him in the night – I begged her to let me come in with her, but she wouldn't, she wouldn't, she said she'd rather be alone; she said if she wanted to cry she'd do it on her own. That was the mistress all over; proud she was, and wouldn't show anyone any softness, not even me that's been with her these ten years or more . . . I begged her, begged her, but even when the master died, still she wouldn't have me. Perhaps she was planning this all along; she must have done it herself or why

didn't she cry out to me for help, I was only in the next
room . . .'

Here, Agnes dissolved into helpless weeping and one of
the maids went to put an arm round her.

I said, 'I know a little about hemlock. I have seen others
die, who killed themselves that way. It takes about half an
hour before the symptoms start. It was how the philosopher
Socrates was executed and it isn't quite the peaceful end that
legend says it was . . .'

I found that I didn't want to talk about the details, but
Brockley took over. 'It takes maybe half an hour to start taking
effect, and then the throwing up begins and there are convulsions and voiding of the bowels before paralysis sets in.'

'And she brewed a drink of it and took it and lay waiting
to die,' said Dale, horrified, while Agnes broke into louder
and more frantic sobbing.

The constable had to be told, insisted Francis. Word must
be sent to him at once. Through her tears, Agnes implored
him not to, for if an inquest was held and the verdict was
suicide, then her lady could not be buried in consecrated soil.
Francis hesitated. Suicide really was the only possible explanation. None of us would have harmed poor Aunt Tabitha, but
the loss of her husband after nearly sixty years of marriage
might have turned her brain.

Privately, I found this hard to believe. As I grew older and
more observant, I had gradually concluded that, for the most
part, her severity was the result of being married to him. It
was what he expected of her and, being Uncle Herbert, he had
made sure that his wife obeyed him. There were moments – as
the time she arrived headlong at my home to beg my help in
an emergency – when I saw a different side of her. As a young
bride she had surely been much softer. The hard carapace was
my uncle's creation.

And I had noticed that yesterday, although she had shed the
proper tears of a newly made widow, and had certainly been
exhausted by enduring such a day, she hadn't shown any signs
of the frantic desperation that must surely precede an act so
appalling as suicide. And yet, what other explanation could
there be?

I suggested that we should start by asking Dr Greene's advice. At length this was agreed upon and he was fetched from the village. Reassuringly, he said that if the verdict was that she had killed herself while out of her mind with grief, then she could lawfully rest within the churchyard walls. Francis and Brockley looked at him and he looked at them, and they nodded. So did Harry. If I had forgotten to protect him from seeing Aunt Tabitha, I thought, I had also forgotten that he was no longer a child. He was a young man now, engaged to be married, old enough to go to war if the queen required it. This was something that I was still learning to grasp.

So, eventually, the constable was informed, and an inquest was arranged. Francis asked us all to remain at Faldene until it was over. This included Master Trent, but he accepted it without protest, just saying philosophically that if he had to stay then so be it, and in what way could he be of use, but could he still get his mare shod while he was here?

'But I'm sorry,' he said, 'that I had no chance to thank my good hostess. Believe me, when I was welcomed in out of the rain last night, and after such a day as she – as all of you – must have had, well, thanks would have been in order.'

A groom was told to take the mare to the smith in the village. Several servants, with cloths tied over their mouths and noses, were set to cleaning the room. The sheets and the one blanket were taken to the stone wash-house out in the rear courtyard and boiled, with soap and rosewater and lye. The pillows and the squirrel-skin coverlet were ruined beyond hope. A bonfire was built in the courtyard and they were burned.

Field pulled himself together, consulted with the house-keeper and, as a proper dinner was unsuited to the occasion, we had the same things as were served at breakfast, except that there was a bowl of preserved plums as well. We didn't sit down to it, but helped ourselves, and in many cases ate while wandering restlessly about.

The inquest was held two days later, in the village. There was an inn there with a large upstairs room which was suitable for the purpose. Master Trent remarked glumly that if only he had found the village and the Horse and Wagon on the night he arrived, and had taken a room there, he would be peacefully in Little Dene by now.

The verdict was suicide in the madness and despair of grief, which had surely turned the poor lady's head. No one knew where she had got the hemlock poison from, but there was no real mystery about that. It grew round about, and she could easily have brewed the poison herself, perhaps at night. Perhaps she had been planning it even before her husband died. She could easily have created the poisoned drink herself. None of her servants slept in the kitchen. The cook, his assistants and the spitboy shared a room beside it, and the maidservants slept upstairs in one of the bigger rooms off the gallery. She had only to work quietly.

The jury consisted of village men who were the tenants of whoever now owned Faldene. They knew what was expected of them and returned that verdict. The day after the inquest, I was a mourner at yet another grave.

Field and I arranged the food for the gathering at the house. It was a repetition of the gathering after my uncle's burial, to the point that – during that afternoon – I felt light-headed, as though I were reliving a past occasion.

The day was drawing to a close, when Francis came up to me and said, 'We still have business to discuss, Ursula. More than ever now, as it happens. Tomorrow morning, immediately after breakfast, in what was your uncle's study?'

'By all means,' I said. The red sky on the morning when my aunt was found had presaged trouble, all too accurately. I could only hope that the will would bring no more.

FOUR
The Gift of the Dead

The next morning, I duly went to the room that my uncle had used as a study. It was in the new wing and it wasn't a small place like the study my late husband had used. This was a big, east-facing room, with mullioned windows and a high, flat ceiling criss-crossed with beams. There was a worktable, set with the usual things, such as a writing set (it was a costly one, in onyx), a pottery holder for quills and another for scrolls, a branched candlestick and a small abacus. The rushes on the floor had been changed, even though the room's owner was gone. I wandered to the window and then away again, wondering, in some puzzlement, what it could be that Francis wanted to tell me. Had I been left a legacy of some kind? Then Francis came in, carrying a polished wooden box under his arm.

'You are punctual, Cousin Ursula. Be seated. This may take a little while.'

More puzzled than ever, I took a seat and Francis sat down opposite. He put the box down, threw back the lid and removed two parchment scrolls.

'I'll hand you these in a moment,' he said, 'but first, I'll tell you what they contain, so that you'll find them easy to understand. My parents both made wills and they did so at the same time, presumably after discussing the matter with each other. No man of business was present but my father himself bought the parchment and wrote the wills in the elegant hand he had learned as a boy. He was educated by a Catholic priest who was cultured and had considerable skill at penmanship. The signatures to both wills were witnessed by the same people, who were Dr Edward Greene, vicar of St Mary's in Faldene, and one Henry Taylor, manservant to myself. I was also present when these wills were made, and by that,' said Francis, looking at me seriously, 'you may rest assured that I approved of them and had no objection to their contents.'

I waited, feeling intrigued, but wary.

'In simple terms,' said Francis, 'my father made modest bequests to various people such as Agnes and Bowyer, and my mother also made a few bequests, especially to Agnes. My father left his savings to me. They are considerable and are in the hands of bankers abroad. I also had a duty to take care of my mother, if she survived him. But in my father's will, Faldene, meaning this house, its contents, its farm and the village, are left in the first place to my mother, but after her death, to you. She repeats this in her own will, to make sure there is no mistake.'

'But . . .!' I was staggered. Whatever I had surmised as possible, it wasn't this. For a few moments, I was speechless. Finally, I said, 'Francis, you're the only son, this house ought to be yours! Why would they want to leave it to me? They didn't even like me, let alone love me! They can't have made me their heiress! I own Hawkswood. My husband Hugh Stannard left it to me. It's a good property. The village rents and the surplus farm produce, and one thing and another – all of them together amount to a good living. I also have the stud of trotters that I have founded. It has become profitable. *And* I own Withysham House, only three miles from here, and in Kent there's Evergreens, which I rent out – last year I had a nasty experience there and I never want to set eyes on it again. At Lady Day and Michaelmas I shall send someone else to collect the rent and inspect the property as I used to do. What I am saying is that I don't need Faldene and I can't *think* why it's been left to me. There must be some mistake.'

'There is no mistake,' said Francis. 'Remember, I was here when these wills were made. They were made with my full consent.'

'But why did you consent?' I asked him, bewildered. 'You are their only son, you have rights! And think what I did to them – running off with Mary's betrothed, getting your father put into the Tower . . .!'

'But later, when they were in trouble, my aunt came to you

for help and you did your utmost to give it, at risk to yourself. Anyway, I'm getting the money,' said Francis, amused. 'I don't want Faldene. I have a fine property of my own in Oxfordshire, including a home farm and five others. If I wanted more, which I don't, I'd want it there, not here. Faldene's yours, my dear cousin. Read the wills.'

I did as he said, with more and more bewilderment. *My house of Faldene, with all that is in it, and the land and Faldene village that go with it, I leave to my wife if she survives me. But after her, and immediately if she has not survived me, I will that they should pass into the hands of our niece and foster daughter Mistress Ursula Stannard of Hawkswood. This is in recognition of the truth that when she was a child, because she was born out of wedlock, we were not always kind to her, and yet, she has never abandoned us. As for certain incidents that occurred when she was young, it is wearisome to keep the past in mind. She has since brought lustre to our family. I wish her well of Faldene.*

I turned to my aunt's will. It virtually repeated my uncle's words. There was no doubt about it. Faldene House, its contents, its land, its village were now my property. I sat there with tears in my eyes, puzzling over the strangeness of heredity, that had bred a kind of love between me and my uncle and aunt, even though, heaven knows, I had suffered at their hands and they at mine.

I brushed the tears away and said, 'But don't you *mind*? I will gladly . . .'

'No, you won't. I won't allow that. It is right and proper that the queen's half-sister should be a woman of property. I know that Faldene is some way from Hawkswood, where you mostly live, but you come to this district often, when you visit Withysham. You can make visits to Faldene at the same time. I have had speech with your son Harry. He says that he is betrothed and that the wedding will be soon. When his children come along, you will perhaps wish him to have a home of his own. Or decide that you wish one for yourself.'

'Yes. I have already thought along those lines. I have decided that eventually, probably when Harry's children begin to arrive, I plan to withdraw to Withysham.'

'You can withdraw to Faldene if you like,' said Francis. 'Meanwhile, you can rent it out, or place it in the hands of a good steward, as you have done at Withysham. Field strikes me as honest and probably capable, though inexperienced. I can lend you an experienced man if you wish, someone who can assist Field until he is ready to be left in command. The man is the assistant to my own butler, but he is quite as well versed in the work as his superior.'

'Thank you. That would be a good idea,' I said bemusedly. 'What happened to the previous butler here?' I wondered. 'Bernard someone or other.'

'He fell down dead with a heart attack. I think he found working for my father a great strain and, as he grew older, a worse one,' Francis said dispassionately. 'Field was a hasty replacement. They had the vacancy cried in Chichester and Field was the only applicant who was halfway suitable. He'll do well enough, once he learns that in times of crisis, a good butler doesn't panic and burst into tears. He isn't used to being in authority yet. But he'll learn – and he won't have to cope with my parents. Don't look like that, Ursula. I have no illusions about my parents. I'll send for my assistant butler – his name is Thomas Archer – and he should be here in less than a week. By the way, I believe that your own butler died recently. Harry mentioned it to me the other day. You have replaced him satisfactorily?'

'I have a ward – adopted son, really – called Ben Atbrigge. Although young, he already understands the duties of a steward and is taking his predecessor's place with the help of Peter Dickson, who was formerly tutor to him and to Harry. It is working well, despite his youth.'

'Hm. You are quite satisfied with this arrangement?'

Francis always did have an officious side to him. 'Perfectly satisfied,' I said coolly, sitting very straight.

'Very well. All right, back to Withysham, as it were. Now,' said Francis, pulling a scroll from the holder, 'this is a map of the Faldene estate. You will want to know the details.'

I tried to shake off my confusion. I must concentrate. I had once known Faldene well, but I had left it at the age of twenty and subsequently made only brief visits. Since then, my uncle had brought some of the common grazing land into cultivation, thus alienating the goodwill of villagers who were accustomed to graze their own animals there. The map showed the area concerned. In addition, new outbuildings had been put up on the farm and old ones dismantled and, of course, I had to consider the occupants of the stables. I asked Francis about them.

'When my parents began to fail, which was some while ago now, they had a carriage made for them, like the one you brought your baggage in,' said Francis. 'They sold the horses they used to ride and bought a matched pair for the carriage. The first pair grew old and died so they replaced them with a pair of chestnut geldings. That wasn't very long ago, about two years, I should think. The current pair were aged five when they were first bought and they're still only seven. Young horses, in fact, and broken for saddle as well as harness. You may find them useful.'

I thought of Splash, the good-natured horse who had pulled our carriage-load of luggage and Dale from Hawkswood. He was getting old now. Yes, I could use those chestnuts.

Francis was continuing. There were heavy horses for the farm, two riding horses for use when there were errands to do or messages to be sent. There were three grooms, 'And, of course, you will have to consider the indoor staff,' Francis said, changing the subject. 'The housekeeper, Mrs Sadler, does tend to bob her head and scuttle about and generally behave as though she is frightened of everything and everyone but, in fact, she is perfectly competent in dealing with the house and the other servants. I think my parents caused that air of fright. She'll eventually get over believing that my father's orders were carved in stone by a higher authority and carried ceremoniously down a mountain. I almost had to wring accommodation for my servants out of her, and all because it went against some order or other that my father had given her, probably aeons ago. If I were you, I would keep her. The same probably applies to the maids and menservants, and the kitchen staff. I suppose one could say that my parents did at least insist on efficient servants.'

'Quite,' I said. A particularly unpleasant episode in my

youth suddenly came back to me, an occasion when one of
the servants, too obedient to his employer's orders, had told
my uncle about some peccadillo of mine. For me, the result
was one of the worst birchings I ever had. I found myself
crushing down an absurd desire to defy Francis, assert myself
and declare that I wanted to dismiss the staff of Faldene in
entirety and then burn the place down.

'Though I doubt,' Francis was saying, 'that you will want
to keep Agnes or Bowyer on – am I right? I have already
promised to help Bowyer if so.'

I pulled myself together. 'Yes, quite right.' I could well
imagine Dale's reaction if I brought Agnes into Hawkswood.
I would have to stay on at Faldene for a while, I thought, to
inspect it and decide about anything arising. Agnes could
remain while I had her need for a new post cried in Chichester
and Guildford. I would see her settled before I went home, and
no doubt Francis would see Bowyer settled as well. That at
least was off my hands.

Francis was folding up the map. 'It's a dull day but not yet
raining,' he said. 'You may care to walk round some of your
new property.'

I would rather have retired to my room to break the news to
Harry, Dale and Brockley in private, but Francis had his father's
dominant nature. Obediently, well clad in cloak, hat and stout
shoes, I allowed myself to be led on a tour of inspection.

When I finally returned from walking round my new domains,
I broke away from Francis in order to take my own companions to my room to tell them the news. I was greeted with
open mouths. At length, Harry said, 'This means that we own
Faldene now, as well as Withysham?'

'It seems,' I said, 'that my uncle and aunt had consciences
– though they didn't owe me anything; for if I was roughly
treated at times as a child, I certainly retaliated once I was
grown-up. However, that is beside the point now. Uncle Herbert
and Aunt Tabitha are no more with us and Faldene is mine
to live in or let or simply keep at will. When you're married,
Harry, and the father of a family, I may decide to live in it. I
can move between it and Withysham as I like.'

It had suddenly struck me that I would like. Deeply as I loved Hawkswood, which had belonged to my very dear third husband, Hugh Stannard, Faldene was where I had spent the first twenty years of my life. It had long saddened me that because my uncle and aunt were so stern with me, I had not had the happy childhood that a beautiful home such as Faldene should have given me. Perhaps now, in later life, I might heal that old sore.

'I will keep Faldene and maintain it and perhaps, in due course, come to live in it,' I said. 'However, that is for the future. At present, I think we are obliged to stay here for some time. I have a number of arrangements to make, especially for Agnes, who will have to find work elsewhere . . .'

'Agnes is not to come to Hawkswood with us?' queried Dale.

'No, did you expect her to? I mean, do you want her?'

'*No!*' Dale was just as emphatic as I had guessed she would be. 'But I think she hopes to come. She said so to me, only this morning.'

'She's wrong there, but I'll see she has new employment before we leave here.'

'But how long will that be?' Harry wanted to know. 'Couldn't I go home ahead of you, Mother? I don't like being so long away from Eleanor!'

'You've only been away for a week,' I said. 'As I take charge here, you can watch and learn. There will be plenty to learn, what with deciding who and what to keep and how to deal with things and people that are not kept. It will be good instruction for you.'

'Oh, Mother, must everything that happens be turned into lessons for me? I am learning all the time at Hawkswood! And I want to see Eleanor. We shall be married soon; why can't I profitably learn how to organize a wedding?'

I groaned, but gave in. 'Very well. Simon can go with you, and return after he has seen you safely back. You can leave tomorrow.'

'Why can't I go on my own? I'm not some timid maiden!'

'No, you are my adventurous son,' I said. I looked at him with affection. Harry was so very like his father. He had

Matthew de la Roche's dark hair and eyes and the same handsome and slightly asymmetrical features, an asymmetry that added rather than detracted from his good looks. He had also, I feared, inherited something of Matthew's . . . no, not wildness. Capacity for passion, perhaps. And a blithe disregard of risks.

Any solitary journey involves a degree of risk: taking a toss in a lonely place, being attacked by footpads, having one's horse go lame.

'You'll go home with Simon or not at all,' I said, and Harry knew I meant it.

'All right. I'll tell Simon, shall I? We can pack and be off early. We can make it in one day.'

'Don't founder your horses!' I barked. Harry's Prince, a light grey, nearly white gelding with a noble head carriage, was full of spirit and pride and would probably let himself be foundered, rather than give in and slow down on his own. Both Brockley and I had on occasion called Harry to order about overtaxing his horses. But, after all, Simon would be there and he would be riding dear old Splash, and dear old Splash, who never shied and would simply come to a stop if he was tired, would probably look after everyone far better than I could.

Harry was no longer a boy. One day, I supposed, I would get used to it.

FIVE

Heavy of Heart

Harry left for Hawkswood the next day. Simon returned shortly afterwards, assuring me that they had arrived there without incident. Two more weeks passed before I felt free to leave Faldene. During that time, however, much was achieved. Agnes and Bowyer settled themselves without help either from me or from Francis. On their own account, they had it cried in Guildford that a lady's maid and a valet, both skilled and of good character, were seeking new positions, and within a few days I was presenting them with severance payments (generous ones, since I knew very well that service with my aunt and uncle hadn't been easy), shaking hands with them and wishing them well.

They had found employment with a recently married couple, who were setting up a new household. Agnes and Bowyer had found posts as a lady's maid and general manservant and would both be working in the same place. They were pleased with the prospect, looking forward to it. I did not need to worry about them now.

During that two weeks, I examined my new possessions in detail, walked round the fields, looked at the contents of the house, talked to Dr Greene and to the villagers, and several times visited my mother's grave in the churchyard. I always shed a few tears when I did so. She had had a hard time as Uncle Herbert's disgraced sister, and she was dead before he ever discovered that his unwanted niece was kin to the queen. It might have made a difference.

I also visited Withysham, the house about three miles from Faldene, which in the days before what was now called the Reformation had been a women's abbey. It had been presented to me by the queen in recognition of services rendered. I was fond of it; had originally planned, in some distant future time, to live there when Harry was established at Hawkswood. Because it was a gift from Elizabeth, I would never sell it. If Harry had a daughter, it might perhaps be her dowry. I inspected it, found it in good order and gave a few instructions. In the care of one of my uncle's grooms, I sent the pair of chestnut carriage horses to Hawkswood ahead of me, along with the news that I had been delayed in returning home but would be setting out shortly, and giving the date when they could expect me.

Francis went home, but he kept his promise to send his assistant butler to reinforce Field, and Field himself had shown encouraging signs of bracing his shoulders and preparing to master his duties properly. I would be back soon, I promised, to see how everyone was faring. Now and then I would make quite long stays, I said. Then, at last, came the morning when Brockley and I mounted our horses, Dale and the baggage were once more ensconced in the little carriage. Splash was in the shafts and Simon had the reins, and we were bound for home.

The month of May was in and the sun was out. We didn't hurry. We spent a night on the road, and by day we rode through woodland tracks overhung with fresh green leaves and past fields where new crops were sprouting and young stock, calves and lambs and foals, were gambolling. May is a happy month. This was not unlike the journey I had made the previous spring, when with the Brockleys I had set out to attend a wedding. That wedding had turned out badly, but I didn't think that Harry's would, and it wasn't far away.

Thinking about that should have made me light of heart, but for some reason it did not, which puzzled me.

Before he left to go home ahead of me, Harry had told me that he and Eleanor had chosen June for their marriage, if her parents and I were agreeable. During the night that we spent at an inn, in the evening, when Dale was helping me into my night rail, she said to me that she had had an idea about the wedding gift for Eleanor.

'It was just before we left Hawkswood, ma'am,' she

said. 'I was tidying the drawers of that tall chest in your bedchamber, and I found some ruffs that I had put away, last year, when we were packing for the court. You said they were too small for court wear, ma'am, and you told me not to include them. But they're so pretty, with those lace-edged pleats. You wear small ruffs at home; they're more comfortable than those great big fashionable cartwheel affairs. You can wear these; I'll spruce them up for you. But I have been thinking, why shouldn't a set of pretty ruffs form part of your wedding gift to Mistress Eleanor? Along with the jewellery I know you're planning for her. I'm sure we could get a set made up in Guildford.'

'Yes. Why not? That's a good thought, Dale.'

Whereupon Dale looked at me gravely and said, 'Ma'am, why do you sound so . . . so heavy of heart?'

'Do I, Dale?'

'Yes, ma'am,' said Dale.

Dale was always intensely aware of my moods, almost to the point of reading my mind, and she had done so now. It was true. I was heavy of heart and I didn't know why. Because this journey reminded me of the one last year? But just because things hadn't gone well then, there was no need to expect the same thing to happen now. And yet, the spark of joy refused to strike.

Dale found an answer. 'You are grieving, ma'am. I can see it,' she said. 'And that's natural enough. Your uncle and aunt were part of you, even though they were sometimes harsh. As you have often said, they did look after you, even educated you. You are bound to have feelings for them. There's no need to pretend. You have a little cry, any time you want to. No need to hide those tears from me.'

'You may be right,' I said. Aunt Tabitha's death had been shocking, after all. An inquest! She herself would have considered such a thing unthinkable.

And it came to me then, the reason for this uneasy feeling.

Aunt Tabitha would also have considered suicide unthinkable.

I knew she would and, in any case, had she ever really

loved my frankly unattractive Uncle Herbert, so much that she would rather die than live without him? I wouldn't have thought her capable of such emotional depths, even if he had been lovable.

And if she did want to die, would she choose such an appalling method? The few drops remaining in the fallen glass had smelt dreadful, and its results were worse still. I had seen them before; had actually witnessed the throes. Perhaps she hadn't realized how nasty the taste would be, and how horrible the consequences. I supposed that she had heard the legend about the execution of Socrates. Perhaps she thought she would just lie quietly and be overtaken by paralysis, and then by sleep. I knew very well that hemlock meant nausea and diarrhoea and convulsions and then a terrible struggle for breath when the lungs began to be paralysed.

But she hadn't cried out. Well, if she had taken the poison herself, perhaps she wouldn't, even though the symptoms would have come as a ghastly surprise. Aunt Tabitha had a great deal of pride. It must also have taken an immense amount of determination and, yes, courage, even to decide to kill herself, let alone actually do it. That pride of hers, that same courage and determination might have carried her through to the end.

But – there it was again, nagging at me – Aunt Tabitha would have considered suicide unthinkable. She was a devout woman. She was a Catholic. Suicide was considered a mortal sin within both the Catholic and the Anglican churches, and perhaps more intensely so in Catholic eyes. Even if Aunt Tabitha had been in such despair after losing my uncle, would she, could she, ever have defied her faith to such an extent?

And yet, what other explanation could there be?

There wasn't one. No one would have wanted to . . . to . . . it was an effort even to form the words in my head . . . no one would have wanted to harm her. She was hard on her servants but since when had that been a motive for murder? Besides, as an employer, Aunt Tabitha was probably better than many. In my childhood she had beaten me, but she never treated the servants like that. She expected good service, but I had known her to be patient with inexperienced maids while they were learning. If they failed to improve, she would dismiss them, but she usually paid them off; they weren't turned out into destitution.

It didn't make sense.

Well, I could think of nothing that would make it make sense. Brooding over it wouldn't help. I told Dale that she was probably right, bade her goodnight and retired to the quite comfortable bed provided by the inn. I was tired and I slept. In the morning, I awoke briskly and got us on the road as soon as we had broken our fast. The inn provided cold meats, bread with honey, and ample small ale. Soon after that, we were ready to leave. Brockley saw to paying the bill, and then he gave me a leg up on to my elderly but handsome and still spirited bay gelding, Jaunty. He mounted his dark chestnut, Firefly, who was also getting on in years, though one would never have known it from his gallant head and tail carriage, and we started. Dale was once more settled in the carriage, if not altogether comfortably, since her feet were on the box containing my ruffs and farthingales, and a hamper full of brocade gowns was half in her lap. Simon took up the reins and clicked to Splash to walk on. We had only a three-hour journey ahead of us, and once more, the sky was smiling.

Before noon, we were in sight of Hawkswood. The last stretch of track led through an oak wood, and then we were riding under the gatehouse arch, which was actually a short tunnel but was always open in the daytime, and into the courtyard. Our two half mastiffs, Caesar and Cleo, beautiful dogs with golden coats, would scent us and begin to bay a welcome before we were through the gate arch.

After an absence, I usually found many of my household in the courtyard to greet me. Half a mile from the house, the track went over a small hill and, just there, the trees were fewer. Someone looking from an upstairs window nearly always glimpsed us as we approached, even before Caesar and Cleo began to announce us. This time, however, it was different. We could certainly hear the dogs, but they seemed to be snarling rather than barking, and around them were human cries of anger and dismay. Brockley and I looked at each other and applied our heels to our horses.

As we clattered into the courtyard, we beheld an astonishing scene. Somebody – by leaning out of my saddle and twisting my head, I managed to identify him as my cook, John Hawthorn – was flat on his face on the cobbles. He was shouting for help, while Caesar and Cleo were apparently worrying him. Harry was trying to haul them off, aided by Ben Atbrigge, my adopted son, who would one day, we hoped, become the new Hawkswood steward. He had come to me after a tragedy in his own family. He and Harry were much of an age and they were friends. Now they were side by side, striving desperately and apparently in vain. Ben seemed to be trying to drag something from underneath the prostrate and bellowing Hawthorn. Hawkswood's other Ben, Hawthorn's assistant Ben Flood, was dancing about and shouting. My senior groom, Arthur Watts, and most of the other grooms were doing much the same thing, and the Hawkswood vicar, bouncy, rotund Dr Joynings, a picture of astonishment, was standing near the gate, as though he had just walked in, and had come to a halt with his mouth open.

This sort of thing was unheard of. Caesar and Cleo were descendants of dogs we had had in the past. They had been born here. They knew all the household members and were no more likely to attack any of us than the sun was likely to rise in the west. They would challenge intruders, but even then wouldn't attack unless ordered.

I all but fell out of my saddle, Brockley did the same and, behind us, Simon had driven the carriage through the gate arch and was now leaping down from the driving seat while Dale was scrambling out of the door. We all ran.

I shrieked, 'Caesar! Cleo!' and rushed headfirst into the melee to join Harry in dragging at Cleo's collar. Hawthorn managed for a moment to lift himself up a few inches and then I realized that what the dogs were after wasn't him, but a linen bag which was attached to his wrist by a thong and had been trapped beneath him as he fell. Caesar had shoved his big head into the aperture that Hawthorn had just made between himself and the cobbles, and was trying to get at the bag.

Hawthorn slumped down again, pushing Caesar's head out of the way with his weight. Caesar whined pitiably.

'There's a bag of something under Hawthorn that's maddened the dogs!' I shouted. 'Get it off him and take it away!'

'Take these bloody dogs away! They've gone mad!' bawled Hawthorn from beneath the double weight of two golden-furred half mastiffs.

Ben was the one who finally managed it. He pulled out his belt knife, somehow got a hand under Hawthorn, hacked through the thongs that attached the bag to my unhappy cook's wrist, grabbed the bag, jerked himself away and stood up, clutching it. At once the dogs were rearing, yelping, still trying to get at it. Ben ran for the kitchen door, got inside just in time and slammed it after him.

Whereupon, all was miraculously peace. The dogs, suddenly quiet, retreated looking disappointed. Hawthorn got up, brushing his clothing, glowering. He was a big man with thick black hair that he wore tied back into a queue. He also had a powerful voice. When Hawthorn was annoyed, everyone knew about it. He was annoyed now. Once on his feet, he stood there on the cobbles, hands on hips and in a voice like thunder, demanded explanations.

'What's the matter with those damned dogs? I've been to the market in Guildford, madam, for some new flavouring that Master Harry's tasted at the Blakes' house, and the moment I get inside the courtyard, these animals act as though they were baiting a bull!'

'Did they bite you?' Harry enquired.

'Of course not!' bellowed Hawthorn. 'Just knocked me over on the cobbles and carried on as if I'd brought back a bag full of a threat to the whole bloody realm!'

Hawthorn showed no sign of being in pain, nor did he seem to be bleeding anywhere, which he certainly would have been if the dogs had sunk their teeth in him. He must have had bruises but, beyond that, he wasn't injured, merely livid. There were exclamations of relief all round.

And yet, for some reason, no one was laughing and, in the nature of things, someone should have been.

Arthur Watts, in a sharp voice, was ordering the grooms to attend to our carriage, to unharness Splash, to take charge of all the horses and take the luggage indoors. Ben had a serious nature but Harry at least should have been amused. Instead, he was solemn, and very pale. And there was Dr Joynings, who seemed to have just arrived and was now greeting me politely but gravely. Dr Joynings was asked to dinner now and then, but otherwise he came to Hawkswood House only if he was needed. And suddenly, I was alert. There was something wrong here, other than the crazy behaviour of our two dogs.

Though I still had to ask questions about that. 'What in the world do you mean by new flavourings? Hawthorn? What was in that bag?'

'Aniseeds. Master Harry has tasted aniseed in wine when he's dined at the Blakes' . . . oh, dear God, at the Blakes' . . .' Hawthorn was no longer thundering. His voice now was just miserable.

I said, 'I am acquainted with aniseed. I too have tasted it in wine, when I am at court. I dislike it. Please make sure that when you use it for Master Harry, there is a separate serving for me, without it. Phoebe can grind some of the seeds and try them in that dandelion wine she's taken to making ever since I began bringing lemons home from my visits to court. I don't care for dandelion wine either, so I shan't encounter aniseed by mistake that way.'

According to Phoebe, my senior maid, lemon juice made all the difference to dandelion wine, which wasn't worth making without it. Lemon juice was also good for the migraines that I sometimes suffered, which was why I had brought lemons in the first place. I sometimes had to protect them from Phoebe.

I brushed these thoughts aside. Standing in the courtyard,

looking at the serious faces around me, I demanded, 'And now may I know what's wrong with you all? There's something amiss. I can see it. This ridiculous scene just interrupted it, or so it seems. Well?'

People had gathered round me. Dale was close by and Brockley was beside her. Also beside me and very grave of face was Peter Dickson, formerly the tutor to Harry and to Ben Atbrigge. Dickson was now the mentor for Harry and Ben alike as they took up the burdens of adulthood. He was becoming bent of back and his hair was completely white, but he was still a capable man and was a valued instructor in music.

Harry and Ben were hovering close to him and beside them was Gladys Morgan. Gladys was a Welshwoman that Brockley and I had rescued from a charge of witchcraft, long, long ago. She was ill-tempered, with a shocking habit of hurling lurid curses at people she disliked, but she was also very gifted with herbal medicines. Her skills in that direction had annoyed vicars and physicians alike. After we had rescued her, she attached herself to my household and she was still there, clinging like a burr. Gladys had not been young when we first met her. She was now heaven-only-knew how old; very lame, gap-toothed, and doubtless as ill-tempered as ever. She wasn't smiling, any more than anyone else. Behind her, some of the maids were clustered. Standing aside was the mightily built John Hawthorn, still brushing at his clothes and shaking dust and dog hairs out of his thick queue of hair. Beside him and contrasting with him was his assistant, the short, bald Ben Flood.

Why was no one smiling? Had my heart been heavy not just on account of Aunt Tabitha, whose death lay behind me, but because of something lying ahead of me, here?

It was Dr Joynings who said, 'Mistress Stannard, I have come because Master Atbrigge sent for me. Your son, Master Harry had need of me, so the message said. I know something of the matter but I think it best if Harry himself . . .'

He looked enquiringly at Harry. I saw Dickson gently push my son forward. And then Harry told me.

'Mother, it isn't the news I'd ever want to greet you with! My wedding . . . there will be no wedding. Eleanor has had a riding accident. She's dead, Mother, she's dead . . .' He couldn't go on. He just stood there and, though silently, he wept.

SIX
The Unreasonable Pattern

It was Brockley who took charge. He led Harry indoors, with Ben following. Dickson said, 'Madam, Dr Joynings, Master Harry is in a desperate state. He heard the news yesterday morning and he went off, already distressed enough, to . . . to see her, to see her body, and to say goodbye to her, and then he came back looking for all the world as though he'd been gazing into hell. He's told me and the vicar what the matter is, but I think it best if I hold my tongue for the moment and let Master Harry tell you himself. He's been frantic to see you. He wanted to ride out to meet you but we somehow persuaded him to wait.'

'That was wise,' said Joynings. 'Such news – oh dear, what terrible news! – is best spoken where there's shelter, ways of ministering to people.'

Around us, the crowd was dispersing. Flood was making for the kitchen door and Phoebe was chivvying the other maids in after him, telling them to get about their work. Dr Joynings, Dale and Dickson came indoors with me, with Gladys at our heels. We went in through the door that led straight into the great hall. It was empty. 'Master Brockleywill have taken Master Harry to his room,' said Dickson.

'So I did.' Brockley came in, from the door to the vestibule and the stairs. 'Madam, your son wants to see you and Dr Joynings. Will you come to him? He has told me something . . . this is serious, very serious.'

Brockley's face was white and few things could do that to Brockley. I stepped past him and out of the hall and took the stairs at a run, with plump Dr Joynings panting just behind me.

Harry was sitting on the side of his bed. As we came in,

he looked up at us, wanly. 'I am sorry, Mother, Dr Joynings, that I made such an exhibition of myself down in the courtyard.'

'Never mind about that. My dear boy . . .' But Joynings seemed lost for further words.

I sat down beside Harry. 'Brockley says you have told him something serious. I understand that Dr Joynings has already heard it. Will you now repeat it for me?'

'I have to. I must.' Whatever had so whitened Brockley's face had done the same to Harry's. I could tell that he was holding himself together with a giant effort. 'It was yesterday,' he said. 'In the morning. Eleanor's elder brother, John Blake, came to fetch me. He had ridden so hard that his horse was blown when he got here. He almost fell out of his saddle in the courtyard; Arthur looked after the horse . . .'

'Harry!'

'Yes, Mother, that's what Brockley said when I was trying to tell him but I hardly knew how to get it out. It's so hard . . . John said that he and his parents knew how much I cared for Eleanor and I had to know at once; that's why he came here in such haste. He told me that Eleanor had ridden out that morning, on her brown mare – Brown Bess is so gentle, no one could understand . . .'

'What happened?' I said, to urge him on.

'She went out to ride for an hour in the morning sunshine. While the dew was still on the grass, she said. She meant to be home to break her fast. She didn't come. John became anxious and so did all the family; Eleanor keeps to what she says, bless her, that's what John said to me. He and his brother Richard went to look for her; they know her favourite rides. They took different directions and John picked the right one. He found her. She was lying under a tree. Brown Bess was grazing nearby, reins trailing. John picked Eleanor up and looked at her and the back of her head was all broken in; he said it was all blood and splintered bone . . . oh, God . . . and he looked about and found blood on the trunk of a tree. You don't usually get the back of your head broken if you're thrown forward, but if a horse rears, John said, then you could be flung backwards. It seemed that Brown Bess must have reared in fright, though she'd never done such a thing in all her life before.

'John said he shouted, and Richard wasn't very far away and heard him. Richard came, and they caught Brown Bess, and laid Eleanor across her own saddle and brought her home. They couldn't imagine what could have made the mare panic. Brown Bess didn't seem upset; she wasn't like a horse that had lately had a terrible fright; she wasn't sweating or nervous; she was easy to catch. Anyway, they got Eleanor home and then John came to tell me . . . I went back to Cobbold House with him. Eleanor had been placed on her bed. She hadn't yet been washed or laid out properly; they'd sent to Woking for women skilled in that, and the women hadn't yet arrived.

'Her younger sister, Margaret – she came running when she heard my voice and she seemed to want to say something to me, but her father pulled her away and hushed her, told her not to talk nonsense. I didn't know what it was all about and I couldn't worry about it then. Master Blake took me into Eleanor's bedchamber. He left me with her to say goodbye.

'Oh, poor Eleanor! There was a towel under her head. I lifted her head . . . I just wanted to see properly what had happened to her. Her hair is thick but it hadn't protected her. It was stiff with blood. The back of her head was all dried blood and splinters. Splinters of bone as well as bark! I felt ill! I laid her back. I was holding her a little awkwardly, with my right hand grasping her crown, and my left at the back of her neck. I was being so careful. I wanted to set her down just as she was before, and my left forefinger . . .'

There was a pause. Harry turned his face away from me so that I might not see his tears. 'It slid into a . . . a hole,' he said. 'Just where her neck joined her head. Something had been driven in there, Mother. But no one had spoken of it. Then I thought, what about Margaret? I went out of the room and insisted on hearing what Margaret wanted to say to me and yes, it seemed that she had helped to lay Eleanor down on the bed and make her seemly, and she had found what I did, only her parents wouldn't listen and her father told her not to imagine things, not to magnify a tragic accident into a great big drama.

'I said that Margaret wasn't imagining things. I wanted her father to come and feel the place for himself, but he shook his head and said it's nonsense, that no doubt there was some protruding piece of broken branch that might account for what I had felt; he wasn't going to poke his fingers into that wound, not for anyone. Then I said I wanted to see where the accident had happened. John took me there. I saw the tree and the blood on the bark, and there was nothing, *nothing* protruding, nothing on the ground – no broken piece of branch – nothing to account for that . . . that hole. It's not so easy to find, as a matter of fact, the whole back of her head is broken in and in all that welter it's true that one little hole can easily be missed. It's just where the head meets the neck . . . I can't bear to talk about Eleanor like this, as though she were just a thing, when it's Eleanor . . . I found that hole by chance and so did Margaret. What do we do, Mother? Dr Joynings, what is one *supposed* to do?'

'If there is anything puzzling about her death, there must be an inquest,' said Dr Joynings. 'That is required by Her Majesty's law. You yourself want any mystery explained, do you not?'

'Did you see any footprints round about?' I asked. 'Hoofprints?'

'Thousands,' said Harry bitterly. 'People ride that way often. For the Blakes, it's a quick route from Cobbold Hall to some common land where the Blake brothers like to go hawking. Visitors to the Blakes often come that way, too. As for footprints, there were mine and John's and, if there were any others, how could anyone tell which was whose?

'The Blakes know now that that . . . *hole* . . . is there, but they don't want to believe that it matters. The women from Woking will find it but if they say anything, Eleanor's father will just go on talking about bits of broken branch. And that isn't all.'

Harry was trying hard to recover himself. 'The mare isn't given to shying or being skittish. I've ridden out with Eleanor, often, and seen for myself how quiet her horse is. When I got there, Mistress Blake was hysterical, wanting the mare to be put down, but her husband was saying that Brown Bess never shied or reared and if she'd done it this time, there must have been a reason. Everyone agrees that Brown Bess wasn't likely to rear without a good reason. But what reason?'

His gaze was flickering back and forth between us, as though he hoped that one of us would suddenly produce an answer.

'It must have been something sudden and frightening,' he said, 'but what sudden and frightening things are there in a quiet English woodland? A bird going up with a rush of wings? A pigeon makes a great whirr and flap, and jays give noisy alarm calls. But Bess would have been used to things like that. A falling tree, perhaps . . . but there wasn't a fallen tree in sight. A stray dog, vicious, attacking . . . but what dog? Whose? There have been no reports of stray dogs. A deer could have burst across the track, there are deer in those woods, but Brown Bess would be used to that kind of thing as well. I asked John and he said that in that case, the mare would just stop and snort. Or flick an ear. She knows all about deer. It makes no sense. There's nothing to explain why Bess should have reared and *what was it that could drive in so deeply?* Whatever it was should have been still on the tree or else fallen to the ground, and it wasn't. There was nothing to account for any of it, not Brown Bess rearing, or the wound that I found. Nothing at all. *Nothing.*'

'You are thinking of a human agency, aren't you?' I said.

Harry looked at me, his dark eyes still bright with tears but also angry. 'Yes. I am. But why? *Why?* She was so beautiful, my Eleanor. And so sweet. All her family loved her. Her father, Reginald Blake, looks as if he has been stunned. Her brothers are . . . are stricken. Margaret is angry too, as I am, and as heartbroken – poor lass, she's just fifteen – she can't stop crying. All the time she was telling me about that horrible hole, she was talking through her tears. The youngest girl, Susannah, she's only twelve and she keeps crying too but, even with tears streaming down her face, she keeps trying to comfort her sister. She's a nice child. They're nice people! Mistress Blake stopped being hysterical in the end, but she could still only sit in the corner of a settle and sob. I think she and her husband feel as if the ground under their feet has fallen away.'

I knew now why my heart had felt so heavy as we rode home. It was said that some of the Faldene family had a trace of what Gladys sometimes referred to as the Sight. Perhaps I was one of them, I thought drearily, though if so, this was the first sign of it. I had sensed something, I thought; the new calamity had thrown its shadow ahead.

Human agency. The moment those words had shaped themselves inside my head, I had known that it was true. Eleanor should not, could not, have met her injuries by accident. Nor could my aunt Tabitha possibly have taken her own life. I had known that all along. There was a pattern here, an unreasonable pattern, but there all the same.

I had no idea, none whatsoever, of its meaning. I could of course warn everyone close to me to be careful of themselves, but even that would be difficult. They would want to know what kind of danger it was that made me recommend such caution, and I had no answers.

For the moment, I could do nothing but cope with the immediate present. I told Harry that I would have his meals sent to him; it would be best, just for today, that he should keep to his room. Perhaps, presently, he would like the company of Ben. Then I left Dr Joynings, as a man of God, to offer the consolations of the church. He would pray with my son and he would know what words could offer comfort. After the vicar had gone, I thought, I would myself have to take on the task of helping Harry through this, his first deep grief. Inside me, there was now a feeling of dread, like a little cold snake in my stomach. I shivered. What could I do about it? Nothing, that I could see.

In the days that followed, we all did our best to help Harry but with poor success. He seemed to have withdrawn himself from us. Even Ben, his close friend, could make nothing of him. Ben was now our steward, but he was still young, as was Harry, and they were old friends. In the past, sometimes, boy-like, in the hall or in the garden, one of them would pounce on the other and they would have a wrestling match. But not now.

'Harry doesn't want to,' Ben said when I mentioned this to him. 'He's too remote. I think he is grieving too much.'

I tried to talk to Harry. I said conventional things like *It will pass one day. You won't always feel like this*, and Brockley, also trying to talk to him, reminded him that he had a lifetime still to come. *You probably can't realize that now, but you will in time.*

When that begins to happen, I told Harry, backing Brockley up, please don't fight against it. It is part of nature.

'If you had been the one to die,' said Brockley, backing me up in turn, 'you wouldn't have wanted Eleanor or anyone else (*even me*, I put in at this point) to grieve for ever.' Harry said he understood and he knew we were right. 'But *what really happened to Eleanor? I want to know!*'

There was no inquest on Eleanor. Someone pointed out to her parents that, although there were no protruding branches or stumps of branches to explain the curious hole in the damage to her skull, the tree she had struck had roots that protruded above ground. These had some knotty points that might account for it, if she had landed on them with force. Her family decided that this was the answer. No other was possible, anyway. The local constable accepted that.

Harry, with savagery in his voice, said he didn't agree; that the tree roots just weren't knobbly enough. 'The Blakes don't feel equal to coping with an enquiry, that's what it is!'

Eleanor was buried. Harry did not attend. If he had already been her husband, custom would have bidden him to stay at home. He did so now, honouring all that might have been. Her parents were there, of course, and her brothers and sisters. Her mother could not stop weeping and nor could Margaret, who was clearly broken-hearted. Kind little Susannah held her sister tightly throughout the whole ceremony.

Meanwhile, the summer weather was effulgent. Crops grew, young stock flourished, birds encouraged fledglings to fly and made ready to rear second broods. I paid a visit to my former ward Mildred, who was now married to my old friend Christopher Spelton and lived at West Leys Farm, two hours' ride away. There was happy news there, of a new child on the way. The whole world hummed with love and procreation, except for Harry.

What should have been his wedding day came and went. Harry remained withdrawn from us all. I thought he was angry as well as grief-stricken and once, finding him alone in the tack room, just taking his saddle from its peg in readiness to take his horse Prince out for exercise, I asked him.

'Angry? Yes, I am! Master Blake just says it was an accident and won't even *think* about that deep wound. I think he's frightened, Mother. And what's more, I think he believes . . . I shouldn't tell you this. I'm sorry.'

I decided that it was time to be bracing. 'Tell me at once! I insist!'

Harry glared at me. 'All right! He let out to me, before you came home, that he doesn't really approve of you; because of the way you have worked for the queen, undertaken duties for her that most women aren't asked to do. I am guessing, but I think that at heart he fears that what happened to Eleanor has something to do with you and he . . . he backs away from that.'

And with that, he seized Prince's bridle as well as the saddle, and marched out of the tack room in a way that said *don't follow me.*

He took Prince out and brought him home two hours later, at a gallop and soaked with sweat. In the stable yard he encountered Brockley. I was in the hall, with the door open and, although I didn't see their encounter, I heard it. I heard Brockley, without any consideration for Harry's state of mourning, bellow, *'What in God's name do you mean, sir, by bringing a horse home in this state? Those are spur marks; there's blood on them! If you were but two years younger, I'd thrash you for this! Get indoors and I'll see to him!'* Brockley then, presumably, led Prince away to unsaddle him and rub him down, because Harry came into the hall almost at once, with a thunderous expression on his face.

Later that day, Brockley said to me, 'We have got to think of some way to distract Master Harry, madam. I found spur marks on Prince. This won't do. He has to begin to remember that there are other things in the world besides his grief.'

'You were harsh with him over the way he brought his horse home. I heard you.'

'Yes, I was. It will do him no good to be treated with gloved hands just because he is in mourning. That won't help him out of it.'

'You are probably right, but what can we do?'

'I'll think of something,' said Brockley.

Then one morning, little Bess, the brightest of our young maidservants, came to me with her eyes full of laughter, and said, 'Madam, you should see what Master Brockley is up to in the tack room. You should just see!'

I didn't ask what Bess was doing in the tack room. She had probably stepped out in the hope of a little dalliance with Eddie. Phoebe had reprimanded her about that, but I hoped it would lead to a wedding – though preferably not too soon, for Harry's sake.

I went to the tack room, and there I found Harry, Ben, and all six of my grooms. I always had a good number of grooms, who acted as menservants when required. Now, they were mostly sitting on the stools that they used while they were cleaning saddlery, or else perching on the edge of the square table in the middle of the room and looking with great interest at what Brockley had pinned up on the wall. This was a sheet on which someone – presumably Brockley – had drawn a life-size outline of a man. He had also marked various points of interest and was busy explaining to his audience that *this* marks the heart and *here's* the throat and, if you are aiming with a bow or using a sword or a dagger, *here* is where you thrust. Get it right and your man will fall like a log. Don't worry about the blood.'

He paused when I came in and said soberly, 'Madam, Master Harry thinks that the death of his lady may point to some kind of spite – against him, or you or this house. I hope he is wrong but there is nothing like being prepared. I was once a soldier and there are things I know that may be useful for Harry and Ben and these other good men to know as well. I know that most of them already practise archery, but I think they should practise with blades as well. Most of them have old swords or daggers, or knives, at least.'

'I agree,' I said. I looked for a spare stool and failed to find one, but Abel Parsons at once got up and gave me his stool, which I accepted. 'Continue,' I said to Brockley.

'Madam,' said Brockley, 'I would never expect that you would yourself . . .'

'Find myself fighting with sword or dagger. I should hope not. But I am still interested. After all, I take it that all this is in case you have to fight in my defence. Please go on.'

Brockley obeyed. It was one of the most interesting and enlightening mornings I had ever spent. It was also one of the most disturbing. Because of my strange career as an agent, I had taken to wearing open-fronted gowns, with hidden pouches stitched inside. In these, I could carry such things as picklocks, a purse of coins and a small but very sharp dagger. It was in a sheath, but I always made sure that it would slide smoothly out of the sheath, should I need it at speed. I carried it in case I ever had to defend myself. I had never had to use it, I hoped I never would, and I had never until that day enquired into the precise details of how to handle a blade.

I now listened attentively to Brockley's instructions on the proper use of weapons. It would do me no harm to know. If any danger were to threaten me . . . Deep within me, the little cold snake stirred again.

Brockley set up archery targets in one of my meadows and arranged regular weapon practices, insisting that my son joined them. After a couple of weeks, Harry did seem more normal. Distraction would work in the end, I thought.

That was two days before I witnessed Harry and Ben chance to come across each other in the rose garden, walk together for a short distance, and then . . .

As so often in the past, Ben said something, probably provocative, and pounced on Harry in the old playful way, and Harry brushed him off with a vicious backhander that knocked Ben backwards into one of Hugh's favourite rose bushes, sending up a cloud of petals and surely shaking Ben's teeth in their sockets.

And that, I decided, was enough. In moments I was in the rose garden. Ben was getting to his feet and Harry was striding away from him, straight towards me. He gave me a nod of recognition and I think would have marched on past me, except that I seized his arm and stopped him.

'My God,' I said, *'that will do!'*

'Mother . . .'

'Don't think polite noises will get you out of this. Listen to me. I know how bitter you are about Eleanor. I understand . . .'

'No, Mother, you don't. I hardly know myself how much I am grieving. What I am mostly is *angry*. No one will heed me when I try to say that she was murdered. I am sure she was, but no one will listen. Nothing is being done . . .!'

'I doubt if anything can be done. There is nothing to get hold of – no trace. But never mind that. What I mind about is you, and I am tired of understanding, and holding off from you because you are distressed. I know about the time you brought Prince home in a sweat with blood on him through your spurs, and I know what Brockley said to you. I heard it!'

'Mother . . .!'

'Be quiet. If ever you do such a thing again, then Brockley has my permission to thrash you as he would have done two years ago. I shall tell him so, this very morning. As for Ben . . .' Ben was still on the path behind Harry, waiting for us to get out of his way, and tenderly feeling his jaw. 'As for Ben, he is still here . . .' I beckoned to him, '. . . and you will apologize to him, here in my presence. If you ever do such a thing to him again, then once more, I will ask Brockley to discipline you. Is that clear? However grief-stricken you are, however angry you are, you don't take it out on your horse or on Ben *or on anyone else*. If you want to rage and curse, retire to your room and do it in private. In the presence of others, you will damn well behave like a normal young man. Here is Ben. You know what to say.'

To do Harry justice, he apologized to Ben as though he meant it, and I expect he did. After that, though he still had silent days, he sometimes smiled and, gradually, it seemed, normal life was reclaiming him.

One thing that certainly did Harry good was taking an interest in our trotters' stud. I had established this some years ago, wanting to add to Harry's inheritance, whenever

the time should come, and taking advantage of the way
that the fast, showy breed of trotters had become so popular
as harness animals.

Whenever I returned from an absence, I always wanted a
report on it. The chief stud groom Laurence Miller had been
sent to me by Cecil and Walsingham, and also had the task
of keeping watch over me. He had to report to them on the
events surrounding me. I didn't like this, or Miller, very much.
He was tall and cold-eyed and never seemed to smile, even
when surrounded by other people all laughing at the same
joke. However, he did happen to be a thoroughly competent
stud groom. This time, once I had drawn breath after coping
with the first stage of Harry's anguish, I summoned Miller
and he had much to report.

We had sold three young, matched pairs of trotters for very
good prices indeed and also sold a number of single animals
at auction and they too had fetched healthy prices. The stud
was becoming well known. One of the older grooms had retired
and gone away. A replacement had been found, a young lad by
the name of Andrew Lomax. He was the son of a horseman
employed by Sir Edward Heron, our county sheriff. He was
one of twelve children. ('At the last count,' said Miller, straight-
faced as usual. 'I believe the number may have gone up by
now.') As soon as he turned fourteen, young Andrew had been
told to make his own way in the world, and a place had
been found for him as a groom at a hiring stables just outside
the town of Reigate. The owner of the stables had lately died
and the business was closed. The horses had been sold off and
Andrew Lomax, bereft of a position, had applied to us.

'I've checked up on him,' said Miller. 'He's who he says he
is. He's asked permission to visit his family occasionally –
seems they find it hard to make ends meet, and no wonder!
– and he wants to help out. Lomax is about seventeen now.
He has a good heart and he certainly has a way with horses.
In fact, I think he likes all animals – he's even made friends
with my dog and Foggy doesn't make friends with everyone.'

This was certainly true. Miller's dog was a lean, leggy
animal of mixed ancestry. It was well behaved among human
beings it knew, but rarely friendly. It would move away from

caresses, though its smooth grey coat invited them. Miller said that his dog was invisible in foggy weather, which was why he had named him Foggy. He often referred to his canine friend in affectionate terms as his Foggy Doggie. It sounded like the name of a cosy, flop-eared spaniel, but Foggy Doggie's yellow eyes were the eyes of a killer. He was a useful dog to have beside you if you feared intruders.

'That's quite a testimonial!' I said.

As well as all this, Miller had been negotiating for a new stallion. We had to change stallions regularly because we often kept promising fillies for breeding and they couldn't, of course, breed with their own sires. He had his eye on a good-looking dapple grey, nearly sixteen hands. He would like Master Harry to come with him to inspect it.

I was in the Little Parlour, reading, when Brockley came to tell me about that. I said, 'While he's having Andrew Lomax introduced to him, and Miller is talking to him about the price of oats and the latest fashions in harness, and taking him along to inspect the grey stallion, he won't be thinking about Eleanor. Good.'

'He's mending,' Brockley said.

'Yes, he is,' I said. Then, suddenly, I heard myself add, 'Brockley, it must have been a very strong feeling that moved you, all of a sudden, to pin up the shape of a man in the tack room and round up nearly every man at Hawkswood and tell them how to get a successful result with a dagger or sword? It was a most interesting morning – but do you really fear that there is animosity against me from some quarter?'

Brockley looked me in the eyes. 'Yes, I do. Madam, as you know, I have never been in the habit of commenting in any way on your family – on things connected with your family. But I am neither deaf nor blind. Your Aunt Tabitha was a devout woman. She had a beautiful prayer book, bound in white leather, and Agnes once told me that there was a prie-dieu in the marital bedchamber and that she had often seen the mistress praying there. Also, I think she was a strong-minded lady. Such women rarely kill themselves when they are widowed. She was one who would accept the will of God and simply carry on. She was not alone, after all. She had a houseful of servants, she had daughters she could go to, she had her son Francis to advise her. I found it hard to believe in that verdict of suicide while her mind was unbalanced due to grief. I saw no signs of excessive grief in her, and certainly no signs of madness.'

'And you can't imagine her getting up at night to brew a hemlock potion for herself?'

'No, madam.'

'I agree, Brockley. Neither can I. But . . . Eleanor?'

'She was not a relative, but she was going to be one, and your son, Master Harry, loved her very much.'

I had laid my book down on my knee. Now I picked it up and slammed it on to the nearest small table. 'Brockley, just what are we talking about?'

'I don't know. But I can't believe your aunt was suicidal, and Master Harry does believe that Mistress Eleanor's wound was suspicious. It's all wrong.'

'But *what* is wrong?'

'I don't *know*,' Brockley repeated, almost fretfully. 'But it . . . it makes a . . . a pattern. And I don't like it.'

Pattern. The very word that had occurred to me. And here was the first sign that the people around me were working things out for themselves.

'I don't like it, either,' I said, in a small voice. 'But it doesn't make sense.'

'No, it doesn't,' said Brockley. 'It's just an unreasonable pattern. It makes me nervous, that's all.'

I agreed with him, wholeheartedly, but because we knew nothing that could explain the mystery, we were forced to leave it there. At the end of July, however, enlightenment came.

SEVEN
Words of Warning

It was the second of July. I was in the East Room, in mid-morning, tackling the necessary but tiresome business of checking the household accounts for the previous month. There had been too much usage of candles, considering that this was the time of bright mornings and long evenings. Nor could I understand why John Hawthorn had bought in so much expensive sugar . . .

Or no. He had done that because he was expecting to prepare a welcome feast for Master Harry's bride, and his assistant Ben Flood would probably want to create one of the marchpane marvels that he so much enjoyed preparing. How Eleanor's ghost seemed to haunt us, I thought. Her shade even seemed to inhabit things like ledgers.

I didn't want to think about Eleanor and I was quite pleased to be interrupted by Ben Atbrigge, who informed me that a stranger had arrived, asking for me.

I laid down my quill. 'What is his name?'

Evasively, Ben said, 'He's alone, madam. He has no attendant, but he is finely dressed and his horse is well-bred, a good dark bay, near sixteen hands . . .'

'Atbrigge, please get to the point.'

'He looks quite astonishingly like Master Harry,' said the respectful future steward, who had been wrestling with Harry in the rose garden before breakfast that morning, imperilling my dear Hugh's favourite crimson blooms. 'Madam, he says his name is Julien de la Roche.'

There was a silence, while we looked at each other. Ben had inherited his father's thick brown hair, though Ben wore his cut short, not tied back into a queue as Atbrigge senior had done. But he had not inherited Daniel Atbrigge's slate-grey eyes. Ben's eyes were dark, not brown, but like deep water. At the moment, they looked very deep indeed. I said, 'I don't think I have ever mentioned Julien de la Roche to you, but I have told Harry about him and no doubt Harry has passed his knowledge on.'

'Yes,' said Ben. 'He has.'

'Julien de la Roche,' I said, 'is his half-brother. It's a complicated tale. I married Matthew de la Roche as my second husband and lived in France with him for a while. We were deeply in love, but he was a Catholic, an avowed enemy to Queen Elizabeth, and it poisoned our union.'

I paused, not sure whether to go on, but Ben said, 'I know all about it. Did you not have to come back to England alone for some reason, and then, while you were here, the queen annulled your marriage? And then informed you that de la Roche was dead?'

'Yes. She also arranged for Matthew to be told that *I* was dead. So I married again, my dear Hugh. You never knew Hugh, but you would have liked him, Ben, I know you would. Meanwhile, Matthew also remarried and Julien is the son of that marriage. Later, I had occasion to visit France again, and there I met Matthew once more, briefly, and Harry is the son of that meeting. And so, they are brothers. But not only that.'

'He was – and presumably still is – one of a trio of pirates who have been robbing English and Spanish ships impartially,' said Ben calmly. 'They are wanted men. I was surprised to see him in this country.'

Ben was younger than Harry, though not by much, but in some ways he seemed older, perhaps because he had been through tragedy, had known danger and betrayal in a way that Harry had not. He sounded now as though he was ten years older than his actual age.

'Quite,' I said. 'And now he is waiting – where is he waiting, by the way?'

'In the hall, Mistress Stannard. I asked Hawthorn to provide some refreshments for him.'

'Quite right. Well, he can't be left in the hall for ever. And nor,' I said thoughtfully, 'do I want to talk to him there. It's too public. I can't imagine why he is here, but it may well be something . . . delicate, private . . . something of that kind, anyway. Fetch him here, Ben. Bring him yourself, and the refreshments as well. I may need sustenance too!'

Ben went away. I waited, trying to compose myself. What Julien de la Roche could want with me was beyond my imagining. I had never met him; I merely knew *of* him. He had been – and perhaps still was – the captain of a pirate vessel with the unsuitably charming name of *Silver Mermaid*. What in Heaven's name could he be doing here in Hawkswood? He would have known about me, that was likely enough, from his parents and also from the Mercer brothers.

Yes, the Mercer brothers. Captain Julien had been their partner. I began to wonder. The Mercers had good reason to dislike me. I was the one who had set the law on their track. I was responsible for the death of their mother and one of their other associates, and I had had a fine haul of treasure seized by the authorities. Could they be behind the hateful things that were happening around me? Just what had brought their partner in crime, Julien de la Roche, here now?

My maunderings had got that far when Ben reappeared, followed by a taller man, Captain Julien presumably. Behind the captain came my head housemaid, Phoebe, with a refreshments tray. I did not rise, but sat back. I could not regard Captain Julien as an honoured guest, entitled to such a respectful welcome. I was Mistress Ursula Stannard, a lady of mature age, receiving an unexpected and probably unfriendly visitor. I would remain enthroned and he would do the bowing. Then I would see what he had to say for himself.

'Master Julien de la Roche, madam,' said Ben, once more the steward of the house, and stood aside to let the visitor enter, which he did with aplomb, hat in hand, bowing as he came. Phoebe slipped past him into the room, without getting between us. Her tray was laden with a wine jug, two glasses, a dish of redcurrant and cream layered dainties (one of Ben Flood's specialities), and a plate of what I recognized as slices of the mutton pie we had had at supper the previous evening. It was as good eaten cold as it was when hot. She put the tray down on a small table and made a quiet exit.

I, meanwhile, was moistening my lips and trying to think

how to address Julien de la Roche. The sight of him had set my mind reeling.

I tried to command myself, to look at him properly. He wasn't actually the image of Harry; Ben had exaggerated. He was neatly proportioned, without Harry's angularity. Both Harry and his father were handsome in the same way, with strong facial bones in which there was a curious and oddly attractive trace of asymmetry. There was no asymmetry in Captain Julien's features. But he had the height and the prominent cheekbones and long chin, and his colouring was the same, for he too had black hair and very dark eyes. He wasn't Harry's double. But there was enough resemblance to stagger me, just the same.

It was he who took the initiative. 'Mistress Stannard, I am happy to meet you.' His English was effortless, though he had a French accent. 'I see that my appearance has surprised you. We met your son Harry in the passageway to this room and I knew at once that he must be my half-brother. Just before his death, my father told me that such a brother existed, here in England. I hope I may talk to him later. Please be easy. May I be seated?'

I found my tongue. One must be courteous to a guest. 'Yes, please do.' From the tray, I selected the dish of redcurrant and cream patties and offered them to him. Ben was still hovering and I told him to pour wine for us. He did so, and then went out, no doubt to find Harry. Resorting to the conventions, I enquired: 'What may I do for you, Master . . . er . . . Captain . . . Julien?'

'Ah, yes. You will have heard of me as Captain Julien. Do please address me as such, if you are comfortable with that. I am not at sea at the moment. My ship is laid up and I intend to change her name. It's said to be bad luck, but I'm prepared to risk it. My friends the Mercer brothers have also laid up their ships; we are not trading this season.'

I noted, without comment, that he had used the word *trading*. As far as the Mercer brothers were concerned, it was a euphemism for boarding ships – any ships, Spanish, English, French, as long as they were carrying treasure – and emptying their holds. Here, in my East Room, drinking

my wine and eating one of Ben Flood's juicy creations, was
a pirate captain.

'Madam,' said this improbable guest, 'I have come on a
distressing errand—'

A knock on the door interrupted us. The door was then
pushed open, revealing Brockley on the threshold. Harry had
no doubt sent him. I signalled to him to enter, glad of his
support. As he came in, I said, 'This is Roger Brockley,
my personal manservant and my right hand. He is in all my
counsels. Brockley, be seated.'

'I know of him, madam,' Captain Julien said to me. He rose
to return Brockley's bow. 'Good morning, Master Brockley.
Madam, I also know of the . . . the duties you have performed
for your good sister, Queen Elizabeth, and of his part in them.'

He sat down again. Brockley sat down too. Brockley's face
was blank but I could feel him exuding silent dislike. Captain
Julien turned to me with a grave face.

'Madam, as I was about to say, I am here on a distressing
errand. A moment ago, I mentioned how I came to know that
I had a half-brother, Harry. Because of him, I have broken
away from my former friends, the Mercer brothers. They are
my friends no longer – though *they* are not aware of it.
All they know is that I have declined to help them in their
scheme – it is the reason why they are not at sea this year – to
avenge the death of their mother, by harming you.'

'And just what do you mean by that?' asked Brockley
ominously.

Captain Julien turned to him. 'It may have already begun.
I don't know. I do know what they were planning . . .'

'What were they planning?' I asked. In my stomach, the
cold snake awoke again, and coiled and twisted. I looked at
Brockley and knew that we were both thinking about the
same things. Aunt Tabitha. Eleanor. Harry rarely spoke of
Eleanor now, but on the few occasions when he had, it was
to speak of her injury and to maintain yet again that a knob
on a tree root hadn't convinced him.

He hadn't pressed the matter because the Blakes, distraught
beyond reason, would not accept any other answer, and it
was most unlikely that an inquest jury would bring in any

other verdict than accident. But I knew he was haunted by the memory of what his exploring fingers had told him. I waited for Captain Julien's reply.

'It is a terrible scheme, madam,' said Captain Julien. 'I want to warn you. I have come to warn you. I swore to the Mercers that I wouldn't do so, but you have done no harm to any member of my family; on the contrary, your family and mine are one. Your son Harry and I are half-brothers. So I have chosen to break my faith with them, to break my word. I am not in the habit of doing such a thing, I assure you. The circumstances are . . . shall we say, unusual. The Mercer brothers, by the way, presently suppose that I am in France, at my chateau, Blanchepierre. You no doubt remember it.'

I did. It was a beautiful place, on the banks of the Loire, a gracious house where I would have been very happy as its chatelaine, if only things had been different; if only Matthew had not hated Queen Elizabeth so much. For a moment, such a pang went through me that I couldn't speak. I nodded instead.

'I was sure you would,' said Captain Julien. 'I said I was going there. They have no idea that I am here.'

'So what *is* this precious scheme?' Brockley barked.

After a pause, during which I said nothing but looked at Captain Julien enquiringly, he said, 'They are angry, madam. You probably didn't know them all that well. They are fond of treasure, oh yes, but they also have passionate hearts when it comes to those they love and they are capable of more remorseless anger than you, perhaps, can imagine. I have worked with them but I have also feared them, believe me. Now, you would be wise to fear them too. Their scheme, madam, is first to break your heart, and then come for you. They intend to break your heart by causing death or injury to people who are known to you and yours. They propose to begin with the outer circle, if I may so phrase it, of your friends and acquaintances, and then to cause the deaths of those nearer and dearer to you, whose deaths will grieve you bitterly. Until, when your life is laid waste, when everyone you have ever cared for, whether much or little, is gone, they will seek you out and you too will die.'

There was a dreadful silence.

After all, what Captain Julien had just said was difficult to take in. Also, he had said it in such a quiet, calm voice. *When your life is laid waste, when everyone you have ever cared for, whether much or little, is gone, they will seek you out and you too will die.*

He might have been saying, *better have that leaning beech tree down before the autumn gales begin,* or *look for fresh lemons when next you go to the market.* His tone was as mundane as that.

But the little cold snake was there. It had a voice. It whispered to me.

Remember Aunt Tabitha, who once looked after you. Harshly, perhaps, but you were clothed and fed and taught, just the same. And remember Eleanor Blake, who should have been your daughter-in-law. The girl who was betrothed to your son. The girl he loved. The girl you were beginning to love, as well.

Brockley was the first to speak. 'They will never get away with it. There is too much of it, too many chances for things to go wrong. And things would go wrong, before long. They would be caught before their scheme was well begun. We are not fools. I will tell you now, Captain Julien, we hardly needed your warning. We have already realized that something of that sort is afoot.'

'Yes,' I said in strangled tones. 'I fancy that their so-called scheme – a plain word for a nightmare plan – has indeed begun. Aunt Tabitha. Possibly Eleanor. That is what Brockley thinks, is it not, Brockley?'

He nodded and then explained them to Captain Julien. 'Mistress Stannard was brought up by an uncle and aunt. The uncle recently died – well, that was probably natural – would you agree, madam?'

'Yes, I would. But after the funeral, his wife, Aunt Tabitha, took poison,' I said. 'A most unlikely thing for her to do; she was a pious woman. A young girl called Eleanor Blake, who was betrothed to Harry, was recently killed by a fall from a horse. There was no inquest; there was no reason, then, for anyone to attack her. But there was an oddity about the injury, all the same.'

'Was there any stranger in the house when your aunt died, Mistress Stannard?' Captain Julien enquired.

'Good God, yes!' Brockley spoke sharply. 'The fellow who lost his way and had a lame horse and came asking for shelter! What was his name, madam?'

'Nicholas Trent,' I said. 'In the employment of Sir Ambrose Walsh, a Devonshire man. He was carrying a message to someone in Little Dene. That is a village near my uncle and aunt's house,' I explained.

'Did he say the name of the person he was going to, in this Little Dene?' asked Captain Julien.

'I don't think so,' I said.

He nodded. 'I fancy that if you were to enquire in Little Dene, you would find that no one there has ever heard of Nicholas Trent, or of Sir Ambrose Walsh. And that if you were to make enquiries in Devon, you either wouldn't find a Sir Ambrose Walsh at all, or if you did, that he would never have heard of Nicholas Trent, either. What did Trent look like?'

Brockley and I consulted each other, wordlessly. Brockley said, 'Dark. Weather-beaten. Very dark hair.'

'Walnut juice,' Captain Julien said tersely. 'Eyes?'

'Light. Sea-coloured,' I told him, and he nodded again.

'I think that was Stephen Mercer,' he said.

Brockley and I both gaped. 'It can't have been!' I said, and then I recalled how I had at the time felt that I had seen Master Trent somewhere before. And now I also recalled that Stephen Mercer had had hazel eyes like his brother and sister, but lighter. Yes, in a face browned by walnut juice, beneath black eyebrows, they might well look sea-coloured. Stephen had been clean-shaven, too. Trent had had a black beard. A beard can change a man's face to a remarkable degree. And it was true; I had not known either of the brothers well.

'It could have been,' I said slowly.

Diffidently, Captain Julien said, 'Did he by any chance encourage you to talk of family matters, and somehow bring Arabella Mercer, their sister, into the conversation?'

'Arabella? No, he didn't. He didn't talk very much at all,' I said.

'Well, it might have been difficult to do without putting his disguise at risk,' said Julien. 'I daresay he thought better of it. It's only that the brothers are anxious to know what has become of their sister. She is widowed now – your doing, mostly, Mistress Stannard . . .'

Just for a moment, disconcertingly, I heard a note of anger in his voice and saw it flash in his eyes. Quietly, I said, 'The law dealt with him.'

'Well, it's all in the past.' He seemed to relax. In injuring the brothers, I had no doubt injured Captain Julien to some extent. I would do well to remember that. He said, 'But her brothers have made a secret visit to their home and found no sign of her. Where is she now?'

'She felt that the crimes committed by her family had tainted her,' Brockley told him candidly. 'She has gone to France to become a Catholic and enter a nunnery. Mistress Stannard helped her.'

'Walsingham wouldn't let me take her to France myself,' I said. 'But he allowed me to find a Catholic couple who were willing to escort her there. She stayed with me until this could be arranged and then left for France early this year.' I added, 'Walsingham would like to make just being Catholic an offence, but the queen will not allow it. Arabella is safe and apparently happy. She is now in the Abbey of St Peter and St Paul, near Rouen. She has been allowed to write to me.'

'I see. Poor wench. Well, let us hope she has found contentment. I will find some way of informing her brothers,' Julien said. 'But now we must get back to the matter in hand. You should know that even though the Mercer brothers could not trace their sister, they are very well informed about *your* family and friends, Mistress Stannard. I believe that when you went to attend Arabella's wedding – alas, poor Arabella, to be married and widowed all in one year! – Harry was with you. He talked to the brothers – quite freely, why should he not? They were the brothers of the bride, and he was a wedding guest.

'They know, for instance, that you have a married daughter, Mistress Margaret Hillman – you call her Meg, I believe – living with her husband George Hillman and their children in Buckinghamshire, in a house called Riverside. They even know whereabouts in Buckinghamshire it is. The brothers also know that you have for many years been on friendly terms with Master Christopher Spelton, a one-time queen's messenger and also formerly a queen's agent like yourself, madam, who lives at West Leys farm, not so many miles from here. His wife Mildred was once your ward. They have young daughters. I think that both families could be in danger and should be urged to go into hiding. Please don't tell me where they are going; you know little about me and I don't expect you to trust me.'

Brockley looked aghast and, no doubt, so did I. Then my mind clarified. 'You are right. I shall do as you suggest. There are other things to be done, as well. Whether the deaths of my aunt and poor Eleanor are or are not the start of this abominable campaign, it might be best to assume that they could be. The existence of the campaign must be reported, and at the highest level. I am the final target and I am the queen's half-sister. Cecil, Lord Burghley, must be informed. He will set the search in hand for the Mercer brothers.'

'The sooner they are in the Tower, the better,' said Brockley grimly. 'It will be the Tower for them, I take it. Since, madam, you are half-sister to Her Majesty.'

'I don't care where they're held as long as they *are* held, and kept from doing any more mischief,' I said tartly. 'They'll have to be caught first. I must try to think of everyone who might be in danger, as well as my daughter Meg and my friend Christopher and their families. You are at risk, Brockley, and so is Dale. So is almost anyone in my employment!'

I said that I spoke tartly. So I did. It was a way of sounding normal. Somehow, I must try to speak and appear as though I were my normal self. I was not. The tartness was a pretence.

Oh, I had been in danger before; I had even been imperilled because someone wanted to avenge what they considered to be their wrongs. But this was different. This was a threat to those around me, to those I loved, as well as to me. It was meant to persist until my heart was broken and then they would come for me too. Ice was running down my spine and my guts were churning. Brockley was looking at me and I knew that he had read my mind.

He said, 'We have to prepare ourselves and fight back, madam.'

I said, 'We will do that. I thank you, Captain Julien, for your warning. But for the moment, I want to be alone.'

EIGHT

Send Them to Safety

I retreated to my chamber, and there, trying to silence the nausea in my guts by lying still, and keeping my face buried in a pillow, I wept. I did it silently, for fear that – although I had told her to stay away – Dale, who was sure to be anxious about me, might listen at the door. I wept out of fear for myself and fear for those around me, and it was private.

At last, the nausea ceased to churn and the tears stopped. The ice water stopped running down my spine. I got up and tidied my dress. There was a jug of cold water on my wash-stand; as ever, Dale had seen that my room was in good order. I found a napkin, dipped it in the water, mopped my face and my eyes until my mirror said that I had soothed away the redness of weeping. Then I went in search of Brockley.

I found him still in the East Room, deep in discussion with Captain Julien and Harry. They turned to me as I came in, Brockley with an air of relief.

'There you are, madam. We have much to talk about, it seems. We are at least forewarned,' he said. 'A blessing that your aunt Tabitha, madam, and poor little Eleanor Blake did not share. We shall have to tell the household that every single one of them could be in danger.' He hesitated. 'Or would they panic? Some of them might leave us. What do you say?'

I was being asked for decisions. I had had my moment of giving way; now I must be practical. I wished my knees didn't feel so curiously weak. It was Harry who said, 'Surely we must tell them something. It is our business to protect them, but surely it's better if they help by protecting themselves as far as they can. They can't do that if they don't know at least something of what's afoot.'

'Yes. That's true.' Harry was right. 'Perhaps, Captain, you

would wait here while I speak with my servants in the hall.
Now, Harry and Brockley, we need to collect everyone together.
Ben and Master Dickson will help you. We must summon
Arthur Watts, as he is the head groom, and Jerome Billington
for the outside hands.' Jerome was my head forester, but
unofficially he was the bailiff as well, keeping an eye on all
the outside staff apart from the stud farm grooms.

'Harry, fetch Laurence Miller from the stud farm,' I said.
'Do it immediately. He is here to watch over me on behalf
of the queen. He must report this to Cecil instantly – I will
write a letter asking that a search for the brothers should
begin at once. Miller must leave today.'

'You've forgotten the vicar,' said Harry, with a glint of
laughter.

'No, I haven't; I hadn't got to him yet.' But the reproof was
gentle, for that glint of mirth was the first I had seen in Harry's
eyes for a long time. 'Certainly Dr Joynings must be present.
The villagers could be in danger as well. When you have sent
Miller to me, then go and fetch Dr Joynings too.'

My heart sank as I saw how wide the threatening net
could be spread. Well, I could only do my best. 'Meanwhile,'
I said, 'I will be in the study, preparing a letter for my daughter
and her husband.'

I had been trying to think of who would be the likeliest
victims, and my girl Meg and her family were certainly among
them. If any harm came to my beautiful, dark-haired daughter
Meg, living so peacefully with George Hillman and their four
children at Riverside, their pleasant house in Buckinghamshire,
I would never forgive myself. I would feel tainted, as Arabella
had. The children ranged in age from three to seventeen.
There had been others that had not survived infancy. Meg
and George had known grief enough. If any of their children
were made targets . . .

Captain Julien had also mentioned the Speltons. Good
God, yes, the Speltons! So happy at West Leys, expecting
another child soon after Christmas.

The brothers also know that you have for many years been
on friendly terms with Master Christopher Spelton, a one-time
Queen's Messenger and also formerly a queen's agent like

yourself, madam, who lives at West Leys Farm, not so many miles from here. His wife Mildred was once your ward. They have young daughters. God's teeth!

I had taken responsibility for Mildred when, because she wouldn't marry the man they had planned for her, her parents had wished to be rid of her. I had witnessed her make what seemed to be a suitable marriage, seen it end in tragedy; taken her once more into my home, and at last seen her married to Christopher. She was happy with him. I was glad. Christopher had once proposed to me and I had come very close to accepting him. I had been considering whether or not to say yes when he fell in love with Kate Lake of West Leys and married her instead. He had married Mildred after Kate's death and both Kate and Mildred were far better suited to him than I could ever have been.

He and Mildred now had four little girls to care for, one of their own, two from Christopher and Kate, and the eldest, Susanna Lake, from Kate's own first marriage. I had visited them only three weeks ago, and I had heard then about their hopes of a new baby. I was suddenly filled with outrage, a colossal hatred of the Mercer brothers, persecuting me because I had acted as a good Englishwoman should, and brought two criminals to justice. If they harmed Meg or any of her family, if they harmed Christopher and Mildred . . .!

While Harry and Brockley were calling the household into the hall, I went to the study. Because the East Room had such good morning light, I usually sat there to do accounts and write letters. However, since it was now occupied by Captain Julien, I would have to use the study. It was a gloomy little room at the rear of the house, but Hugh had made it his study because it was small and he said that to use a bigger room for dull things like adding up the household expenses and penning the occasional letter was a waste of space. It was impossible to work there without at least one lamp or candle, no matter how bright the sunlight.

I lit every candle in a four-branched candlestick, for the letters I must now write were so very important.

The first was to Cecil, setting out the alarming deaths of my aunt and Eleanor Blake – Miller had probably informed

him of these things already but they had a new significance
now – and describing the warning that Captain Julien had
brought me. I asked that a search for the brothers should be
set in hand. Cecil would not fail me.

The second letter was to Meg. That was more difficult.

*To my best beloved daughter Margaret and to her husband
George Hillman, greetings from Ursula Stannard. You already
know that through my service to my sister the queen, I have
made enemies. This is to warn you that among those enemies
are two brothers, Stephen and Hector Mercer, who are now
trying to avenge what they think are their wrongs, by attacking
my family members and my friends.*

*They know of your existence, and that places you and
your family in danger. They may not know very much about
George's family, however. I urge you to go into hiding, perhaps
with George's brother Bartholomew and his wife Thomasina
in Devon. If strangers do come into that district, they will
be noticeable. But with luck, the brothers know nothing of
George's family and Devon will be safe. But wherever you
choose to go, go immediately. The danger is real and there
have already been two suspicious deaths in my circle: that
of my aunt Tabitha, and my son Harry's betrothed, Eleanor
Blake. In haste and urgency, your loving mother, Ursula
Stannard.*

I signed and sanded it, rolled it into a scroll and sealed it. I
hesitated. My mind was racing. Were my neighbours
Christina and Thomas Ferris at White Towers, which was
actually the nearest house to ours, also in danger? They were
certainly our friends. They bred mastiff crosses and we had
bought the parents of Caesar and Cleo from them. Hastily, I
prepared a letter for them as well. Then I went to the hall.
I had taken time over the letters and I found my people
assembled. Their faces were frightened. Ben in particular was
as pale as chalk, and Dickson looked as though another ten
years had been piled on to his already considerable age.

'I have told them the state of affairs, madam,' Brockley
said.

More people had come than I had asked for. All the

grooms were there, not just Arthur. He was the oldest, and did more supervising than riding these days. Simon was middle-aged and steady, a family man whose wife Netta had once been one of my maids but had given that up as her family increased. Taciturn Joseph Henty was also a family man, but his wife Tessie did still lend a hand in the house. She had once been Harry's nurse. They were both present. The brothers Jack and Abel Parsons were young, healthy, and as yet not married, though Jack was courting a girl in Hawkswood village. Eddie Hale was also single, though he was now over thirty. He had come to Hawkswood as a shy sixteen-year-old and had matured into a brisk and intelligent fellow who had once or twice shared danger with me.

The grooms and Netta were standing in a group, staring at me. Billington, beside them, stood with his arms folded, somehow impersonating the word Resistance. Plump Dr Joynings, usually so bouncy, hadn't looked as grim as this since the time, two years before, when I had gathered my household and told them what to do if Spain invaded. The maids, who had clustered together like the grooms, just looked terrified.

I said, 'If Brockley has done the explaining, then you already know of the campaign that threatens me.' There was a chorus of agreement, of voices shouting *Aye* and, *Yes, we do*, a few dissenting *Don't believe it*s and one tremulous, female, *no, it can't be true.*

'I am sorry,' I said. 'But it *is* true, and any of you could fall victim to it. Anyone who wishes to leave my employment may do so and I will pay them off.' Gratifyingly, there was no response to this. 'My married daughter, in Buckinghamshire, is at risk too, and so are my good friends Christopher Spelton and his wife Mildred, who was once my ward.'

Ben nodded. Mildred had for a while been his stepmother and he had grown fond of her. 'Eddie,' I said, 'Come forward. I must send an urgent letter to my daughter and her husband. You know the route.'

For a moment I paused, reviewing the occupants of my stable. In the last two years, several of my horses had died or been retired to grass. I had now replaced them with Ruby, a sprightly young bay mare, and Smoke, a sturdy dapple grey, not as fast as Ruby, but with more stamina. I also had the two chestnuts from Faldene, Ginger and Sovereign. They were so alike that they could only be told apart because Ginger had a tiny white star and a few white hairs in his off fetlock. They were broken to the saddle and were good horses, but Smoke was the best weight-carrier. Eddie was a fairly big man.

'Take Smoke,' I said. 'After dinner; it's about time for that; best not to start off hungry. Ride to Riverside, as fast as you can, but don't change horses. That leaves a trail that a clever killer could follow. You should still do the journey in two days if you nurse your mount. Pause for rests but use the light evenings. Go armed! I am also concerned for the Speltons at West Leys, but I intend to go there and deliver my warning in person. I shall take Jaunty as usual and Brockley, you will ride with me.'

I didn't glance at Dale. She never liked it when Brockley and I went off anywhere without her. It was many years since the time when we nearly became lovers, but she knew about it and could not forget it, and we had had serious trouble once, on account of her jealousy. But this present emergency was too important to be hindered by such things.

'I am also sending a warning to White Towers,' I said. 'I have the letter ready. Abel Parsons, after dinner, take Ruby and deliver it. Here it is.' I held it out to him as he stepped forward.

I said, 'Brockley and I will also leave immediately after dinner. It's a two-hour journey to West Leys as a rule and, if the Speltons are to get to London today, as I want them to, that's another ten miles. There is no time to be lost. Arthur, get the horses saddled. Eddie, pack your saddlebags with whatever you need for a few days away. I will give you a purse for expenses. Brockley, will you lend him your breastplate . . .?'

'A breastplate, madam?' Eddie looked startled. 'Madam, do you really feel . . .?'

'Yes, I do. It's protection against one form of attack, at least. I said, go armed. Sword and dagger.'

*   *   *

John Hawthorn sensibly and very quickly provided us with a brief dinner of cold meat, bread and fruit. Eddie and Abel left on their errands immediately afterwards, followed within minutes by Brockley and myself. I was glad to be doing something active. I had never been good at staying quiet and letting events unfold. It was a cloudy day, not too hot; we could canter for long stretches. We were halfway there, cantering steadily along a track through a wood, when Brockley suddenly remarked: 'Madam, you haven't said how you feel, but I am angry.'

I turned my head to look at him. 'So am I. Very angry. We have done nothing wrong; we behaved as honest citizens should. That because I did my duty, our lives should now be disturbed, and harmless people who happen to be our friends and relatives threatened – perhaps two of them already murdered – is outrageous. And that's a feeble word compared to what I really feel. Eleanor in particular! Just a young girl with all her life ahead of her and only part of my . . . my endangered circle . . . because she and my son were in love and wished to marry! Will Harry ever quite get over it, I wonder.'

Brockley didn't answer directly. Instead, he said, 'We're out of the trees now and there's a straight track ahead, good firm going, and Firefly wants his head. Madam, I suggest we gallop, and eat up a mile or two.'

'I find it hard,' said Christopher Spelton, 'to believe what you're saying, Ursula. If I didn't know you so well, I don't think I would believe it. These two brothers are out to take vengeance on you because you have put a stop – probably only a temporary stop – to their career of piracy, and brought other associates to justice – all right, one close relative, but even so! Because you have done this, they are now setting out to destroy your friends and family members, presumably to cause you as much grief and fear as possible, before they come for you. That is what you are saying?'

'Yes. And you do know me well enough, Christopher, to know that I wouldn't be here, telling you these things, unless I were sure of my ground. Brockley will confirm everything.

He was in the room with me when Captain Julien described these nightmare plans.'

'And you trust this captain?' Christopher's friendly brown eyes were kind, as ever, but also reproving. 'He could still be part of the enemy. He could have been sent to tell you the plans so that you would know that a succession of distressing deaths were intentional and not just unhappy coincidences. So that you would be afraid, and so that you would grieve doubly for the dead, because you would feel you were responsible.'

'I have considered that. I'm still considering it. He doesn't want to know what precautions I am advising you and my daughter to take. That at least looks honest,' I said. 'And he is Harry's half-brother. That seems to be his principal reason for coming to warn us. Also, I haven't been responsible for the execution of any of *his* family.'

Mildred, who had been listening in silence, now spoke up. 'There's sense in that. This man is Harry's brother and, in a way, Ursula, you are his stepmother. And he isn't a Mercer.'

Grimly, I said, 'I already had suspicions of *something* even though I hadn't quite worked out what. So had Brockley.'

Brockley nodded, also grimly.

I said, 'It was wildly improbable that Aunt Tabitha would ever kill herself and Harry noticed something about Eleanor's fatal injury that couldn't easily be accounted for.'

'I see,' said Christopher.

We were sitting in the West Leys kitchen. It was a big room, stone-walled and stone-floored, with a high ceiling criss-crossed by blackened beams from which hung bunches of herbs. Within the immense fireplace, hams in the process of smoking hung from hooks around the chimney and, as well as the spit for roasts, the hearth held trivets for pots and a stone oven.

In the middle of the room stood a whitewood table and stout benches, and there were several basketwork chairs as well. The kitchen had always been the centre of the house, where the family and any visitors would sit to talk. Only the most important guests were invited into the somewhat stiff parlour, and even some of those preferred the kitchen.

Lord Burghley, otherwise Sir William Cecil, had visited

West Leys once and, having heard all about the kitchen from me, frankly asked if he and his companions (two guards, a valet and a secretary) could sit there instead of in the parlour. It had been congested but comfortable, as Mildred afterwards told me. There had been much merriment, she said, and a sudden evening-up of everyone's station in life. The guards had laughed and talked as if they were Lord Burghley's brothers, and the valet, who was interested in cooking, complained openly that in my Lord Burghley's household, the cooks wouldn't let him into the kitchen, and then began to talk recipes with Mildred.

At the moment, because there were pots on the fire and the July day was hot, the back door was wide open to provide a draught, and a couple of hens had wandered in to peck at some breadcrumbs left over from the morning's baking. Most of the children were upstairs with their nurse, but Mildred had her tiny daughter Anna on her knee.

The two maids were also upstairs; now and then we could hear their voices and the sound of swishing brooms. Joan Janes, the hearty and masterful woman who kept the maids in order, was with us in the kitchen and had been paying attention to us, even though she was looking after the stockpot and keeping an eye on the oven where a meat pie was baking.

Now she glanced back over a massive shoulder, gave an aggressive stir to the stockpot with her long wooden spoon, and observed, 'Sounds to me like this captain might be trustworthy, but better not put a wager on it.'

'That makes sense,' said Christopher. 'But now, Ursula, what is all this about us getting out of harm's way? How can we? At least, I can't. The sheep shearing is over but there is still haymaking to be done. It's late this year; just as we were about to start it, last month, rain chose to set in. It poured for two days and left the hayfield soaked. It has only just got dry enough to cut.'

'You have a competent bailiff,' I said. 'I know perfectly well that John Ross once actually told you to your face, and with a big grin on his, that you were surplus to requirements. He always runs this place for you when you step back into being a Queen's Messenger or an agent, as you sometimes do.

This is a matter of your life and the lives of Mildred here
and the children. I think the danger is urgent and real. My
suggestion is that you ask for shelter with Sir William Cecil.
He will know the situation; Laurence Miller is on his way
now to inform him. And when you act as a Queen's Messenger,
you work for him. Go to him; take the family; say you have
come on my advice and ask for shelter.'

'He will offer protection to you, surely, Ursula.'

'He may want to but I do wonder how. I am not in immediate danger. At present it is those around me who are at risk.
He can hardly gather up everyone I know . . . I can't guess
where the Mercers will strike next. Except that I think you
and yours are likely victims. For God's sake, Christopher, you
must take me seriously. Do you know where Cecil is at the
moment – at his home in the Strand or on his country estate?'

'He is at his house in the Strand,' said Christopher.

He nearly always did know where Cecil was, just as Miller
did. I could see that he was thinking rapidly. 'I think we ought
to go,' said Mildred. 'Christopher, my love, would Ursula have
come here in such haste, urging us to go, if it didn't matter?'

'Well . . .' Christopher looked at me questioningly and I
said, 'It does matter. I am serious. *Believe me!*'

'*I* believe you,' said Mildred. She had changed greatly from
the diffident girl I had once met at her parents' home. Mildred
had since then acquired much experience of life and her
manner now was authoritative. 'I for one am not willing to
delay. We have the children to protect. We won't be able to
travel fast, anyway, because of my condition, so the sooner
we set off, the better. We'll need to use one of the carts, for
the children. Their nurse and I will travel in the cart with
them.' She hoisted herself to her feet. 'I must put together
food, milk for little Anna, flasks of water. The children will
need food and drink on the way, even if their elders don't. I'll
set about it now. Joan! Leave that stockpot for a while; lift it
off the trivet. I need your help.'

'My good lady seems to have made her mind up,' said
Christopher, with a faint grin. 'I fancy Mildred will insist on
going, even if I don't go with them. I've never known you
talk nonsense yet, Ursula, so we'll do as you wish. I must see

John Ross. You and Brockley were so intent on delivering your warning and getting me to act on it that you have refused refreshment. You can take your ease now while we're getting ready. There are honey cakes in the crock on the sideboard, and cider in that demijohn in the corner. Help yourselves while you're waiting.'

NINE

The Third Strike

We saw them off. Mildred, the nursemaid and the children were settled in one of Christopher's covered farm carts. Mildred was seated on a chest in which her best clothing, her jewellery and some money had been stowed; the others were perched on an assortment of boxes and hampers. There was plenty of food and drink for the journey. There had to be. Mildred said that the children were like baby blackbirds. 'Always with their beaks wide open, wanting something to eat.'

There were four children altogether. The eldest, Susanna, had been born to earlier occupants of West Leys, Eric and Kate Lake. After Eric's death, Kate had married Christopher and the next two, eight-year-old Christina and two-year-old Elizabeth, were theirs. But Kate had died in bearing Elizabeth and after a while Christopher had married Mildred. Little Anna, now seven months old, was theirs. Mildred had been unable to feed Anna herself and said (but laughing) that this was the reason why she was now two months into another pregnancy. Christopher was concerned about her and had padded her chest-seat with cushions and, despite the urgency of the journey, had put the most stolid – and slow – of his farm horses in the shafts. He was driving the cart himself, with a sword and firearm in readiness beside him, a dagger in his belt and a very sharp knife alongside it. His saddle horse, Jet, was in the party too, but was tethered behind.

As they left, I could only say Godspeed and hope that God would put some sort of energy into the hairy-heeled, plodding gelding who was dragging them all along.

'With luck, we moved quickly enough,' said Brockley. 'They'll be there before nightfall, God willing, and Cecil won't let any harm come to them.'

We saw them out of sight, exchanged a few words with the bailiff, John Ross, who assured us that nothing would go amiss on the farm if he could help it, and then we set off for home, reaching it safely during the evening.

The next day, Laurence Miller returned and said that the search for the Mercers was in hand, and that Cecil was sending me protection. The day after that, two soldiers, mounted on sturdy cavalry horses, rode in and announced themselves as being sent by Lord Burghley to guard me. The soldiers presented themselves as Captain Alan Banks and Sergeant Thomas Wooller. Captain Banks, respectfully handing me a letter with the royal seal on it, said, 'You will not know me, madam, but my elder brother rode with you nine years ago, when your son Harry was kidnapped and we set out to rescue him.'

I smiled, recalling his good-natured brother. I opened the letter, which commended Captain Banks and Sergeant Wooller wholeheartedly to me and urged me to use them in whatever way I thought best, to protect myself, my household and my property from danger.

Brockley and I conferred, with the soldiers, with Laurence Miller, and Jerome Billington, and we arrived at a plan. We were sure that no one had actually infiltrated my employees in the house, on my land or in the trotters' stud. 'I'd like to see anyone try!' said Miller, looking as if he *would* like it, but the infiltrators would not. That being established, it seemed sensible to guard our boundaries and make sure that strangers could not enter.

Unlike Christopher, we had got our hay in before the downpours that delayed his haymaking so badly. Things were quieter for a while before the corn harvest was ready. Jerome Billington said that he could easily arrange for farm hands to be working in strategic places during the hours of light.

'There's always something to do on a farm, wherever you are. A length of fencing to check over, and for sure there'll be a weak place somewhere that needs shoring up, or else there's a ditch that wants clearing or a tree that's better felled and turned into firewood, madam. We can have every yard of your boundaries under scrutiny, madam, no trouble.'

'I can safeguard the boundaries of the stud,' said Miller, almost rubbing his hands at the prospect. 'I ride round them anyway, most mornings, and there's always someone out there, working on the training track, looking the young stock over and what will you. A mouse couldn't get in that way, I promise you. And I'm as handy a fellow with a longbow as any archer in the queen's army.'

'Yes, well, don't shoot the Blakes if they come to call,' I said. 'Or the Ferrises from White Towers. It's strangers we need to worry about. Now, during the night . . .'

It was agreed that the two soldiers should guard us during the night. During the hours of darkness, they could patrol the boundaries. Abel and Jack Parsons, who looked after the two half mastiffs, Caesar and Cleo, suggested that the dogs should be turned loose to run wild on my land after dark. They taught the soldiers the whistle that would summon the dogs in an emergency. We made sure to introduce the dogs to Banks and Wooller so that there would be no mistakes during the hours of darkness. I had spare rooms in the house and gave one of them to the soldiers to sleep in during the day.

I had done my best, I thought, rolling into bed in the knowledge that my borders were now being guarded and hoping now to sleep in something resembling peace and safety.

Some days passed, then a week, then another week. Captain Julien was still with us and seemed to be relieved by the presence of the soldiers, but not yet free of worry.

'Perhaps they've given up on the scheme. Perhaps they've found it too difficult. You've fairly built a wall round this house, anyway. But we need to be anxious about Harry and Ben. I can tell you this, those two Mercer brothers – Hector especially – are tenacious. They are the sort who can wait a long time. There were treasure ships that we knew about and wanted to seize, but it wasn't easy to separate them from their fleet. Mostly, such ships sail in company. But Hector would plot and plan and *wait*. I think we must wait as well. A year at least and even then, be cautious. When those two, and especially Hector, have a quarry in view, very little except a serious wound, or death, will stop him.'

I tried not to let him see that I was shuddering. 'Are the Mercers really so . . . so . . . Are they killers?'

'We used to try to use the captains as hostages so that we could board and seize the cargo without too much resistance. It often worked. But if it didn't . . . I have had to fight for my life on a deck slippery with blood, trying not to trip over the casualties.'

I didn't know what to say to that. *How awful!* would sound foolish, inadequate, the comment of a woman with no conception of what such a thing would really be like. Which was untrue. My long experience of danger and now, the knowledge that somewhere *out there*, someone was planning my destruction – my inch-by-inch destruction – had taught me much. Finally, I said, 'I have always dreaded the idea that I might one day have to kill someone. It has never happened yet, and I hope it never will.'

'To save your own life, or the lives of those who depend on you, I fancy you would do whatever you had to do, Mistress Stannard,' said Captain Julien.

During this time, soldiers or no soldiers, I rarely slept well. More often than not, I lay awake for hours, listening to the darkness, alone in the big four-poster where once I had slept in Hugh's comforting arms. The darkness wasn't quite complete, for neither Hugh nor I had ever wanted to close the bedcurtains, nor to curtain the windows. From where I lay, I could see a patch of stars and sometimes the full moon. I could hear, too. I could hear the haunting calls of hunting owls, occasionally the murderous screech of squirrels quarrelling, the hoarse bark of foxes; in wintertime the scream of vixens seeking mates.

During those fear-ridden nights, these sounds were oddly comforting, just because they were not human. For I would imagine the Mercer brothers trying to creep on to my land, trying to reach the house. Once, deep in one moonlit night, thinking that I heard a sound in the house, I rose and put on a bedgown. Better to face a danger than to lie and wait passively for it to come to me. I crept out of my door, went to the top of the stairs and peered over the banister. I saw

Brockley, lantern in hand, cross the moonlit vestibule below. And remembered that since Banks and Wooller would be out, patrolling the boundaries of my land, he and Simon Alder had agreed to take turns in patrolling the house at night. Brockley had asked Julien to help but Captain Julien very firmly said no.

'If something were to happen in the night, if someone were to get in, how would you know that I didn't let them in? Choose someone you know is completely trustworthy!'

I slipped back to bed and lay thinking of Captain Banks and Sergeant Wooller, out in the night, armed not only with swords but with whistles that would summon the dogs and would also carry to the house, to call the grooms from their beds. If I were to open the window and put my head out, I might catch a glimpse of their distant lanterns.

Eventually, because I was tired and nature usually has her way in the end, I would sleep, but never long enough. I would wake in the morning still tired, though I would privately give thanks to something or someone because I was still alive and unmolested and, to judge from the sounds of the house, so was everyone else under my roof. I should be grateful, I thought, that I was surrounded by people who wanted to keep us all safe.

Word came from Christopher, to say that he and his family had been sent to Theobalds, Cecil's Hertfordshire estate. They had travelled under a heavy guard, had arrived safely, and were now waiting until the world should become normal again and they could all go home. The children were enjoying the wide grounds, but were always watched. It was to be hoped that the Mercers' knowledge of me and my friends didn't extend to an awareness of Theobalds, but one never knew.

'No, one doesn't,' said Julien. 'Harry admits that he talked freely to them when you all met at Evergreens before their sister's wedding. He can't remember what he said, but it could have included mention of Theobalds. In the year of the Armada, wasn't there a man who was stopped and killed when he was taking information about the Spaniards to Cecil at Theobalds? You were there when the news came to the queen, were you not?'

'One thing Harry has yet to learn,' I said, 'is to keep a still tongue in his head!'

'You can hardly expect him to watch his words when he is making friends with fellow guests at a wedding.'

'In view of my unusual occupation, yes, I can. Beware of strangers is a rule I keep by instinct. I will have to see that the same applies to Harry.'

But it was not Christopher or any of his family who suffered the third strike.

It was the last day of July, a pleasant day; sunny but fresh, with light clouds drifting across the sky. We might start the wheat harvest early this year I thought and then, with the usual thud in my chest that reminded me of our constant danger, remembered the harvesters who would be out in the fields, out in the open . . . were they likely victims in the minds of the Mercers? There had been a report from Cecil about the search for the brothers, but not an encouraging one. It was thought that they had been sighted once, but they had disappeared before they could be apprehended. *As elusive as a pair of slippery fish* were Cecil's words.

My harvesters might well be at risk. Also, Harry and Ben would be out there with scythes as well, and my grooms would lend a hand now and then, and the farmhands' wives, and probably Netta and Tessie too would follow behind the cutters, putting the wheat into bundles. I had better tell the grooms that their wives must not join the harvesters this time and that two men at a time were not to cut wheat, but to stand guard, armed.

Oh, dear God, how long must I live like this, under siege, trying to defend everyone in my world from an attack that could come from anywhere?

Dale came to dress me as usual and, as always, I put a cheerful face on for her. Brockley was up already, making sure that all was well in the stables. Breakfast was being prepared. Many households didn't trouble with it and others provided a few things on the table that could be picked up and eaten while people were on the move, but I liked to see that I and my household started the day with something solid inside, and a chance to eat it in comfort, at a table. Everyone came to it, including the grooms, except for the married ones, whose wives saw to it.

We breakfasted, therefore, in the hall, with the outer door open to let in the soft wind. It also let in a few stable smells, for our courtyard was the stable yard as well. Hawkswood was no great house, but had started life as a small manor house and grown haphazardly into its present, somewhat unconventional shape. Hugh had often said that we really ought to separate the stables from the house, as everyone else did, but neither of us could see how this could be done without an upheaval, so we left things as they were.

Breakfast over, an ordinary day began. Jerome Billington came to talk about the harvest, and suggested that the wheat needed ten more days to reach perfect readiness, and he hoped the weather would hold. Peter Dickson and Harry went into the garden to enjoy the sunshine and practise the lute at the same time. Brockley went off to Woking to order some stable supplies. Ned Dodd from the village came to work in the rose garden, as he did three times a week.

When Billington had gone, Dale and I decided to sit in the little parlour with the window open and have a quiet morning doing embroidery. I was making a new pair of sleeves to go with my favourite tawny gown, and Dale was putting decorative corners into a white tablecloth. We had plenty of work to keep us occupied. And, I said to myself, to keep my mind from fretting.

Midday came. A clatter of pots in the kitchen announced that preparations for dinner were well under way. Voices from the courtyard and the sound of hooves proclaimed that Brockley had returned. Dale and I folded our work away and I called for a jug of cider and three glasses.

And then, suddenly, there were more hooves, urgent ones. The voices in the courtyard swelled to a babble and I heard feet running into the adjacent hall, and Brockley calling my name. Dale and I ran and met him in the hall doorway. Behind him was a man in riding clothes, a tired man with sweat running down his temples. I recognized him at once. He was a thin, wiry fellow, with a shock of fair hair straggling over his ears, and his name was Walter Horne. He was one of Meg and George's grooms. He was holding out a letter.

'They wanted me to get to you as fast as I could. I left at five, changed horses four times, pressed on hard as if the devil was behind me . . . this is from Mistress Hillman . . .'

'From my daughter? From where? Not Devonshire, if you started out this morning?' I was breaking the seal as I spoke but my eyes were on Walter's face.

'No, madam. I came from Swindon.'

'Swindon? But you should have got to Devonshire a week and a half ago, maybe sooner, surely!'

'The plans went wrong, madam. We left Riverside the day after your letter arrived. I was one of the grooms who went with them. We couldn't travel fast, because of the children. Master Hillman has a carriage, so that the nurse and the little ones – John is six and Philippa is three – could ride inside along with the baggage. Mistress Meg travelled in the carriage as well, this time. It's a good two-horse affair and it gets along at a fair speed. Only, we couldn't go fast because little Philippa seemed to be ailing. We kept having to find an inn and stop sooner than we meant to, so that she could be carried indoors and put to bed and given drinks of milk or water. Everyone was worried. It slowed us down so much. It was three days till we got to this place called Swindon, and then we really had to stop because Philippa suddenly became very ill and it was chicken pox. All the rest of us have had it but poor little Philippa . . . and the inn where we stopped, well, Master Hillman had to pay the innkeeper a fortune so that he would let us stay. Innkeepers never like illness in the house. Philippa is still too weak to travel but she'll be all right, only . . . oh, read it, I beg you, mistress, I can't bear to tell you, thinking what could be happening – it's not for the tongue of a rough groom like me.'

While Walter was talking, Julien and the boys had joined us. I was listening to Walter but only with half an ear, for I was scanning the letter. It made a brief mention of Philippa, but this was not a tale of a journey halted because of chicken pox. I could see why Walter Horne didn't want to speak of it himself.

'It's the eldest girl,' I said. 'Ursula Mary, the one who was named for me, only they call her Ursula Mary, using her second name as well, to avoid confusing everyone. She's vanished. She disappeared from the inn over a week ago. She had been looking after Philippa while her mother took some rest; the child cries if she is left alone. The nurse was taking care of the other child – that's their six-year-old son, John. Their elder boy, Nick, is away in another household, learning fashionable manners. It hasn't been possible to get him to Devon. As for this present calamity, it was late afternoon. Meg came back to the sick room, said she would take charge. Ursula Mary should go down to the parlour, read, or sew; call for some refreshment, as supper time was still some time away and they had eaten very little dinner. George was with the landlord, explaining that it would be at least another week before they could travel on. He came back from that, went into the parlour and found the book that Ursula Mary had been reading flung down on the floor, as though she had rushed away in great urgency. There was no sign of Ursula Mary herself.'

I looked round at them all and then began to read aloud.

'*George ran upstairs thinking that something dreadful must have happened with Philippa, but the child was sitting up with me beside her, and taking a meal of bread and milk. No one knew where Ursula Mary was, and then they found that one of the inn's own grooms had seen a horse tethered outside the inn, at the roadside, where there are a few small trees to use as tethering posts. The groom saw a man come out of the inn, supporting a girl who hardly seemed able to walk. He loosed the tether, got on to the horse, perched her in front of him and rode off. That's all. It's over ten days ago now. We have searched and searched; had the cried in the streets of Swindon, done everything in the world to look for her. Half Swindon has turned out to help us search; people here are kind and good, but it is all no use. No one has seen or heard of Ursula Mary since that afternoon. We did not want to tell you, Mother, but we think you will have to know. Our poor daughter is only fifteen years old. We are frantic.*'

'Christ almighty!' said Brockley and, in his horrified eyes, I read the same monstrous possibilities that were in my own mind and certainly in the mind of the exhausted messenger in front of us.

Captain Julien said, 'It's the third strike.'

TEN

Hard Riding

'Of course I'm going to them!' I snapped. 'Meg is my daughter; Ursula Mary is my granddaughter – my first grandchild. Who should go to them except me? We'll have to ride fast. Put a cross saddle on Jaunty, Brockley; I'll wear breeches. Dale, put three plain gowns and two nightgowns in one saddlebag for me, tooth cloths, four changes of under linen and two pairs of shoes in the other, and a couple of ruffs in a shoulder pack. I'll borrow a farthingale from Meg if I want one. Brockley, why are you just standing there? Do I have to saddle Jaunty myself?'

'Madam, I can't allow this. It could be a trap. They could be lying in wait for you to do just what you are proposing to do.'

'I doubt it. Not yet. You might be the target this time. You had better not come. I'll ride with Simon and Captain Julien.'

'My God, you will not!'

'Are you giving me orders, Brockley? Who pays your wages?'

We stood simmering, like two cats disputing the right of way along a fence. Then Brockley said, firmly, 'I am coming, madam. With or without your consent. I'll saddle up. Fran, you'll stay here. We'll be riding too fast for you.'

'No, please! I want to be with you! I can manage. Blue Gentle can go fast, she just doesn't move her legs the way the others do.'

'Dale,' I said, trying to be patient. 'From here to Swindon is at least as far as it was from Whitehall to Faldene House. You couldn't face that distance in the saddle.'

'I will manage! I'd be frightened to stay here. You talk about traps, Roger – suppose I'm the victim and all this is a trick to get all of you out of the way?'

'There is some sense in that, Mother,' said Harry. 'Dale could be right.'

'Oh, very well. Let Fran come. If you agree, Brockley.' Let Brockley take the decisions. I had known him in this mood before and I knew he would probably take them anyway.

He said, 'I doubt if it's wise, but . . .' he looked reprovingly at his wife, '. . . I know you, Fran. I daresay you would be nervous if I left you behind. Perhaps, after all, it's best if you come. Blue Gentle can move like lightning when necessary, and if you get too tired, I'll take you up with me on Firefly. I agree.'

'Captain Julien,' I said, reclaiming my authority, 'you will stay here, please. Harry, you are the master of the house and Ben, you are the steward. One of you must inform Dr Joynings of this development and ask him, next Sunday, to offer special prayers for us in this dreadful situation. Explain it all to him. Do your best here. Dickson will advise you if need be. Keep the guards in place. Jerome Billington and Simon Alder can patrol the house at night.'

Harry and Ben declared willingness to attend to all this and Captain Julien set off at once to see Joynings. I turned to Horne. 'You know the road and I don't. Can you face the return journey at once? We'll travel fast, though we'll still have to spend a night on the road. I can vaguely remember where Swindon is and how far away. I stayed there once when I was on my way to visit Devonshire, but I couldn't find it easily without a guide. If you have a wash and take some food and wine now, will you be able to lead us?'

'Certainly, madam,' said Walter Horne, with a trace of indignation at the suggestion that he was too tired. 'But my horse is tired,' he said. 'It comes from the Old Bell in Windsor and I rode it hard.'

'When it's had time to recover, we'll send it back to Windsor,' I said. 'Eddie will see to that. We'll lend you a horse. Ginger will do. I suppose we had all better eat before we go. Ben, go and warn the kitchen to serve us something as soon as possible. And arrange some hot water and a meal for Horne, including a glass of wine. Do you like aniseed in your wine, Horne?'

'I have never heard of it, madam.'

'It's a new thing. I know that my senior maid Phoebe has put half a dozen aniseed-flavoured bottles of wine on our stillroom shelves. But not everyone likes it. Ben, see that Master Horne is served plain Canary. Horne, what's the name of the inn where you left the Hillmans?'

'The Plough and Wagon, madam.'

'So, saddling up can wait while we eat and prepare ourselves,' said Brockley with a glint of humour. 'I never like to pack in too much haste; it's so easy to leave out something that matters. Horne, do you need me to lend you anything for the night on the road?'

We couldn't leave instantly as I wanted to do at first, but we still wasted no time. My chief cook, John Hawthorn, was used to sudden excursions and requests for food to start people off with full stomachs. Two plump hens that had ceased to lay were on the spit, but they could now be eaten by the servants later, and the dinner the servants should have had – which was fried veal slices with fresh baked bread and redcurrant tarts – was provided in haste for us and also for Horne.

We ate therefore, made ourselves comfortable, saw that our packing was properly done, and gathered in the stable yard. Horne didn't seem to be at all exhausted. I had changed into the old pair of Hugh's breeches that I used for emergencies, topped off with a shirt and one of his doublets. I clapped a hat on my head, mounted and looked round to make sure that Brockley, Dale and Horne were in their saddles. Julien had returned from the village by now. He, Harry and Ben were standing in a row, watching us anxiously.

I said, 'Take care of everything while we're gone, and pray that there is better news when we get there.' Gladys at this point came hobbling out of the house and I picked up my reins in a hurry. Gladys had come to prophesy disaster; I knew it. We were away.

The Plough and Wagon was an attractive place, modern looking, its white walls criss-crossed with brown timber beams,

its tall brick chimneys elegantly patterned. It seemed to be
extensive, and it had a sizeable stable yard, standing across a
side lane from the inn itself.

'I'll go,' said Brockley, slipping out of his saddle. 'I'll see
if they can find room for us.'

'I'm so glad we're here,' said Dale. She was wilting where
she sat, on Blue Gentle's back, exhausted by the hard riding,
just as I had feared she would be. It was late afternoon on
the second day of the journey. Yesterday, we had ridden
on until dusk began to fall and we had started out at six
that morning.

There was a long wait, during which I feared that Dale
might actually topple out of her saddle, but at last Brockley
returned. 'All right. I found the landlord and he's a philosophical soul, with an eye to business. If we don't mind attic
rooms, he can squeeze us in. Horne, you and I will take the
horses to the stable. Someone's coming from the inn to
take our baggage – here they come – and there's room for us
and, oh . . .'

Two menservants were just then emerging from the
entrance but, behind them and then overtaking them, at a
run, came Meg. 'Oh, Mother . . . Mother . . . I am so glad
to see you . . . it's so terrible . . .!'

I was down on my feet and opening my arms to her. 'Meg,
is there any news?'

'Nothing. God help us, nothing! We didn't send to tell you
until everything anyone could think of had been tried. Here's
George!'

She had pulled me indoors, into a vestibule from which a
staircase led upwards, and her husband, good, steady George,
was descending the stairs. He grasped my right hand. 'I am
glad to see you; you will be a support to my wife but oh, my
God . . . we have tried everything! *Everything!* We called the
constable – he organized a search. Dozens, scores, fifty, sixty,
of the townsfolk joined in. All along the tracks, questioning
people who lived near them, going into their houses to
search. We had the news cried, not just in Swindon, but in
Malmesbury, in Cirencester, Chippenham . . . and all in vain.
Nothing. *Nothing!* She might never have existed, our beautiful

eldest daughter. Wherever she is, if she is alive, she must be so frightened . . .'

His voice broke in a sob. We stood together, taking what comfort we could in each other's arms.

ELEVEN
All That They Hoped

We were all very tired and my memory of that evening is blurred. I recall accepting the attic rooms for myself and then insisting that the Brockleys should have the bedchamber next to mine. They were not to share the servants' quarters downstairs. Dale was hopelessly exhausted and I remember telling Brockley to take care of her, and saying that I would get one of the inn's maidservants to help me change out of my breeches and into a gown and ruff. I recall doing so. By then, Dale was asleep.

After that . . . I presume that we ate supper and that Dale woke up for it. This must have happened but I don't recollect it. I suppose I talked to Meg and George, and no doubt at length, but I can't recall that either. I do remember once more seeking the help of a maidservant when I wanted to undress. My room had a ceiling that came down to the floor on one side, and the bed was a narrow tester. Its mattress was comfortable enough but, even so, I couldn't sleep for a long time, until at last – I fancy it was around midnight – exhaustion had its way and I crashed into unconsciousness.

I woke to a racket: voices shouting, dogs barking, Meg screaming *Oh my God!* and feet clattering everywhere. There was a faint dawn light in the air. I toppled out of the bed, looked round wildly for my dressing robe, saw it on a hook on the door, snatched it off, flung it round me and ran out of the room. The hubbub was now climbing the stairs. Looking over the banisters, I saw George and Meg and the philosophical landlord, all of them with dressing robes round them, just like me, coming up the stairs, supporting someone between them, a girl, drooping between them but still using her feet to walk, if weakly . . .

'*Ursula Mary!*' I shrieked, and started down the stairs to meet them.

We got her up to the Hillmans' room. She seemed to be semi-conscious. Her eyes were open but apparently unseeing. But she was murmuring something and suddenly her eyes seemed to come awake as she looked at Meg; she had recognized her mother. I helped Meg to pull the bedcoverings tidy and we laid her on top of them. I looked at the landlord. 'What time is it? How did she come back?'

'It's barely dawn. It was the dogs, barking, as woke me,' he said. 'So up I got and went to the front door, and would you believe it, the door wouldn't open, had something in the way. I had to use a side door and go round the house to see what was on my doorstep and I found this poor lass, tied hand and foot and gagged . . .'

'Oh, how wicked!' Meg burst out, sobbing.

'But alive,' said the landlord. 'So I get the nasty gag off and carry her inside. Servants were all awake by then, so I said someone go and fetch her parents and I got a kitchen knife and sawed through the bonds and by then Master and Mistress Hillman were down and between us we stood the poor wench on her feet and got her up here. I'd guess she's been drugged somehow. You awake yet, lass?'

There was life now in her eyes. She was looking round at us. She moistened her lips and one of the inn servants, a sensible young man with forethought, appeared with a glass of milk. George held it for her while she drank. Weakly but clearly, she said, 'I'm home.'

Then she dissolved into tears and Meg took her daughter into her arms. George sat down on the edge of the bed, trying to embrace both of them at once, and the rest of us moved away and would have left the room, except that Meg put out a hand and pulled my sleeve, so I stayed.

Through her tears, Ursula Mary said, 'I want to talk.'

The story that emerged came out in bits, and there was a point at which she looked piteously at her father and George left the room, because he could not bear what she was telling us, and in his presence she could not bear to say what she knew she must. Shocked, frightened, damaged, Ursula Mary was nevertheless an essentially strong-minded girl, not unlike myself at her age. She well understood that there were things she had to say and she also understood that there were things that should not be said between father and daughter. Therefore, she wouldn't speak until George had gone. Then, though it was horribly painful for her, she explained.

She had been reading in the inn parlour, she told us, sitting on the window seat, when two men walked in. They were strangers. They didn't hesitate. They sat down, one on either side of her. One put an arm round her and the other produced a flask and forced her to drink from it. It was something sweet and cloying, with honey in it but something else as well. They dosed her with the same thing before they brought her home. In the inn parlour, one of the men moved away and the other pretended interest in the book of verse she was reading. No one, either inn servant or fellow guest came into the room, but the man beside her showed her a dagger and said *if anyone comes in, just one squeak and you're dead, lady*, and she was too frightened to move. Then she began to feel very sleepy. Her head swam. She realized that she was being got to her feet and walked out of the inn but she couldn't protest. 'I was too mazed; nothing was real,' she said.

'Juice of the poppy, I expect,' I said. I was well aware of the properties of one species of poppy. It came from some Eastern country, but there were people in England who grew it and no doubt the much-travelled Mercer brothers knew all about it anyway.

She had a dim recollection of being on a horse. 'Someone was holding me in front of him. The horse was going fast. I'd been blindfolded and there was a gag in my mouth – ugh!'

Then she was transferred into a cart and, eventually, when she woke up properly, she was lying on a bed in a strange bedchamber. The gag and the blindfold were gone. She didn't know where she was. The two men were in the room, waiting for her to come round.

'The awful thing was that they were smiling, behaving as though they were being kind,' she said.

They brought her food, with small ale. She asked questions but soon became too afraid to go on asking. She knew, of course, why the family had had to leave Riverside and seek shelter in Devonshire. She asked her captors if they were the Mercers and they grinned at her and one of them said she was a clever girl and yes, they were. The older one was Hector and the other one was Stephen. They said they didn't mean to harm her. Well, not really, Hector said. She didn't understand what that meant but, somehow, what he had said and the way he had said it frightened her so badly that she asked no further questions in case the answers frightened her even more.

It was late afternoon by then. She thought she must have travelled a long way, by horse and by cart. Evening approached. She was allowed to use a necessary house, but one of her captors took her there and stood outside the door all the time; she had no chance to escape.

'And where could I escape *to*?' she said, crying. 'I didn't know where I was. I could have been on the moon, for all I knew!'

She was taken back to the bedchamber. She was given an excellent supper with wine. Her captors clearly didn't mean to starve her. At dusk, they came with candles for her room. They left her there with the candles lit and she thought they might be going to leave her alone until the next day.

But when night had truly fallen . . . that was the point at which Ursula Mary looked at George and he left the room. When he had gone, she told us that after dark, they came to her again, together, and raped her, both of them, the elder one of them first.

'I fought them!' Ursula Mary wailed. 'I kicked and bit and struggled, but all they did was laugh, and they hurt me so; they were so rough. I bled!'

Horrified, Meg flicked up her daughter's skirt and pulled out a fold of her petticoat and we all saw it – the patch of dark, dried blood.

I said, 'It looks old. I mean, the bleeding hasn't persisted.'

'No, but *they* did!' said my granddaughter bitterly. 'Every night; not always both of them, but always one, night after night. They always gave me good meals. But they laughed at me when they brought my food, and said I must eat well and be strong or I wouldn't enjoy it. I knew what they meant by then. *Enjoy* it! Could anyone? It always hurt me and I would cry and plead, but all they said was that I would soon get used to it; I should try to imagine I was on my honeymoon. They said I'd get to like it. *Like it!*' said poor Ursula Mary.

I was beside her immediately, taking her into my arms. 'Hush now, it's all over. You will heal.'

'Will I?' asked my granddaughter with bitterness. 'I'm ruined. No man will ever want to marry me, and I wouldn't dare to marry anyone, anyway. I don't want ever, ever, to . . .'

There was something that had to be said, and at once. Meg seemed too stunned to say it, so I did. 'Believe me,' I said, 'between real lovers, it's not like that. Do you think it's like that for your mother, who loves your father and has had many children, and retires at night into the room she shares with him and is happy to do so? What those vicious brutes did has nothing to do with honest love.'

I tried to sound calm but inside I was shaking with rage. The Mercers had done more than hurt my granddaughter physically; they had put poison into her mind, and would her mind ever be cleansed of it?

George came back. Meg said to him, 'They both had her. Over and over.' I saw his jaw tighten and then he came to the bedside and took his daughter's right hand in both of his, and began to cry, openly, without any attempt at pretence.

'My poor little girl. My poor little girl.' He said it over and over. It was a long time before he stopped and mopped his eyes and tried to be practical and said, 'It's all over, darling, and we will take care of you. We won't journey on until you feel better. One mercy is that little Philippa is now well on the mend, and her spots will leave no marks.'

Somewhere nearby, a child's wail came to us. 'There she is,' said Meg. 'She is always upset if she is left alone. The nursemaid has to sleep sometimes, poor soul. The inn is a strange place to Philippa; she wants her home.' Meg herself looked ready to drop, but she smiled at us and went out, presumably to tend her smaller daughter.

'I only hope all this disturbance hasn't woken my son,' said George. 'Our little John is in the care of Anna – she's our nursemaid – but he is well grown, with a mind of his own, and there are times when he is almost too much for her. Even when she's awake, though presumably she isn't just now. Thank God that John has already had chicken pox. At least we haven't had to look after two of them. Now we have to look after Ursula Mary . . . oh dear God, what future does she have now, her innocence gone, my poor little girl . . . my poor little daughter . . .'

He kept on repeating himself, over and over. If Meg had been there, she would no doubt have tried to hush him, but without her, he just raved on, until Ursula Mary said, 'I think I want to sleep. I couldn't sleep much, not in that cottage, not knowing that soon, again . . . yes, Father, I have lost my innocence!'

It was Ursula Mary herself in the end who stopped George from repeating his dreadful litany. 'But it can't be helped now, can it?' she said, almost sharply. George fell silent.

'You are safe now,' I said, and I gave George a keen look.

She sighed wearily and turned on to her side. Meg came back. 'Philippa is settled now, but George, will you go and sit with her? I'll stay here.'

Ursula Mary was already sinking into sleep. I withdrew. I called the Brockleys into my room. Briefly, I explained the situation to Dale, and Dale's slightly protuberant blue eyes became more protuberant than ever, while her old smallpox scars suddenly seemed more noticeable, as they always did in times of stress. Brockley listened in silence, his jaw muscles growing tighter and tighter as the horrible narrative unfolded. Meg joined us presently, saying that Ursula Mary was now fast asleep in her bed. 'I would like a physician to look at her,' she said, 'but I think – well, a man – she wouldn't like it.'

'They're probably not diseased,' I said, recalling the very fit and healthy young men I had met at their sister's wedding. 'Let us see what nature will do for her. Let's wait a day or two, anyway.'

*   *   *

Ursula Mary was a strong girl. She had been treated very badly but she had not been starved. Her captors had apparently wished her to be in good health and they really had fed her well. On her side, Ursula Mary had the hearty appetite of youth, and so she had eaten what they gave her because she was hungry. Now, freed from their attentions, she was even hungrier.

Before she woke from that first sleep in safety, Meg returned to her, pulled the coverlet over them both and slept for some hours at her side. When Ursula Mary woke again, it was fully, without the haze of whatever medicine her captors had given her. She asked for hot water and a tub for her to sit in. Meg gave her a bath, washing away the stains of her ordeal, and providing clean clothes for her afterwards. She went back to bed then and slept again for most of the day. That night, the landlord provided a truckle bed for George so that Meg could share the big one with her daughter. The next day, the girl insisted on taking another bath. The inn servants cursed as for the second time they had to carry the tub and numerous jugs of hot water upstairs, but Ursula Mary was adamant. She was a strong-minded girl, as I said. Afterwards, she asked for her dressing robe so that she could walk about inside the bedchamber. The morning after that, she dressed and came downstairs.

George began to show signs of pulling himself together. 'I believe she is going to recover,' he said. 'She may have a future, after all. Give it a few years, and by the time she is twenty, she will have put all this behind her. She will forget.'

Meg and I exchanged glances. George was a good, kind man, but imaginative he was not. What had happened to Ursula Mary had left – must have left – not just physical damage but also damage to her mind, to her emotions. George had only the most shadowy understanding of that. He was thinking of her experience as an accident, her injuries something that would heal, and now what filled his mind was his duty as a father to settle his daughters in life, and he was wondering how to keep the disaster quiet, so that it need not prevent her from making a good marriage. In fact, he was saying so.

'There is plenty of good society round Riverside,' George

said to us. 'We had no trouble in finding a household where
Nick could learn manners and get some polish, and we've already
noticed some young sons who will be ripe for marriage when
Ursula Mary is old enough. As for this episode, we need never
speak of it. If it does get known and anyone rejects our
daughter because of it, they will get the rough side of my
tongue and no mistake.'

'I hope it's as simple as that,' said Meg. 'She may not want
to marry, not after this.'

George looked nonplussed and didn't reply.

Ursula Mary had been torn and bruised but, at the end of
a week, she declared herself able to sit on a horse. I said that
surely she would prefer to ride in the carriage, but to my
surprise, she was insistent. Philippa was now quite well again
and would travel in the carriage with Meg and the nurse and
her small brother, but Ursula Mary would ride. I decided that
I and the Brockleys would go with them to Devonshire, as
extra protection. Brockley said cynically that it looked as
though the Hillmans had had their turn, but I asked him who
could be sure of that. We would travel on with them and we
too would be riding.

This plan was carried out. There were no more alarms, but
the journey to Devon was long and took us over a week.
During that time, I saw that Meg seemed anxious and somehow
watchful, while Ursula Mary was tight-lipped and silent.

Before we reached our destination, which was a house
called Ladymead, in a village with the curious name of Zeal
Aquatio, we made a final overnight stop at a hostelry in the
Devon town of Okehampton. Meg came to my room that
evening, closed the door behind her and said, 'Mother, I think
something dreadful may have happened.'

I was there with Dale, who was brushing my hair. We both
looked at Meg, startled. She sat down on the side of my bed.
'We hoped it wouldn't happen,' she said. 'But I think *they*
hoped it would. They meant it to! They did their best to make
sure that it did. A damnable fate has done well by them, but
not by my girl. May they burn in hell for this.'

Dale said, 'But what . . .?' in a bewildered voice, but I
already knew. I had begun to guess some days ago. I had, for

one thing, noticed Ursula Mary keeping her horse to a fast trot when the rest of us were cantering. I had already faced the worst when Meg said, 'Those bastards have got my daughter with child. She is going to have a baby by one of the men who raped her. I think it's what they intended. All that they hoped, damn them, has come to pass. My poor, poor Ursula . . .'

And then I had to hold my own daughter close and make comforting noises, while all the time I was thinking *oh, my God, what do we do now?*

TWELVE
Smoothing the Path

After a while Meg drew herself away from me and said, flatly, 'What now? and the three of us sat there staring at each other.

Finally, I said, 'I reckon that this was part of their plan, though they couldn't be sure it would work. If they failed to get her with child, well, they would still have harmed her, in body and mind. They could be sure anyway that it would cause both her and us great distress if she was delivered like a tied-up parcel to the doorstep of our inn in the chilly dawn.'

'Ma'am,' said Dale, 'they brought her here the very morning after you reached the inn yourself. Do you think they were . . . watching for you?'

'Yes, Dale, I do. I don't know who is doing it or how, but I am under surveillance. Well, one thing we *can* do, and that's keep very silent about this new development. That will disappoint them.'

'But how can it be kept silent?' Dale protested.

I said, 'At home, our old Gladys knows a thing or two about potions. I suggest that we take Ursula Mary to Hawkswood and let Gladys prescribe for her. I know it's against the law, but I'm fairly sure that she has obliged a wench or two in Hawkswood village. We can set Ursula Mary free of this.'

At which, Meg drew herself sharply out of my arms and snapped, 'No! Absolutely not! It's against the laws of God and man, for one thing, though maybe I wouldn't let that stop me, except that I know it's dangerous. Girls have died, taking things to rid themselves of unwanted burdens. We all know that!'

'I don't believe Gladys's potions, whatever is in them, have ever killed anyone,' I said. 'I nearly asked for her help once, myself.'

'You what?' Meg stared at me in horror.

'Nature did the work for me,' I said calmly. 'I was never sure whether I had been pregnant or not. Anyway, I had no need to resort to Gladys. But those who do haven't complained.'

'But what happened? How did you . . .?'

'It was years ago. You know very well, Meg, that I have not lived a safe life. I have been in danger, often. I have been attacked. That is what happened and there is no need to upset yourself over it. We have Ursula Mary to consider and—'

'She is not to take any kind of clear-out poison!' said Meg fiercely. 'There is another way.' And, unexpectedly, she smiled.

Dale and I stared at her.

'If I am heartbroken,' she said, 'it is because I grieve that my poor girl must go through the pain of bearing a child she does not want. But it need not stain her reputation. I have been thinking and I have had an idea.'

Her smile broadened. She said, 'I came on this journey inside our carriage. Normally, I would have ridden my good old Bay Beauty. I enjoy riding. But it is dangerous when one is with child, and I have recently begun to think that I may have conceived again. I missed the course I should have had just before your message arrived, warning us to flee, Mother. I think I shall give birth quite shortly before my daughter does. Maybe just under a month. If George can be brought to agree, and if Bartholomew and Thomasina consent to shelter us, we can pretend that Ursula Mary – no one in Zeal Aquatio has seen her since she was a tiny child – is a young widow who has come to stay with us. We can make up a suitable story about that. She can have her child quite openly. So can I. Then, as soon as possible, we will leave for home. When we get back to Riverside, I shall announce to everyone there that I have had twins. If one is noticeably larger than the other, it won't matter. It's sometimes that way with twins. No one's good name will be at risk and the unfortunate infant, who has not committed any crime, will have a home and be brought up as Ursula Mary's much younger brother or sister.'

'But could it really be done?' Dale asked. 'Will the men agree? Will the Hillmans agree?'

'I hope so!' said Meg. 'George, and Bartholomew and Thomasina. Somehow we will have to make them! We shall be there tomorrow. We'll have to start with George.'

George did not agree.

The scheme had struck me as essentially a good idea. George didn't see it as a good idea at all. He seemed determined to scuttle the whole notion like an unwanted rowing boat. We called him into the room and explained the plan to him, whereupon George, usually so solid and sensible, turned crimson with anger, slammed a clenched fist down on the table by the bed and spluttered *No!* in a voice almost loud enough to disturb the entire inn. I opened my mouth to protest but Meg nudged me, and we waited for the first outburst to subside. When shouting and thumping with his fist produced only silence, he finally turned to words, of outrage and misery mingled.

'My daughter, my poor little girl . . . I can't bear to think of it! She is little more than a child herself. If I could get my hands on those brutes, I would choke the life out of them and enjoy it! And now, Meg, my wife, do you seriously mean that we should welcome the offspring of one of these . . . these murderous pirates . . . into our home, and adopt it as a twin of the one you may be carrying?'

In a very quiet voice, a contrast to his, Meg said, 'It will still be our grandchild. And it isn't responsible for its father's sins.'

'It will be a cuckoo in the nest!'

'George,' I said, 'I was once a cuckoo in a nest. My mother was sent home from court in disgrace, pregnant with a child whose father she wouldn't name.'

'But your father was a king! Not one of a pair of piratical miscreants!'

'No one knew that at the time. The truth, that my father was King Henry, didn't emerge for years. All those years I spent in the care of my uncle and aunt, and I was lucky to have any care at all. It was my Faldene grandfather who insisted that my uncle Herbert and his wife should take my mother in and, in due course, me. Even so, I was not always

kindly treated. I would hope that this unfortunate child will
not only be taken into the care of his or her mother's family,
but will be kindly treated too.'

'Yes, indeed!' Dale spoke up. 'Terrible to be cast out,
ill-used for something one can't help!'

'Does your tirewoman often speak out of turn?' enquired
George, addressing me but glaring at Dale.

'My friend Dale often gives me good advice,' I said,
countering the glare by smiling at her. 'If my uncle and aunt
hadn't taken my mother in, I can't think what would have
happened, either to her or to me.'

'She would no doubt have appealed to the king who
would probably have taken steps to see that she was looked
after. He acknowledged his son Henry Fitzroy. He would
probably have acknowledged you and made provision for
you and your mother.'

'I think my mother was afraid. I believe she had been
threatened in some way, by friends of Queen Anne Boleyn,
or possibly friends of Jane Seymour. I don't know for sure.
It's all in the past now, well in the past. I was lucky to
have a home and an education, though I could have done with
a little more love. George, how can a baby be guilty of
anything? When this child is born and you see it, well, you
will just see a baby. Helpless, innocent. If you and Meg won't
care for it, what will happen to it? What will happen to
Ursula Mary? What if she wants to bring it up herself?'

'I hope she won't be such a fool. She is not to keep it. She
must hand it over to someone else as soon as it's born, and
forget it!'

'Women rarely forget their own children,' I said. 'She will
wonder about it all her life.'

'I sincerely hope she won't.' Poor George was visibly in a
state of turmoil. His face was red with rage but there were
tears in his eyes. He rounded on me. 'Care for it yourself if
you feel so tender towards it! It can't be reared in our house,
and that's final!'

'If you reject it, I will have to care for it,' I said. I had
feared that it would come to this. Well, I supposed it could
be managed. I said, 'I will not tell the poor child anything

about its father but, if Ursula Mary so wishes, I will tell him or her who their mother is.'

'Ursula Mary will request no such thing!'

'That decision will be hers. There are things I understand, George, that you evidently don't. I repeat: I was a cuckoo too. I know what it's like. Cuckoos have feelings, especially when they are defenceless children.'

'Tchah!'

But he was weakening. I knew it and Meg knew it, simply because he had replied this time with a snort instead of words. In a soothing voice, Meg said, 'Come, George. Let us talk it over in private. Let us go to our bedchamber.'

George grunted and said if she thought she was going to talk him round, she should think again, but Meg, giving me a wink that he didn't see, led him away. What happened between them after that, I don't know, except that I heard their voices late into the night. The wrangle no doubt resumed once they were alone together and continued long. But by morning, George had given in.

'As long as Bartholomew agrees,' he warned, across break- fast next morning. 'And Bartholomew may be difficult.'

I hoped he wouldn't be as difficult as George.

That last ride was lengthy and we didn't reach Ladymead, the rambling house on the hillside above the village of Zeal Aquatio, until late in the evening. Just before we left Swindon, George had hired a courier and despatched a detailed letter ahead of us, and I too despatched a letter early on that last day of our journey, just before we left Okehampton. We were therefore expected. The sound of our arrival, the carriage rumbling, the chickens, which always got everywhere, scattering from its wheels with loud and indignant clucks, the sound of hooves and voices, brought people out into the courtyard at once.

I looked at them all with a rush of affection. I hadn't seen them for years. The children were growing up now. Their parents had changed very little. Thomasina, with the glossy brown hair and the kind blue eyes, had become very plump. She was a cosy woman, but sharper of mind than most people realized until they got to know her. Tall, dark Bartholomew,

very sharp of mind indeed, with a disconcerting sense of
humour which showed itself rarely and usually took people
aback, hadn't altered much except for the grey hair at his
temples. Nineteen-year-old Tom was a younger image of his
father . . . and there was seventeen-year-old Ann, pretty
as could be, though she took after her mother; her shape was
already becoming rounded.

The twins, Alice and Katharine, had Bartholomew's
colouring. They were fifteen now, angular and dark, shrill of
voice and identical in appearance. The next in line was yet
another Susannah, like Eleanor's sister and the firstborn
daughter at West Leys. This Susannah was ten now and
resembled Thomasina's mother, or so Thomasina had once
told me. She was ginger, though she had Bartholomew's dark
eyes. Four-year-old Daniel and Ninian, another pair of twins,
came last, tumbling excitedly out of the house, pursued by a
harassed nurse. They were identical twins like Alice and
Katherine, and very much Thomasina's sons.

Descending from our horses, getting Dale and Meg out of
the carriage, we found ourselves surrounded. The babble
of voices was deafening. I shook hands with Tom, hugged
Ann, tried to embrace Alice and Kat both at once and was
then drawn away by Thomasina, who was calling to her
offspring to come back indoors; they could talk to the visitors
later. We had serious things to discuss. Tom was helpful.
Evidently in his parents' confidence, he began to collect his
younger siblings. Servants were whisking the luggage out of
the carriage and into the house, grooms were taking the horses
and running the carriage into a shed, and we were being guided
indoors. Thomasina was saying that luckily they had no one
else staying; there was room for us in the guest suite.

Bartholomew embraced his brother, kissed his niece and
his sister-in-law and shook hands with me. With these polite-
nesses fulfilled, he rounded us up like an efficient sheepdog:
his brother, sister-in-law and niece, and then me and the
Brockleys, separating us from everyone else and steering us
into his study. This was a little different from the last time I
had seen it. The Turkey carpet was still on the wall, but there
was much more seating this time. There had only been two

visitors' chairs then. Now there were cushions on the window seat and a settle squeezed in between the side of the hearth and the set of shelves which accommodated books and papers. It had been made ready for a crowd. Us, in fact.

'Seat yourselves, I beg you,' Bartholomew said, and then noticed that one sheep had evaded the sheepdog. 'Where is Thomasina? Haven't we servants enough to see that the luggage all goes to the right rooms?'

Thomasina's arrival placated him. 'Ah, there you are, my dear. I have been looking for you. Come and join us. Now . . .' he looked round, sternly, '. . . what about these extraordinary letters I have received? One from you, George, saying that you are in danger because you are related to Mistress Stannard – who has accompanied you here – and that Ursula Mary has already been the victim of an attack. And then another, that arrived today, from you, Mistress Stannard, saying that a grave trouble has arisen and you will be seeking our help. Just what is all this?'

'It's about me mostly, Uncle,' said Ursula Mary quietly. During the last part of the journey, she had acquired a remarkable self-possession. It was as though she had grown up, suddenly, and now had a mental age beyond her years. 'The first letter, I know, was from my father, explaining that we needed shelter because we might be attacked in some way as a means of hurting my grandmother, and that an attack had already been made, on me. That was why my grandmother sent you the second letter, early today. She wanted to warn you that we might need help. Is that not so, Grandmother?'

She was sitting beside me, on the cushioned settle. She turned to me and I put a hand over hers. Then I told Bartholomew the whole story, in detail. George tried twice to interrupt but I asked him, sharply, to desist, and the second time, Bartholomew also bade him be silent until I had finished my tale. Bartholomew and Thomasina both listened without moving or interrupting, but I saw tears in Thomasina's eyes, and I knew from the set of Bartholomew's mouth and the hardening of his eyes how appalled he was.

At the end, addressing his brother, he said, 'Well, George,

here is the situation. Your daughter was stolen from you by
these Mercers and returned to you carrying the child of one
of them. You, along with Meg here and your children, wish
to take shelter with me, and Ursula has advised you to do so,
even though these charming people, the Mercer brothers, might
wish to wreak more havoc still on the Hillman family. And
so, very likely, on mine.'

Gently, Thomasina said, 'Bart, dear . . .'

'Facts are facts,' said Bartholomew, in tones of steel.

I had expected Bartholomew's challenge, however, and was
ready for it. I said, 'I very much doubt if the Mercers knew
we were coming here. They knew that George and Meg
had fled from Riverside, but I doubt if they knew where they
were going. They have probably never heard of you,
Bartholomew, or of Ladymead or Zeal Aquatio. They struck
when my daughter and her family were at Swindon, and very
likely they finished with them there. My own feeling is that
their next attack may take place at Hawkswood. I intend to
return there as soon as I can. I simply wished to see my
daughter and her family safely here first. Only, before I leave,
we have to settle the matter of Ursula Mary's condition.' I
looked at George.

George opened his mouth and then closed it again because
his brother, ignoring him, had turned to Ursula Mary. 'My
child, are you sure about this? There is no chance that you
are mistaken?'

'I don't think so, Uncle.' Her new self-possession was plain
to him as well as to us. It was startling him as much as it had
startled me. 'I have been sick twice,' she said unemotionally.
'And I have missed. I am well overdue. That has never
happened, not since I turned fourteen. Not once.'

'I see.' Bartholomew seemed lost for words. Until George
said, 'There may be a solution. Meg and I have talked it over
– we were awake most of last night, in fact.'

He looked at me. 'We have embroidered a little on the
scheme that you and Meg first invented. The news that Meg
had for me has made things simpler. Bart, will you let us
shelter here for a few months? No one here has seen Ursula
Mary for years and we can say that she is a young ward of

ours, who was married young but has lost her husband almost at once and has returned to our care. We can perhaps borrow a wedding ring from someone . . .'

'You can have mine,' I said helpfully. 'I have three. The other two are in my strong box at home.'

'Thank you, Ursula. As it happens, Meg tells me that she too is expecting a child. It will be born no more, we think, than four weeks before Ursula Mary's, but if you will agree, Bart, we can wait until both new mothers are recovered and the babies are both a few weeks old and then we can go home, hoping that having been targets once, we will not be so again – and say to everyone at home that the babies are twins. Meg's twins.'

'The child has done nothing,' said Meg strongly. 'It will be my grandchild, however it was conceived. I will nurture it. Ursula Mary, my darling, you can remain innocent in the eyes of the world. There will be no bar to your marriage, one day.'

'I will never marry!' Ursula Mary was suddenly fierce. 'And as for *it* . . . well, thank you, dear mother, dear father, dear uncle. If you will consent to all this, well and good. Though I shall find it hard to be an affectionate sister to it.'

'I may find it hard to be an affectionate father to it,' remarked George, 'but it seems that I shall have to try. So will you, my girl. Well, Bart? Will you and your family assist us? It will be for a few months, and you will need to be wholehearted about it. The world is a clever guesser. But if we succeed, we can preserve Ursula Mary's good name and her chances of marriage.'

'If I ever did marry, I would tell the man the truth first!' Ursula Mary snapped. She flung her head up and stared us all in the face. 'Why should I live a lie? Why should I be forced into living a lie?'

'It would be better for the child, and a good deal better for you, whether you realize it or not,' said her mother reprovingly.

'Much better!' George chimed in. 'Listen, Ursula Mary, there is to be no question, ever, of the truth being told. You had better understand that, at once.'

'What if one day those . . . Mercer creatures . . . are brought to face justice? How will we hide the truth then?'

'They've done damage enough to bring them to court, without mentioning you, darling,' I said. 'And by maintaining secrecy, we protect the child as well as you.'

'Why should I care about the child? I never wanted it!'

'Someone has to care about it,' Meg remarked. 'It can't look after itself. This isn't ancient Rome where unwanted babies could be exposed on barren hillsides.' The Brockleys, who had both been listening in silence, now looked scandalized. Meg said, 'Be calm, my dear daughter. We only want to keep our family life peaceful and not a subject for gossip. Things will shape themselves, no doubt.' She glanced at me. 'You will be a great-grandmother,' she said. 'Will you mind?'

'I won't mind,' I said, and pulled my wedding ring off my finger. I did so with regret, for it was the ring that Hugh had given me. However, I still had Gerald's. I would wear that instead. It would still fit my finger. I tested the fit of my rings now and then. I handed Hugh's ring to my granddaughter, who tried it on her hand. It was a little loose. 'You can put another, tighter ring on as well, as a keeper,' I said. 'Something that looks like a betrothal ring.'

'I can lend you something that will do,' said Thomasina. 'I have an amethyst ring that won't fit any of my plump fingers now.'

Bartholomew had listened to all of this in a thoughtful silence. Now, across the width of his study, he caught my eye. 'Tell me the truth now, Ursula. Is there any likelihood that these Mercers will attack anyone in my household? You have said that at the moment they are finding their victims among what you call the outer reaches of your family and acquaintances.'

'I have already said,' I reminded him, 'that I think they have finished with your part of my family. I rather expect their next attack to take place at Hawkswood. They have spaced their onslaughts out in a certain fashion so far. My aunt Tabitha, at Faldene. My son's betrothed, near Hawkswood, though not actually at it. Now my granddaughter, away in Swindon.

I feel they are likely now to begin closing in, to come nearer home; that is more or less what Captain Julien has implied will happen. Yours is the Hillman family; you are not closely connected with me and . . .' I caught Brockley's eye and remembered his cynical remark, '. . . you have, so to speak, had your turn.' I saw Brockley smile, just a little.

'Our turn. What a way to put it,' said Bartholomew, and then that fugitive humour of his showed itself. 'I don't mean any offence, but what a harbinger of trouble you are! Once before, you brought danger to my door. On that occasion, I ordered you away, but this time the danger you have brought is tangled round my own kinsfolk, and for the sake of kinship I suppose I have to help them. Ursula Mary, here, is my niece. I am in honour bound to protect her. Though, once more, Ursula, I frankly wish you away. You are like a tall tree that summons the lightning.'

'If only we can stay here until the children are born,' said Meg pleadingly.

I rose to my feet. Brockley and Dale, who had remained silent, looked at me enquiringly.

'I am anxious to leave as soon as I can,' I said. 'I want to get back to Hawkswood. I think that the threat may well shift in that direction. If I am right, you will be left in peace. I think the brothers intended to get my granddaughter with child. If they have followed us and are lurking nearby, they may hear of a very youthful widow living here, who is expecting a child. That will make them hug themselves and, of course, there is the possibility that they will start some gossip going. You will have to deal with that. With luck, they'll let ill alone, and turn their attention to me or to someone in my Hawkswood household. I will then be the one having to deal with things. Master Hillman, we are all tired and so are our horses. If the Brockleys and I may rest here for a day or so, we will then take our leave and start for home.'

THIRTEEN
The Net Draws In

Because we had to pace our horses and also take care of Dale, it was fifteen days before we at last returned to Hawkswood. Even at that, both we and our horses were very weary by the time we arrived. Dale had actually been heroic, doing her best to sit on Blue Gentle as though she were on a padded settle in a lady's parlour, and trying to keep her back straight. But every time we stopped at an inn, she would sit down at the first opportunity and visibly sag as she did so. When we stopped for the night, I always made a point of sending her upstairs to rest as soon as I could. A few times, Brockley took her up behind him on Firefly, but the double weight was hard on the horse if continued for too long.

If anyone was following us, we saw no sign of it, and when at last, late one afternoon, we came through the gatehouse at Hawkswood, we found that nothing untoward had occurred while we were away.

I had despatched couriers from Devon to announce that we were starting for home, and also from our final stop at Windsor. All was in readiness for our arrival, and everyone was smiling. That included Harry and Ben, and I saw with relief that, although Harry was quieter than he used to be, he was now very much himself, wounded by the past but healing.

Captain Banks and Sergeant Wooller were still there. They had been regularly patrolling my boundaries, augmented at times by Captain Julien, who was still with us. They had nothing to report. Harry and Ben had various household matters to explain to us. As soon as he knew that we were on our way home, John Hawthorn had had a calf slaughtered and the meat hung, and after the arrival of the Windsor courier, Hawthorn had marched out to tell our poultry keeper, Etheldreda Hope, that chickens were required for the spit and, if she hadn't any bad layers to offer, then good layers must be sacrificed. There would be roast meats for supper, he declared, and his assistant Ben Flood was creating a spiced sauce to go with them, sharp and hot with verjuice and peppercorns, and then there would be apple pie accompanied by a custard flavoured with cinnamon and dusted with nutmeg.

'And your favourite Canary wine, madam; I have taken the liberty of having a keg of it broached and it will be served in a flagon and there's no aniseed in it.'

'Has there been any message from Cecil?'

'To say that those black-hearted villains have been caught? Alas, no, madam.'

Caesar and Cleo had bayed their usual noisy greeting, but had been restrained from rushing up to us and getting under the hooves of the horses. Though the horses were soon out of the way, for my grooms had unsaddled them within minutes and whisked them into their stalls to be rubbed down, while bran mashes were prepared. Brockley went with them to the stables to make sure that there was no neglect.

He returned to find me in the hall with Dale, Harry and Ben, and Peter Dickson joined us at the same moment. 'We are all thankful for your safe return,' Dickson said to me. 'We received your letter saying that your granddaughter had been returned to her parents. How is she?'

I was ready for that question. Before we left Ladymead, I had discussed it with the Hillmans and with the Brockleys and we had decided on a suitable story. It was necessary because never, ever, must anyone but ourselves know what had really happened to Ursula Mary. That was a secret to be lost and forgotten, as though it had been dropped into the deepest ocean or cast into a volcano crater.

Calmly and untruthfully, not catching the Brockleys' eyes, I said, 'By the grace of God, Ursula Mary is unharmed. Her parents had to pay a ransom. She had been frightened, of course, but she wasn't ill-used.'

'Held in an attic somewhere,' said Brockley laconically. 'In a house somewhere isolated – or so she thought from peering out of a window. It seems that she was properly fed.'

I nodded. 'Her parents paid up and, early the next morning, she was blindfolded and put on a horse in front of one of her captors and left on the doorstep of the inn where we were staying with my daughter and her family. She looked grubby and she had been scared, but nothing worse. I could almost believe that the worst sufferer was – is – her mother! My daughter is expecting again and all this did her no good. However, we hope that all will go well now that Ursula Mary is home.'

I hoped I sounded convincing. 'The whole family is now safe in Devon,' I said. 'How have things been here?'

'Captain Julien has made himself useful. He has kept an eye on the maids just as Wilder used to do,' Harry told me, and we both spent a sad moment remembering the former steward, Adam Wilder, who had been such a mainstay in the household and had died the previous year.

Then Harry added, 'And when we invited the Blakes over to dine one day, and there was so much to do in the kitchen, Captain Julien turned the spit! You don't mind that we asked the Blakes to dine, do you, Mother? They had asked me, just the week before, and I felt I should return the invitation.'

'No, that's quite in order, Harry. You did right. We should keep on friendly terms with our neighbours. We share their grief for Eleanor.'

'They might well have blamed us for what happened to her,' Harry said. 'We are fortunate that they haven't!'

That evening of our arrival, we ate well, and the talk round the table was cheerful. Banks and Wooller had eaten earlier and were back on duty, walking round the boundaries of my land in the dusk. Captain Julien, who had done his best to replace them while they supped, was able to join us. Across the supper table, we heard tales of amusing things that had happened in our absence. Etheldreda Hope's chickens had escaped from their run one day and the whole flock got into the kitchen, said Captain Julien, and oh how furious John Hawthorn had been! Harry told us how a pedlar had come to the house – 'he came in by way of the courtyard, driving a donkey cart, Mother' – and had refused to believe that he, Harry, was in charge and kept on demanding to see 'the master'.

'But I got him to see sense, Mother, and in the end he came into the hall and the maids all crowded round and bought ribbons and needles and such things from his tray, and I bought three big balls of good strong twine and I agreed that John Hawthorn should have two new saucepans. The pedlar had a little cart with him, for his heavier goods. But the way he kept calling me *boy* . . .!'

'I overheard it all,' Julien said. 'But I didn't want to interfere. Harry had a right to deal with the situation himself and not depend on me or Mr Dickson to cope with it. And deal with it he did, too! But Gladys got mixed up with it. She'd been in the courtyard, sitting on that bench by the hall door and snatching a taste of sunshine. She came inside to see what was going on and you should have heard her berating that pedlar!'

Our arrival, therefore, was blessed with merriment, and that night I think we all slept well. In the morning, Dale, who last night had helped me out of my breeches and into a pretty gown for supper, and later helped me into my nightgown even though her eyes were trying to close from weariness, now insisted that I ought to wear a truly dignified gown, with a bigger ruff and farthingale. 'As befits the lady of the house,' she said.

Thus attired, I swept down to a breakfast of small ale, chicken pies and fresh bread, with butter from our own cows. And with that, the business of a Hawkswood day began. The first thing I always wanted to do, after an absence from home, was to hear a report on the trotters' stud, and I therefore summoned Laurence Miller.

And now came the first hint of something untoward. Brockley took my message and returned to say that Miller could not come until midday. When I asked why not, he replied that Miller was asleep.

'*Asleep?*'

'He was awake and on duty between two in the morning and seven o'clock, madam.'

'On duty?'

'Yes, madam. He and his deputy Jem Higgs share a night watch in case of trouble at the stud. In view of the danger that we all know our household may be in, they thought it wise to have the stud guarded at night. Miller's dog is always with them, and just as well, for last night there was a prowler. The dog saw him off.'

Brockley said, 'Miller says that he caught a glimpse of him, but not to recognize; the prowler was just a shape in the darkness, and when that dog was on his trail, he was a shape that moved off very fast, vaulted a fence, and was gone.'

'I don't doubt it,' I said, thinking of the killer in Foggy Doggie's yellow eyes. The shadowy prowler had been wise to flee.

I didn't like it. Nothing like this had ever happened before, never in all the years that the stud had existed.

A word shaped itself unpleasantly inside my mind. *Mercers.*

Meanwhile, however, there were other things to consider. Harry, who had apparently taken to talking household matters over very seriously with Ben, suddenly wanted to know why we had so few servants.

'Mother, the Blakes have at least twenty, though Cobbold Hall is smaller than Hawkswood by far. They have footmen and a spitboy. Why haven't we?'

'I have enough grooms,' I said. 'They lend a hand if any furniture needs to be moved or baggage carried about, and they run errands. I have already noticed the Cobbold Hall arrangements, and what they come to is that they have menservants standing about and doing nothing and no doubt eating heartily at mealtimes. Here, we are more careful with our money. Flood and Hawthorn turn the spit or call one of the maids to do it if necessary. Or let Captain Julien do it, as I gather he did on one occasion.'

'We ought to have a spitboy at least,' said Harry obstinately. 'And the grooms are outside men. We ought to have at least two indoor menservants and more maidservants. We only have Phoebe, Bess, Jennet and Margery at the moment, with Tessie giving a hand at times. We should have a dozen maids, to help in the kitchen and form separate groups for attending to the different floors.'

I sighed. I knew that my thrifty habits went back to a time when Hugh had lost money through a failed business venture and we had had to retrench, cutting down on the number of horses in the stables and making do with a skeleton staff inside the house. Since then, I had always been wary of expenditure. It now seemed clear that Harry had other ideas and that times would change once he was really the master. I led him into the study and proceeded to explain to him why I was so careful.

'But I'm not very interested in business ventures and buying into merchants' voyages,' he said. 'Hawkswood pays its way very well and we can afford more help now. I think we ought to have the spitboy, anyway. He can be a trainee in the kitchen and learn to assist Ben Flood one day, perhaps.'

This was fair enough, I supposed. 'Very well,' I said. 'Find out if anyone in the village has a lad who would like to work in our kitchen. The lad can expect some instruction in cookery, a chance to win promotion, in time. Send Ben to enquire.'

A week passed and then we acquired the spitboy. He was Tommy Reed, now aged about thirteen. When younger, he had been one of the most diabolically ill-behaved urchins ever seen in Hawkswood village, but he had grown up somewhat since then and was in need of a trade. His mother, as it happened, had taught him how to make pastry. He was to be our spitboy and would also be instructed in cookery. 'The boy's bright enough,' said Hawthorn, who knew him (and of him). 'He'll make a chief cook one day.'

He wasn't expensive, since he worked for his keep plus a penny a day and, as he had never had any money of his own before, to him this was riches.

I resisted the idea of indoor menservants, although I could see that once Harry had the power, he would no doubt flood Hawkswood with well-paid and probably under-worked footmen. I wondered whether his wife, when he had one, would have any say in the matter. For the time being, of course, I didn't speak of such things. Eleanor's death was still too near.

I had been home eight days when my forester, Jerome Billington, came to the house asking to speak to me. Ben put him in the study, where I joined him. Billington was middle-aged, a squarely built man, very steady, full of good sense. I was surprised, and disconcerted, to realize that now, as he stood holding his cap in one square brown hand, he was obviously seething.

'I have never known such a thing, madam, never! I could have been killed. I was meant to be killed! I'm sure of it.'

I felt my heart turn to stone and begin to sink. So here it was again. Another attack. As I had feared. 'What happened?' I asked.

'There's that big old fir tree out on the edge of the wood, towards the lake, you know it, madam.'

I nodded.

'I reckoned to have it down; the next gale would likely knock it over anyhow, and it's overshadowing some good beech saplings. There's plenty of timber in it, too, firewood for the house here and a good load to take to market. So I settled to deal with it. I could work on my own. My assistants are busy.'

I nodded. Jerome had two assistants, but he didn't always need them. He was a great one for sending them off to tasks elsewhere while he worked alone.

'That tree could only fall in one direction. Everywhere else there are other trees in the way. Still, that's no matter. When I'm felling, I always decide in which direction a tree should fall. I make a cut to weaken it on that side, and then work at the other side, until it falls. Only, when I got to the tree this morning, there was something not right. It was leaning a bit, which it hadn't been yesterday. So I squatted down and took a look. I'd marked the place where my saw would make the weakening cut. I mostly do that in case I want to show one of my apprentices, like, where to position a cut. Well, just there, there was a cut already. I don't know what it was done with. It was a thin cut; hadn't disturbed the bark much, if at all. I wouldn't have seen it if I hadn't been looking closely. It was thin, like I said. I don't know how deep it went, but when I inspected it, I could see that someone had tried to brush away any wood dust from the ground.'

He looked at me, with serious brown eyes. 'Someone had worked there, patiently, for it must have taken time. But if it went deep . . . well, that fir has a slender trunk. If I'd just set to work with my saw to make my own weakening cut, and hadn't noticed that there was this one there already, I reckon that tree might have come down a lot sooner than I expected. I think the cut had gone deep, from the way the tree was beginning to lean already. Chancy, but it might have killed me.'

'Surely not!' I shied away from the implications. 'You would hear the tree creaking, sense its movement; you're experienced. You wouldn't have been caught that way. Or the tree might have stood after all until you were ready for it.'

'No doubt. I'm none the worse, madam, and you'll have your load of firewood and your cartload for sale. But whoever made that cut meant mischief, madam. And we are all aware of the danger that you fear. We all know that you have urged Master Spelton and his family into hiding, and that you have been away so as to help your daughter and her family to safety.'

'Yes. I see. Billington, I am sorry. Sorry to have brought this danger to my people. You were very right to report it.' I found myself rubbing my forehead and silently asking *will your agents never find those Mercers, Cecil?* 'Miller guards the trotters with the help of Jem Higgs and Foggy. But how on earth can I guard *all* my grounds, my woodland, the gardens, the fields? Even with two soldiers prowling round the boundaries at night, the boundaries are too long. Two men just can't keep it all under surveillance.'

'Well, I know that while you were away, Master Harry insisted that your two half mastiffs went on being loosed at night. I have a dog, too, my terrier, he's excitable enough and has sharp teeth. Some of the other hands, the ones that live in your grounds, not in the village, have dogs too. We will all loose our dogs at night henceforth. At the least, their barking may wake someone in time to prevent trouble.

It was the best that we could do.

Three more days passed, and nothing further occurred either to disturb our present peace or relieve our future fears.

On the fourth day, Gladys disappeared.

It was some time before her absence was noticed. Gladys had few regular habits. She pottered about, now doing a little helpful dusting, now wandering into the herb garden to pluck herbs for her potions and sometimes even to weed the beds. She was old and lame, but with the aid of her stick she could still climb stairs, and she was still capable of kneeling to get at dandelions or tufts of grass.

After picking herbs, she would probably invade the kitchen to create one of her brews. John Hawthorn was used to her and had learned to accommodate her. I had provided her with a shelf of her own in my stillroom, and in the kitchen she had the use of a couple of basins, some utensils and two pans, which lived on a small shelf that I had had put up for her. I had said that certain times of day should be set aside as times when she could come into the kitchen if she had any brews to make. Hawthorn, albeit reluctantly, had agreed that she could do so very early in the morning or for an hour after dinner. On the day that she vanished, she hadn't used the kitchen. Her only other regular habit, at least on warm sunny days, was sitting on the bench in the courtyard to watch the grooms working. Ben Flood said that he had seen her there just after dinner. But no one knew where she had gone since then. No one saw her go; and if anyone came to fetch her away, the dogs failed to bark.

She could be relied on to appear for meals. When dinner or supper were served in the servants' hall, Gladys would be there. On that day, it was her failure to appear for supper that sounded the alarm.

I learned later that Bess, the lively young maid I had brought back after a previous visit to Devon, ran upstairs to see if Gladys was ill, perhaps lying down in her little attic room. She returned to say that Gladys wasn't there, and there were no signs that she had been. Her bed was tidied, as it would have been when Gladys rose in the morning, and that was all.

Ben who, by his own choice, now took his meals in the servants' hall, said that the maids should finish their supper; he would look for her himself. Later, he came to where Harry, Julien, the Brockleys, Peter Dickson and I were. Having finished supper, we had not yet heard of Gladys's disappearance and were preparing for an evening of music. Dickson was a skilled musician and had taught both Harry and Ben to play the lute and the spinet. Ben, in fact, had expected to join us for the evening anyway. When he came into the East Room, where the spinet was now kept, and where the rest of us had gathered, we turned to him, smiling, with Harry saying, 'We were only waiting for you!'

Then we saw his anxious face and I said sharply, 'What's amiss, Ben?'

'No one can find Gladys, mistress,' Ben said. 'She didn't come to supper and she's not ill and in her bed, either.'

'Had a fall in the garden and she's still lying there, I would wager anything,' said Harry.

'And it's cold tonight!' I said sharply. 'If she's left there long, she'll take a rheum and very likely a lung congestion!'

Harry, looking startled, was halfway out of the room before the sentence was finished. Brockley said, 'I'll go after him. There's plenty of the outside to search; not that she ever goes beyond the gardens, but they're big enough. You are very likely right, madam; she's had a fall or a seizure out there.'

He hastened away and I rose to my feet. 'I'll walk through the rooms on the ground floor. The rest of you go through the bedchambers. The kitchen quarters are all in use, except for the washroom, and if Gladys is in there, of her own free will, it's the first time in history. Still, Ben, make sure.'

'I did, before I came upstairs,' said Ben. 'She wasn't there. I'll join the search in the gardens. Shall I call Banks and Wooller in? They're out patrolling just now.'

'Yes. As many people as possible,' I said.

An hour later, what had begun as a simple search for someone possibly injured or ill had taken on a more sinister tone. We all came together again, this time in the long, stone-walled room that was the servants' hall. It was dark by then, and there were candles on the table. Our numbers were now increased by the grooms, who, like Banks and Wooller, had been called to join in the search of the grounds. No one had found any trace of Gladys.

I began to ask questions, seeking to find out when she had last been seen. Gradually it emerged that she had been at dinner, had eaten some veal and a bread roll, and had then taken an apple outside to eat in the courtyard, while she sunned herself on the bench. Ben Flood had seen her there. But no one at all could testify to seeing her later. She had left most of the other servants still at their dinner and, by the time they dispersed, she was gone. After that, there was a complete blank.

'It's plain enough,' said Julien, sounding very worried. 'During that quiet time, someone slipped into the courtyard and took her.'

'She'll be terrified,' I said. 'She's so helpless. There's nothing of her; she's so old and shrunken . . . she couldn't fight them. She's . . .'

She had lived with me for years and years. She hadn't been young when she more or less pushed her way into my household, and God alone knew how old she was now. For all that time I had, I thought, endured her out of pity. Brockley and I had once rescued her from a charge of witchcraft, and later on, even though she was in my household and under my protection, she had only just escaped from another such charge. She loathed washing herself; she cursed people she disliked – her curses were imaginative and forceful – and she did in fact dabble in witchcraft. I knew that, discouraged it and kept silent about it. She regularly foresaw disasters and announced them like a croaking raven, and she was often right.

And I now discovered that I loved her, was as stricken by her disappearance as I would have been at the disappearance of a child or grandchild of mine, and in any case, that wasn't all, for this had come after the deaths of Aunt Tabitha and Eleanor and the abduction of Ursula Mary. It was, it had to be, part of the Mercers' campaign. It was all too much. Poor Gladys, to be dragged into that! I lost my dignity, sat down on the nearest bench and helplessly began to cry.

I felt a hand on my shoulder and looked up to find Brockley there. 'I thought I loathed her,' Brockley said. 'But now . . . if she's been abducted, she'll curse whoever's taken her but she'll still be terrified. I can't bear to think about it!' His voice was trembling.

Brockley had often – no, frequently – been infuriated by Gladys, and now, I thought, he too had found out that he loved her. Perhaps, because in her cross-grained way, she had loved us. She had also been helplessly dependent upon us. We must not fail her now.

Furiously, I rubbed my eyes on my sleeve and said, 'I feel as though there is a net of steel all round us, all round me, and it is closing in on me. Aunt Tabitha. Eleanor Blake. Ursula Mary. Someone prowling round the trotters' stud. Someone trying to kill Billington. Now this.'

'I know. Mistress Stannard, I must warn you further,' said Captain Julien. 'You must be prepared. I know how those boys think. They may hope that you will surrender to them before they wreak any more havoc among those you care for. They may offer you an opportunity. You must consider how to respond to that. I would counsel you not to give in!'

'I feel ashamed,' said Captain Banks. 'We have been so anxious to guard the bounds of your land, madam, that we haven't taken enough care of the main entrance through your gatehouse. But there is usually someone about in the courtyard and there are the dogs . . .'

'We are both sorry,' Wooller echoed. And then added, 'But there aren't enough of us.'

'All the men on the premises and in the village are armed,' said Brockley. 'And I have kept up regular practices with weapons.'

Captain Julien burst out, 'But they all have their duties to perform. It's quite true that there aren't enough men to guard this place, but I am beginning to feel that I shouldn't be one of them.'

He looked at me and there was pity in his eyes. 'Madam, you are truly having a dreadful time and so, my brother Harry, are you. It has been a happy thing for me to meet you; I had no idea what a joy it can be to have a brother. Before, I had only the brotherhood of – well, you know.' He turned back to me. 'Madam, I think I should leave you. I did wrong in coming here. I did so because I thought I might in some way help or protect you and my brother. I failed to realize how close a watch the Mercers would probably keep on you. By now, they surely know I am here. That will make them furious – and it will make me a target too. I would be wise to get out of the way. Harry, my brother, you must take care of your mother – and don't let her go and sacrifice herself. I think she is capable of it.'

'Is that really what they want?' I said in bewilderment.

'It could be. I don't know. But I think it would please them if you did. Madam, I will leave in the morning. Unless there is anything more that we can do tonight. Did no one see anything?' He looked round at the gathered household. 'Have any of you seen any strangers about – in the woods, in the fields?'

We all shook our heads. Captain Banks said grimly that if he or Sergeant Wooller had seen any strangers anywhere near Hawkswood, let alone on its land, they would have accosted said strangers and made them give an account of themselves. Brockley said, 'I doubt if we can do any more till morning.'

But dreadful things were going through my mind. The Mercers were hardly likely to use Gladys as they had used Ursula Mary. So why had they seized her? Would we find her dead, perhaps after some miserable days? Or – because Julien's words had now put the idea into my head – would word reach me that it was her life or mine?

Harry was saying, 'But if strangers came into the courtyard to snatch Gladys, why didn't the dogs bark?'

'*They* had a nice afternoon sleep, same as I did,' said Arthur Watts. 'They were fast asleep when I woke up; didn't rouse until I called them. My sleep was natural. I'd wager money that theirs was a case of drugged meat.'

I said, 'Captain Julien, please don't go. If as you say, the Mercers now know you are here and it makes you a target – well, you'll still be that wherever you are. Meanwhile, here, you are one more man to help guard the premises and I know that Harry likes having a brother – is that not true, Harry?'

'Yes, it is,' said Harry.

Captain Julian shrugged and smiled. 'If you wish it, I will stay.'

The smile seemed forced, though. He didn't look happy. Harry, however, took his arm and led him away. These were dreadful times for them as well as for me. The brothers would help each other, I thought.

FOURTEEN
The Outrageous Bait

However it had been done, Gladys was gone. Brockley went to Guildford and arranged for her disappearance to be cried in its streets; we visited the Blakes and also my friends Christina and Thomas Ferris at White Towers and asked if they could help, or if they had heard or seen anything that might concern Gladys. No one responded to our crier, and neither the Ferrises nor the Blakes had any useful news for us. The Ferrises reported – which was a relief – that they had not themselves suffered any form of attack, but as for word of Gladys, there was just a blank. Our neighbours were sympathetic up to a point, but there wasn't much real sympathy for Gladys. The Blakes had met her while Harry was courting Eleanor, and been disconcerted by her, while even Thomas Ferris, a hard-headed man if ever there was one, regarded Gladys as a witch and wondered why I kept her about my household.

The only person among them all who really seemed to understand was Eleanor's younger sister Margaret, who said, 'But she's so old. She must feel that this is too much, that she has nothing to fight with. An old woman can't go saving herself by climbing out of windows, or running away. She must be so frightened, just longing for home.' Margaret was a nice girl, I thought.

Meanwhile, in that ruthless way it has, life went on. I might cry myself to sleep at night; in the daytime I might fret about Gladys to everyone who spoke to me, but life still went on. It always does. Tragic things happen. People may fall ill, be injured, die, vanish, but meals must be prepared and eaten, bedlinen changed; people need to eat, sleep, wash, buy provisions; night follows day and day follows night in relentless procession. First of all, Gladys had been missing for several hours, then it became since yesterday, then since the day before yesterday. Eventually, it would be a week, a fortnight, a month . . .

That the Mercers were behind this, I had no doubt. Their horrible scheme was closing in on me and I wondered how I could live with so much fear, continually in dread of what horrible thing was going to happen next. And yet, I did just that. I lived with it, doing from day to day whatever needed to be done. I wondered how I could seem so outwardly stolid and the answer, of course, was that I wasn't stolid at all, but food must be cooked and eaten, rooms must be dusted, one must wash, dress, eat, sleep . . . it was all quite impossible, but I did it just the same.

Once Brockley said to me, 'Madam, you could take refuge at court, you know. The queen would shelter you.'

'While I closed Hawkswood and took you all to court with me? Including the stud? Can you imagine? No.' I shook my head. 'There's no escape that way.'

Gladys had vanished on Friday the fourteenth of September. On the following Tuesday it was market day at Woking, and we were due to attend it.

We went to Woking market once a month or so. I liked to go, with Dale and Brockley in attendance, and Ben Flood usually came with us, armed with a shopping list created by John Hawthorn and Phoebe. Sometimes Phoebe came too. We would travel in our mule cart, leave it at the Barlow Mow hostelry, and walk round the market on foot. Dale and Phoebe, if she were there, would have large baskets while Flood had a sack for his purchases and we usually lost sight of him until we all met again at the inn, to refresh ourselves with ale before setting off for home.

This time, however, things were different. It was as though the disappearance of Gladys had done something to Hawkswood, shaken up its pattern of living. Phoebe said she would come, as there were things she wished to buy for the maidservants' clothing. Brockley, however, said he didn't wish Dale to go to the market.

'It's not safe for her to be out and about, madam,' he said.

'She is as likely a target as any, and neither you nor I could bear that – and if Fran were to be snatched or hurt . . . *she* couldn't bear it. I am sorry to deprive you of her company, madam, but I am her husband and I have the right to protect her.'

So my bright young maidservant Bess accompanied me in Dale's place, while Brockley and Dale stayed at home and Ben Atbrigge came with us as our escort.

The day was warm and sunny and Woking was packed. We edged our way through the crowds among the stalls, searching for the ones we wanted. The air rang with raucous exhortations. Come and buy remedies for every ailment from ingrowing toenails to headaches; come and buy the freshest and tastiest cauliflowers, cabbages, carrots, apples, plums, cherries!

Other stallholders declared that they were offering everything anyone could possibly want in the way of kitchenware, tableware, workboxes for ladies, jewellery (the prettiest and the cheapest, come and buy!) or saddlery for the tack room. The qualities of various cloths – velvet, wool, silk or linen, plain, brocaded or embroidered – were being stridently bawled, in competition with bellowings about leather goods – gloves, shoes, cloaks and hats – and silken thread for a lady's workbox, fit to embroider a queen's best gown. Come and buy! Come and buy! Come and buy . . . buy . . . buy! The noise was deafening.

Further on came the livestock pens, where the human shouts were augmented by the squeals of frightened pigs, the agitated clucks of poultry, the bleating of sheep and the blaring – one couldn't call it lowing – of nervous cattle. This early in the day there were not many horses, except those being ridden by haughty individuals who cleared a path for themselves by the vigorous use of their whips. There would be a horse sale later on, at the far end of the market.

'Don't worry, madam! I shall not let any pickpockets near you. You can rely on me!' Ben assured me, in a shout, so that I would hear him. I wasn't actually worried, since the purse at my belt was empty. I did have a little money on me, but it was in a velvet bag hung round my neck and dangling under my gown. Nor had I put on any earrings.

We all made some purchases. Phoebe and I chose some holland cloth and red flannel to provide my servants with new ruffs and warm underskirts for next winter, and some linen thread for the stitching. The roll of flannel completely filled Phoebe's basket, while the holland cloth made Bess's basket bulge. I hadn't brought a basket of my own, so I purchased one and then bought a roll of sky-blue velvet and some silk thread for embroideries. Bess was attracted by a couple of cheap but pretty earrings made of copper and tinted glass and Ben, laughing, bought them for her.

When Flood joined us at the inn, his sack was bulging. Proudly, he showed us his purchases. He had cauliflowers, a bag of sugar, a box of assorted spices (peppercorns, cinnamon, powdered ginger, cardamom), two dozen candles of the type that I liked for my bedchamber, and two pounds weight of the new vegetable, potatoes, which were gradually gaining popularity in England. 'Master Hawthorn thought we might try them, madam. He says they're supposed to be easy to cook.'

Ben made a mild fuss over seating me comfortably in the public room, and sat beside me. 'Not for impertinence, madam, but I mean to be careful with you. What would Brockley say if harm came to you while you were with me?'

The room was full of people talking and laughing, but it was not quite as noisy as the market and Ben really didn't need to speak so loudly.

'You'd make a fine stallholder,' I said, though I smiled, not wanting to hurt his feelings. He probably did feel responsible for me. 'I didn't know you had such a powerful voice.'

'Sorry, madam.' But when we had refreshed ourselves with tankards of the Barley Mow's excellent ale, he once more seemed to feel that he must reassure me, and I had to shush him. He really didn't know the strength of his own voice. In fact, he made me nervous and Bess even more so. On the way home, she whispered anxiously to me that the whole world must now know that he was my self-appointed guardian, and she hoped he hadn't put himself in danger.

We returned home from Woking in time for a late dinner. We ate, and then I showed my purchases to Dale. 'There's

some work here for us,' I said. 'The servants can make their
own petticoats, but I'll have to have the ruffs made by the
ruff-maker in Guildford, and we must use this velvet. There's
enough here for a gown each.' I wished I didn't sound so
listless.

'Yes. It will take our minds off . . . things.' Dale was listless too. Our fears for Gladys had leached our energy away.
'What did Bess buy?' she asked.

'Earrings,' I said. 'She has taste. They were copper and
glass, but very pretty. She has an eye for that sort of thing. I
think we should teach her embroidery. I fancy she might enjoy
it. She enjoyed the market; I'm glad we took her.'

'You need to do something pleasant as well, ma'am. I think
that for you, the market was just part of work. Why don't you
go out to the stud and see how the youngsters in training are
progressing? Didn't you say you were hoping to sell those
two dapple greys as a matched pair?'

'You may be right, Dale,' I said.

The sky had clouded and the day had cooled. I put a cloak
round my shoulders and set out.

I had established the trotters' stud in some leased fields out
beyond the home farm. One of the fields had a wide track all
round its perimeter, where young horses could be trained to
harness and taught to trot at speed. A good fast trot could
match a canter easily and it looked stylish. For that reason,
trotters were popular. As I had hoped, training was in
progress. I leant on the railed fence, watching. At the far side
of the field, I could see Captain Banks, on guard, I supposed,
but also watching. The dapple-grey pair that Dale had
mentioned were on the circuit, driven by Jem Higgs, the
senior groom who was Miller's chief assistant. He pulled over
when he saw me.

'They're doing well, madam. They can go to the next horse
fair if you wish, unless we hear of a private buyer.'

'I like private buyers,' I said. 'We can make sure that they
understand what trotters are and how to manage them. Tell
me when you have this season's new entry quite ready for
sale and I'll have them cried in Guildford.'

'And keep the fillies for breeding?'

'All but the flea-bitten grey with the long back and the goose rump. Can't think how she inherited conformation like that, but we can't have her passing it on. She trots all right; she can go to the sale. Where is Master Miller?'

'In his house.' Jem, still on the perch of his lightweight training cart, looked down at me with anxious eyes. 'Madam, he is up to something. He's doing some kind of weird experiment in his kitchen! Says it's something to do with training his dog, the one he calls his Foggy Doggie. Not that I'd disagree with giving that beast all the training it can use. I think it ought to be kept under control. I don't like it. It's never done anything wrong, never chased any of the mares or foals, never even scared them, but I've seen it look at them and I don't like its eyes.'

'I'll go and see him,' I said. 'Take good care of those greys, Jem. They're going to make money.'

I left the field and took the short path that led to Miller's house. It was in fact a fairly large cottage, thatched, timbered, limewashed, with a door that Miller had painted a vivid green. The door was ajar, as it often was, and I went in, calling Miller's name. The moment I was inside, my nostrils were assailed by an extraordinary smell, a mixture of the sweet and the pungent. Miller called to me in answer to his name and his voice came from the kitchen at the rear, so I made my way there, noticing that the smell grew stronger with every step I took. I stepped through the kitchen door and stopped short.

'Good day, Miller. And may I ask, what on earth are you doing?'

'Experimenting with smells, Mistress Stannard.' He had the fire lit in his kitchen hearth, and he was standing in front of it, using a long wooden spoon to stir something noisome in a saucepan. He glanced round at me and grinned. 'It's too strong, of course. I shall have to dilute it, and very thoroughly at that. I want it so that humans can't smell it but dogs can, especially my dog Foggy.'

'Whatever for?'

'I want to train his nose to the utmost degree, just in case there are any more prowlers. Our trotters are valuable. The idea is to smear the stuff about on the path round the stables. That's where I saw the prowler and it's the likeliest place for a mischief maker. If I see any more shadowy figures that run away; well, they'll get this on the soles of their shoes and Foggy can track them. They won't get away! Only I've got the mixture much too strong as yet.'

'Have you tried aniseed?'

'Aniseed, madam?'

'It excites dogs. When my cook John Hawthorn brought some home from a market in Guildford, Caesar and Cleo jumped on him, knocked him down and tried to get at the bag it was in. Hawthorn grinds it up very fine and adds it to soups and stews and sometimes even sprinkles it on a roast. Though not over all of it. He leaves a bit free of it and carves that for me. I don't like it and insist on separate servings. We have a supply, though. I can let you have some. It would save you from all this.' I waved a hand at his saucepan. 'What have you got in there?'

'Everything I could think of that smells strong. Garlic, lavender, excrement – I'm using my own – some meat that's gone off, rosewater . . . can you think of anything else?'

'You'll make Foggy sneeze. I'll get you some aniseed. We have it in the herb garden now. You can grind the seed to powder, and then I should think you could mix it with oil. That would spread smoothly and stick to an intruder's feet. There haven't been any more prowlers, have there?'

'No, mistress, though I have been watchful. Jem Higgs and I take turns during the night. I watch from ten in the evening until one of the clock in the morning, and then wake Jem and he watches until four. Then I take over again until six. The grooms are about then. Nothing will happen to our beautiful trotters, mistress, if I can prevent it. Although . . .' He turned to me, looking grave, and let his wooden spoon fall slack. He hesitated to speak.

'What is it, Miller?'

Laurence Miller was a tall, lean, laconic man with a long face, in both senses of that phrase. When he came to the house to make one of his regular reports on the fortunes of the stud, he usually did so in a stiff manner, with no expression in his pale eyes and I always felt that, to him, I was a tiresome and inferior woman whose requirements were a nuisance to a busy and important man such as himself.

All the same, he was Cecil's watchman, placed in my household to watch what I did, who I saw, what events surrounded me, and report on them to Cecil. Over time, I thought that he had acquired more respect for me. Now, although he was as usual standing tall and looking over my shoulder rather than straight in the eyes, I sensed genuine concern for me.

'This business of kidnapping Gladys Morgan,' he said, 'I don't like it at all. I can't see the point of it and that is a serious worry. It looks like a change of tactics. I know that although I have been with you now for many years and have, I hope, given you good service, you still resent my presence here. You don't like being watched. But you are the queen's sister, after all, and she wishes to keep you safe. Until Lord Burghley's agents get hold of the Mercers, you need protection, for her sake as well as yours.'

I said nothing. I loved my royal sister and more, I knew her for a protector of England, a guardian of her people's freedom of thought, which Mary of Scotland would have taken from us and Philip of Spain probably still hoped to take. I also realized that although I had been useful to her in many ways, I was also a weak point. I was her sister and I could be threatened as a means of putting pressure on her, to do this or not do that. Except that in that extremity, she would put the safety of England first and, if necessary, sacrifice me. She had at times sent me into danger, or allowed Walsingham to do so. I understood all this and did not complain, but there were times, and this was one of them, when I devoutly wished my royal blood out of the way.

Miller was continuing. 'I am part of the business of keeping you safe and, believe me, I am now wondering anxiously what I should do to assure that safety. I don't like this development of taking an aged servant and following it up with nothingness. I don't like it at all. I can't see what it means.'

'Neither can I. It worries me night and day. I daresay we'll find out eventually, and probably in some unpleasant way. For the moment, even speculation raises demons in our minds. Let us talk about horses instead. I've just been watching that dapple grey pair going round the track. They look splendid.'

'As you know, their dams are full sisters. I took one look at those two foals when they came into the world, and I thought at once, if those two turn out to be good high-stepping trotters, there's a matched pair there worth a deal of money.'

'Get the highest price you can,' I said, 'and as soon as you can. The sooner they are sold and away from here, the better. I wouldn't like those two to come to any harm, and it has occurred to me that my horses could be targets as well as people. As you have said, there have been prowlers. I'll fetch some aniseed for you. You have a grinder?'

'Yes, of course. I dry ginger root, chop it, and grind it ready to make a medicine for colic. Apothecaries and grooms have much in common.'

I went back to the house and despatched Ben Flood with a packet of aniseed. I hoped that Foggy would approve.

Two more days passed. Ben seemed to have little to do, beyond watching over the service at mealtimes. On the second morning he took Eddie for company and went into Guildford to buy a more ornamental bridle for his mare, Windfall, and on both afternoons he went to the stud for a while to lean on the fence as I had done, and watch the young horses in training.

Eddie, who had grown from an insouciant sixteen-year-old to a good-natured and sensible man in his early thirties, told me confidentially that during the expedition to Guildford, Ben had worried him.

'He was boastful, madam. We went to the Tun Inn for some ale before we started for home and dinner, and he kept telling everyone how valuable he was to you and how much you had come to depend on him. I began to think . . .' his voice dropped to a murmur, '. . . that he wanted to draw attention to himself; to make himself into bait! It was outrageous. I had to stick an elbow in him to make him quieten down.'

'Indeed! Thank you, Eddie!'

I was horrified. Eddie was watching my face.

'Madam, there is one thing. He did talk to me about old Gladys. He is very troubled for her. Well, we all are, and we all keep talking about Gladys; I didn't think then that it meant anything. But now I am wondering. Master Atbrigge is a decent man, madam, able to pity a frightened old woman. Suddenly, I'm wondering . . . does he want to become bait, so that perhaps he may be taken to where she is and try to help her to escape?'

'The same idea had crossed my mind, Eddie,' I said grimly. 'I must speak to him.'

Though I wasn't at all sure what I wanted to say to him. If what he was doing was an attempt to rescue Gladys, or even just to find her, could I reasonably order him to stop? It was honourable, even if it was also insane.

Muddled in mind, I let opportunities to speak to him slip past. That day, he spent all afternoon at the stud and on return was much occupied in the kitchen, discussing future purchases of supplies with Hawthorn, and after that, he spent a long time with Harry, poring over the household accounts. I thought of calling him away, but hesitated.

At supper, there were people all round us and after supper, there was music, with Ben playing the spinet while Dickson and Harry played the lute and Harry sang. No one felt much inclined for music, but normal life had to go on somehow. Then it was bedtime.

In the morning, once breakfast was over, Ben decided to supervise the maids – I rather thought so that he could do a little courting with Bess. She still flirted sometimes with Eddie, but I had noticed of late that she seemed to be attracted to Ben. I was inclined to encourage them. They were much of an age and it would be a good match for both of them. They would stay in Hawkswood and work as a couple. I would have a cottage built for them, I thought. Ben would be far better for Bess than Eddie, who was something of a philanderer. I knew that he had one girl in Hawkswood village and another in Woking. Therefore, I left Ben and Bess alone. I still hadn't had a chance to talk privately to Ben.

I had tasks of my own before dinner. I was landlord of Hawkswood village and the vicar, Dr Joynings, came to me and wished to discuss some repairs needed to the church and also to two of the cottages. When he had gone, Dale said hopefully that perhaps we could spend a quiet hour together over some embroidery, or perhaps start work with the blue velvet. It would calm our minds, she said.

I doubted if anything would calm my mind, which was now in a permanent turmoil, but Ben was in the kitchen again, where Hawthorn was apparently planning something unusual for next Sunday, as a way of putting heart into us all, only there were ingredients to be bought for it. Ben was planning to go out forthwith and buy them. I was still making excuses to myself for not peremptorily summoning him to me. I let him go out and tried to settle down with Dale in the little parlour.

Ben came home for dinner but, the moment it was over, he said that he was going off to spend an hour or so at the stud, watching the youngsters.

Secretly cursing my own indecision, I went back to the little parlour with Dale and we started to sew, but less than half an hour later came a clatter of hooves and voices, one of which I recognized as that of Jem Higgs.

I sprang up and ran to the window, which overlooked the courtyard. Jem was out there, dismounted but still holding the bridle of his sturdy bay cob. He was talking rapidly to Arthur Watts and Eddie. Then Eddie broke away and ran for the door into the hall and at the same moment, to my astonishment, I saw Brockley running from the tack room with a bridle and my side saddle over his arm. The Parson brothers were out in the courtyard and he was shouting at them. The sound reached me faintly and I thought he was telling them to saddle Firefly. I ran to the hall to meet Eddie.

'Your horse is being saddled, madam. It's urgent. Master Atbrigge has been taken but we know the direction and Mr Miller's dog is on the scent. Please come.'

'What? What scent? What do you mean, taken?'

'Madam, just *come*,' pleaded Eddie, catching my sleeve, pulling me.

Five minutes later I was in the saddle. So were Brockley and Eddie. Together with Jem Higgs, we were making for the stud at a gallop.

FIFTEEN
Seizures

On that headlong ride, I had no chance to speak to Jem; he was in front all the time, leading the way. I heard hooves behind me and glanced back to see Brockley and Eddie following but I couldn't exchange any words with them either. The four of us arrived together at the place where I had seen Ben leaning on the fence to watch the training. A training trap was drawn up to the fence, with one of my stud grooms in it, looking bewildered. Miller was there, on foot, with Foggy straining at a leash. Captain Banks was also there, visibly angry, and also breathless. In the adjacent field to the right, a flock of sheep were bleating noisily and moving restlessly about, disturbed by something.

'I saw it happen, mam, I saw it happen, but I was too far off to do anything about it!' Banks was grim. 'I was over at that far boundary, the other side of the training field, due south. *That* field . . .' he pointed towards the agitated sheep, '. . . there to the west, has a gate into it from here and another one opposite, opening on to the public track to Woking, and there's a path between the two gates.'

I nodded impatiently. I was acquainted with the west field, which belonged to the farmer who leased me the fields used by the stud.

'Sergeant Wooller is guarding the east boundary of your land – from the start there haven't been enough of us!' said Banks. 'I saw a cart turn in from the Woking track and come across that field there, following the path. It disturbed the sheep . . .'

'Mercifully they're not in lamb just now or there'd be aborted lambs,' Miller put in grimly.

'It just came quietly across; no one thought anything of it. It would be a delivery of some sort for the stud, I thought,

though it shouldn't be coming across that field. There were
two men in the cart . . .'

Banks stopped, shaking his head. Brockley and Eddie had
both dismounted, but I remained in my saddle, surveying
the terrain and seeing all too clearly what had happened. Ben
had been here, leaning on the fence. The cart had come from
the Woking track. It had approached soberly, not attracting
much attention. One man had presumably got out to open
the gate from the track and then again, to helpfully open the
opposite gate into the field where Ben was, where we all
were now, and then . . .

'Master Atbrigge saw the cart arrive, turned to hail the
driver and ask him his business,' said Banks angrily. 'And
then the driver swung the horse round to face back the way
it had come, and the second man leant out of the cart and
flung a great noose of rope over Atbrigge and dragged it
tight. I saw it happen. I started running, but I was too far
away to do anything! Master Atbrigge fell over, arms pinned
to his sides, and that second man – must have been strong
– jumped out, picked him up and threw him into the cart
and scrambled in after him, and then it started back the way
it came and this time it went like blazes. There was a fast
horse in those shafts! I could do nothing, nothing . . . I was
within bowshot but I don't carry even a longbow, let alone
a crossbow. I only have a sword and a dagger. With a bow,
I could have knocked the horse out, anyway, and if we'd
once got our hands on the men in the cart, we wouldn't
need to track them to wherever they'd come from. They'd
soon have told us! I'd have seen to that!'

'But we'll get them anyway,' said Miller, reaching down to
pat Foggy's head. 'I used that aniseed you sent me, mistress;
I made a good, smelly liquid with it, and you were right,
Foggy adores it. He'll run for ever with his nose down to
an aniseed trail. Every day now, Master Atbrigge has
had aniseed smeared all over his shoes. We can follow to
wherever he's been taken. We'll find out where they're
taking him, and maybe where they took Gladys. They've had
a fair start, Captain Banks, but we haven't lost them. We'll

have them soon enough, with Foggy's help. You need not come, mistress. We'll be back soon, I'm sure of it. With luck, we'll have Master Atbrigge, maybe Gladys Morgan and – we all hope – a couple of prisoners with us.'

I was absorbing all this in, so to speak, a series of gulps, as though I were swallowing a series of gigantic pills. Certainly, as the implications became plain to me, I nearly gagged. Then I said, 'Do I understand that this was planned? That Ben Atbrigge really did, deliberately, intend to get himself seized?'

I had suspected it, of course, ever since Eddie told me of the way Ben was behaving, but to have it confirmed like this still came as a monstrous shock that filled me with outrage. Why had I hesitated so long about speaking to Ben? I could have stopped all this before it began. I could have . . .

Miller was shrugging. 'Master Atbrigge volunteered himself. This persecution has to stop, mistress. If Foggy can follow the scent to wherever these vicious enemies of yours are hiding themselves, and very likely are holding old Gladys, then we have them. We'll outnumber them . . . ah, here come the Parsons brothers. We shall be a force to reckon with.'

I rounded on Brockley. '*You* knew about this? And never said one word to me?'

'Yes, madam,' said my good friend, my loyal manservant and almost – in some remote time – my lover. 'I knew you would forbid it, and so you had best not know of it. Fran doesn't know either; I have deceived her too. She would have told you and begged you to prevent it; I know her!'

Abel and Jack Parsons had arrived on Ruby and Windfall. They slipped to the ground and threw their reins over a fencepost. 'We're here. We're ready. It's happened, has it?' That was Abel, steady, reliable Abel, apparently not at all concerned that he had let himself and his younger brother become involved in madness.

Yes, madness. 'You are all out of your minds!' I shouted. 'And Ben most of all. What made him, what made you, think he'd be seized? He could well have been killed instead, like my aunt, like poor Eleanor!'

'Your granddaughter wasn't, and nor, as far as we know, has Gladys been,' said Brockley, not at all disturbed by my furious face. 'Ben said he thought their tactics had changed, entered a new phase. He thought he was more likely to be kidnapped than murdered and, as you see, he was right.'

'It was an insane risk! You're all insane! Ben above all!'

Yes, Ben above all. Sick at heart, stomach clenching, I remembered that Ben's father, in his final hours, had been not only insane but dangerously so. Ben himself had always seemed to be balanced, steady, but who knew what seeds of madness might not lurk within the son of a crazy man? To offer himself as bait like this, not knowing whether he would be simply murdered instead of snatched . . .

But Miller was saying calmly, 'No, mistress. We are all in our right minds. Just prepared to take a chance in the hope of putting an end to all this. Granted, it is a chance, but it could work. Mistress, you must now return to the house and wait. You at least must take no risks.'

'You planned this . . . you are all in it . . . you, Brockley! You, Miller! And Jem and you Parsons brothers. Every one of you. In secret, keeping it from me . . .!'

'I didn't,' said Eddie ruefully. 'I just worked out for myself what Ben was up to. He didn't tell me it was part of a plot. He just said he was worried about Gladys and that was natural enough. But if he had told me the truth, I would have held my tongue.'

'I *said* he should have been in it,' Brockley remarked to the air.

'I wasn't in it either,' said Banks dourly, and then, brightening up: 'But it might work!'

'You would have done all you could to prevent us,' said Brockley reasonably. 'This way, it has gone too far for you to halt it.' Maddeningly, he grinned up at me. 'Can you really dismiss us all? Madam, now, please, go home.'

Foggy was pulling at the leash in Miller's grasp. He was already on the scent. I was still in my saddle. I had been addressing my disloyal servants from the back of my horse. I turned Jaunty's head for home, and went.

*   *   *

Once indoors, I stormed into the little parlour in the hope of finding Dale there, and there indeed she was, seated near the window, embroidery frame in hand.

'Did you know about this?' I thundered at her. 'Were you a party to it as well as Brockley?'

Dale dropped the frame into her lap and stared at me in such alarm and bewilderment that I realized at once that I had made a mistake. I sank on to a settle. 'No, I see that you weren't. I am sorry.'

'Ma'am, what are you talking about?'

Briefly, I told her, and she listened to me with increasing astonishment and finally with an open mouth.

'Ma'am, I knew nothing. Except that Roger has been . . . thoughtful, quiet, these last few days. But you say that he has gone, that they have all gone, following that nasty dog's nose. I've always thought him a nasty animal, the few times I've seen him. He looks at you as though he's wondering what you'd taste like. Not like our dear friendly Caesar and Cleo. Those yellow eyes . . .!'

'It's his nose they're relying on,' I said. And then, as I heard someone shouting outside in the courtyard, 'Now what's happening?'

Dickson appeared in the doorway. 'Mistress, the boy Andrew Lomax from the stud is here, very anxious. He says you must come quickly – you are needed!'

I went out to the courtyard to see him and found him hopping from one foot to the other, full of impatience. 'Madam, I'm so sorry to disturb you, but Master Brockley said to fetch you back at once. Please come. He's hurt. There's no time to saddle your horse. I have a horse waiting – please come now!'

Brockley was hurt and there was no time. That was how they did it, of course. By giving me no time to think, no opportunity to ask questions. I shouted to Arthur Watts, who chanced to be crossing the yard, that I was going off in haste with Andrew Lomax, and as I got into the side saddle that had been so thoughtfully provided, Arthur ran after me with a cloak. Then, with Lomax, I went straight out of the courtyard, under the gate arch, out on to the track into the oak wood.

Once into the trees, I was seized. Riders emerged from the trees and jostled me from either side. A hood was thrust over my head, blinding me, and a hand was slammed over my mouth. I tried to struggle, but found myself being wrapped tightly in the cloak, pinning my arms. A gag was being forced into my mouth. Cloth, I thought; it had no taste or smell but still I heaved, and then made myself stop, afraid that if I actually vomited, I would probably choke. A rope was being fastened round me, making the cloak tighter still. I was helpless, a well-wrapped parcel. I was being lifted out of my saddle and carried. But not far; suddenly I felt myself being heaved up and then dumped on to something hard, like boards, and a covering of some kind was thrown over me. I was trying to kick, but strong hands hold of my ankles and they too were being tied.

Whatever I was lying on creaked as someone – or maybe more than one – came to sit near me. I could smell things: wood, horse . . . one of my captors chirruped and whatever I was lying on began to move. I must be on a cart. It was gathering speed, too; I could sense it and I could hear the hoofbeats of the horse. It was cantering. The cart lurched over ruts in the track and threw me about. I hoped again that I wasn't going to be sick.

I wasn't, but I came perilously near to it. What saved me was that the horse finally slowed down to a more dignified trot and the cart stopped lurching. I heard voices and realized that there were probably people about, who might take too much interest in a cart that was being driven too wildly.

The nearest village – or rather, hamlet – to Hawkswood lay to the north, and it was a tiny place called Eddings. It had a dozen or so cottages and a cobbled street through the middle of it and three or four smallholdings. Some of my farmhands lived there. But we hadn't gone far enough for the voices to come from there. The voices were masculine and might have come from men working in one of my outlying fields. In that case . . . we must be on the track that bypassed White Towers. And therefore, we were heading towards Woking.

No. We were slowing down. We stopped. I was being lifted, heaved over the side of the cart, I thought, and deposited on the ground. Hands were busy about my bonds. My feet were freed and the ropes around me were unfastened. My hood was whisked off.

I was standing, unsteadily, in a woodland clearing, in front of a dilapidated-looking cottage. It was vaguely familiar; I knew my own land well enough. I knew where I was. The cottage had once belonged to a charcoal burner, who had died and left it vacant.

I had tried to find a tenant for it but no one wanted it and, in the end, I forgot about it. It had been abandoned. Some creeping plant was making its way up the walls and on to the steeply pitched thatch of the roof. The thatch swept nearly to the ground. It was untidy and streaked white here and there with bird droppings. I shook out the folds of my cloak and a voice I somehow thought I knew, said, 'You're a heavy load to carry, mistress. Kindly walk indoors on your own two feet.'

I looked round. Stephen Mercer was there, looking at me. And there beside him was Lomax. So, Lomax, I thought savagely, he was in with the Mercers. Miller had trusted him and therefore I had trusted him too. Stephen, addressing me as politely as though we were in his mother's parlour at Evergreens, said, 'We've made a temporary base for ourselves here. You'll find it's fairly comfortable. Do please go inside.' He gestured towards the door of the cottage. It was open.

There was nothing to do but to do as he said. If I didn't walk, I knew I would be pushed. Or carried. Trying to run would be useless. I'd be outdistanced and fetched back in a few seconds. I went in.

I found myself in a small, stone-walled room. There was some meagre furniture: a wooden settle, shelves with various things on them – cooking gear, mostly – and a couple of ironbound chests on the floor beside the settle. There was a hearth, empty and cold.

There was also Hector Mercer, as instantly recognizable as Stephen. He held out his hands, as if in welcome and said,

'We must regret the undignified form of transport, mistress. How are you feeling now?'

I couldn't think of an answer; at least, not in terms that a lady ought to use. He smiled. It was not a pleasant smile. 'Welcome to our lodgings, Mistress Stannard,' said Hector.

SIXTEEN
The Meaning of Hate

I ought to have been terrified but, to my own surprise, I wasn't. Except for the fact that he was carrying a sword at his side, Hector looked much as he had looked when I met him at Evergreens. His younger brother Stephen had come inside as well, and was now coiling ropes tidily and placing them in a wicker basket. Stephen too wore a sword, but otherwise seemed unchanged from when I had seen him at Evergreens.

They both, in fact, looked like the suntanned young men I had first seen, just home from a profitable trading voyage, and back in time for their sister's wedding, bringing gifts to her and to their mother.

Hector had brought a jaguar skin rug for their mother. Stephen had brought his sister a wedding present in the form of a pendant with an emerald that was at least three times the size of any emerald I had ever seen before, even at the court of Queen Elizabeth. Her brothers had brought a roll of light green velvet for her, too: beautiful stuff; soft, rippling, and as light in weight as any silken cloth.

I tried to straighten my back, to look dignified, and to tidy my rumpled skirts. As usual, I had that morning put on an open-fronted gown over a pretty kirtle, and inside that open skirt, I had my usual hidden pouch. Also as usual, the pouch contained some objects which the lady of a respectable manor house didn't usually carry, but were convenient if the said lady had for years been an agent of the queen. They included a purse containing a few coins of various denominations, a set of picklocks and, sheathed, a small but very sharp dagger. As I tidied myself, my fingers brushed against their hard outlines. They were comforting.

Then I found that I needed comfort because at that point, to my shame and anger, the gag and the jolting cart finally took effect on me. Suddenly I started to retch. I staggered to the settle, sat down, and a moment later I was sick.

Hector, tutting, was there at once with a basin grabbed from a shelf. He got to me in time, just before the retching became vomiting, and held it for me until the spasm stopped. Over his shoulder, he said, 'Steve, bring some water.' To me, he added, 'It's good, deep well water, clean as can be.'

Stephen brought the water. I wasn't entirely surprised to see that it was in a silver goblet. The Mercer brothers had, after all, made a fortune out of piracy, with treasure ships as principal targets.

I drank the water thankfully. I said, 'I am disappointed in Andrew Lomax.' I felt queasy again but this time not for physical reasons. If Lomax was their creature and had been planted on my premises, then they knew about Ben's perfumed footwear. Hector's next words confirmed this.

'Yes, Lomax. An excellent lad. He really does come from that big family in Heron's employment, but he never worked for any hiring stables. We found him in an inn yard in Sussex, trying to get work there, thought he looked likely and asked him if he fancied a life at sea. He jumped at the chance. The hiring stables was real, by the way, and it really was sold up. It provided us with a useful story because there's no one there now to confirm or deny our tale about where Lomax went after he first left home. He's grateful to us; doesn't mind what he does to please us; knows what will happen to him if he betrays us. He's seeing to the horses now. He really is an excellent groom. The old charcoal burner had a couple of nags and he built himself a stable; so convenient.'

Hector was smiling as he spoke and then, after all, I did become afraid, for it was a smile to induce terror.

But his voice was calm, almost friendly, as he said, 'I daresay you have surmised that we know all about the aniseed scent on Ben Atbrigge's shoes. We took him a good distance and well away from here, took his shoes off, left them where they were and then brought him here. This cottage has an attic – that's where he is now, along with Gladys Morgan, in case you're wondering. I'll take you to them in a moment.

We shall feed you properly while you're with us, of course. Unfortunately, there's a bird's nest or something in the chimney so we're having to cook outside or, now that Lomax will be staying with us, he will. A lad of many talents is Lomax. He is a much better cook than we are. He'll make us some flatbread over a charcoal brazier. Proper bread is a bother to make so we don't go in for it. Flat unleavened bread is surprisingly good. We have butter and eggs, and Lomax plans omelettes for this evening. The old man left a good stock of charcoal behind, in sacks, in here.'

Miller and the others would have found Ben's shoes by now, I thought. They would know that – somehow – their scheme had been betrayed. Lomax would hardly go back to them; they would soon realize who was responsible.

As I sat, still mechanically wiping my wet mouth, Hector said, quite conversationally, 'The little Hillman girl. Is she pregnant?'

'By the grace of God, no,' I said, shortly, untruthfully and, I hoped, convincingly.

He looked disappointed, which pleased me. 'Too young, perhaps. They don't always breed until later.' He might have been talking of a young mare. 'Ah well, we did our best with her.'

I felt furious but preferred not to pursue the matter. Nor did Hector, apparently. In any case, I had a question to ask. It had been hanging in the air unspoken ever since I was brought here.

'Why have you done this?' I asked, and for the life of me I couldn't keep the tremor out of my voice. 'Why have I been brought here? Why Ben and why poor old Gladys?'

'Poor old Gladys be damned,' said Stephen. 'She has curses fit to freeze the blood. If we were timid men we'd be cowering before her like mice before a tomcat.'

'I daresay,' I said. 'I know all about Gladys's curses. But what did you want with her? And Ben, and me?'

I was looking at Stephen, and realizing that in him, yes, I could see the black-haired and black-bearded Nicholas Trent. I could recognize those light hazel eyes. In some lights they could look sea-coloured. He had killed my aunt Tabitha. One or both of them had murdered Eleanor Blake, a young girl, beautiful, looking forward to marriage with my son, doomed only because she loved Harry Stannard. And although poor Ursula Mary wasn't dead, they had set out to ruin her life, and had it not been for the love of her parents and that excellent family in Devonshire, they would have succeeded. As it was, they had done damage enough. I was afraid now, but it was not only fear that seethed inside me. Hate was there too. Hate of a kind that was quite new to me. Knowing what these men had done . . .

But to tell the truth, I still didn't really know what hatred meant. Not until Hector, smiling sweetly, answered my question.

SEVENTEEN
The Straw Staircase

Much later, I heard from Brockley how the pursuit with the aid of Foggy's nose had gone. Ben's captors had travelled a long way, mostly on side tracks that led through woodland or along the edges of pasture. It seemed to lead in the general direction of Cobbold Hall but then veered away south-west.

The pursuers had decided to go on foot. Foggy was on Miller's leash, but it was the dog who was in charge of the hunt. He was sure of himself, tugging at the leash, wanting to go much faster on his long legs than his human companions could manage.

Until, just as the track had gone past a field of wheat, with no human witnesses in sight, and they slipped into the shadow of a small wood, the trail stopped.

Foggy stopped, four legs stiff, nose questing, turning this way and that but without result. Then he seemed to start afresh, but plunged nose first into a clump of bushes. There he halted.

'What the . . .?' said Miller. Still holding the leash, he went past Foggy, parted the bushes and leant forward to peer into them. Then he reached down with his spare hand and stepped back. In his hand, he held one of Ben's shoes. He set it down, reached once more into the depths of the bushes and brought out the other.

Brockley told me that although he was not in the habit of swearing, as he was sure I knew, he had nevertheless heard plenty of it in the vanished days when he was a soldier, and now he let out all the curses he could think of. Even Laurence Miller, who was far from mealy-mouthed, looked shocked.

When, eventually, they were relating the story to me, Miller

was still seething. 'We had come so far; we thought we would
find him, rescue him, perhaps rescue Gladys too and only for
this! Those . . . those buggers knew. I beg your pardon, madam.
They knew of our plans all along.'

'Of course,' I said. 'Andrew Lomax.'

'And meanwhile, that same young brat, that lad with the
charm of an angel and the mentality of Lucifer, was enticing
you, madam, out of the house and into their hands.'

And in their hands I was.

I had never felt so desperate. Sitting there with the silver
goblet in my hands, I heard Hector Mercer out and I could
hardly believe what I was hearing. I would have fainted, I
think, from shock, from horror, from terror, except that my
anger was so intense that it sustained me. I just sat there,
staring at him, letting my angry eyes do the talking and
keeping my mouth tightly closed. It was best to say nothing
aloud. But I remember huddling my cloak round me, as if
for warmth, or protection.

Whatever my eyes may have said, it didn't impress Hector.
'The others are upstairs,' he said, smiling again. 'Come. Give
me the goblet.'

I rose to my feet and handed it to him, and now I did
speak, and I was surprised to hear that my voice sounded
quite normal. 'You clearly haven't gone voyaging this
summer,' I said.

'We have wealth enough to get by for a season,' said
Stephen, in reassuring tones, as though he feared that I
might be anxious about it. 'We didn't want to lose our crew
members, though, so we have employed them to help keep
watch on you. It has all worked out very well.'

'And now,' said Hector, 'Mistress Stannard, I am sure you
would wish to join your friends, young Atbrigge and that
dreadful old woman with the mouth so full of curses. There
are the steps.'

I hadn't noticed the steps before. They were in a shadowed
corner. They were narrow and steep and made of stone, with
a twist in them. 'Up you go,' said Hector, taking my right
wrist in a hard grasp and leading me to the foot of them.

'Take your time. They're a bit on the steep side for a lady your age, but you're too damned heavy for us to carry you up there.'

I climbed, aided from behind by pokes in the back. It was difficult. There are moments when, as the years go on, one suddenly notices that what would once have been easy is now a struggle.

At the top, breathless, I emerged into the attic and brushed sweat out of my eyes. The room was quite large as far as floor space went, but the thatch was close above and sloped to the floor on two sides. The two ends were triangles of stone. The light was poor but there was a little, from two very small windows, one in one of the triangular walls, the other a dormer window in the thatch. I could see well enough.

They were there. Ben was lounging on a bench and Gladys was slumped in a corner on a bale of straw. There were some other straw bales, arranged roughly like a large bed, and on them lay a piece of sheeting and a few fleeces. We would have to sleep there, I supposed. Ben gave me a brave smile. Gladys looked utterly wretched. I went to her and took her in my arms. She felt so frail, her bones so like the bones of birds, that I feared to hold her tight in case I hurt her. I let her bury her face in my shoulder and felt her tears; if she still smelt as unwashed as usual, I didn't notice. Then, gently, I let her go and turned to Ben, who was watching us. His feet were shoeless. He gave me another smile but I could read nothing in his young face.

Whoever had been behind me on the stairs – Hector, probably – had gone downstairs. 'As you see,' I said, 'they got me too.'

'I have feared for you ever since they tore my shoes off, laughing, and then started off again, leaving no trail behind,' said Ben. 'How did they know about my shoes?'

'Lomax,' I said. 'He was planted on us.'

'Yes, he was!' said Gladys pugnaciously. 'It was him come to me when I was a'sunning myself in the courtyard, said the mistress wanted me to see summat in the wood. Led me outside and then them great hulks of Mercers grabbed me.'

No wonder the dogs hadn't barked. I said, 'He told me a

tarradiddle about Brockley being hurt, and could I come. Like a fool, I went with him and I was grabbed too. Lomax will have to be here from now on, I think. Dale saw him fetch me away and so did others. As soon as they realize that I've been snatched, they'll know that Lomax was in on it. He's the Mercers' creature.'

Gladys, now sitting upright in her corner, said, 'I have laid every curse I know. None of them will die in peace.'

'The point is, rather, will any of us die in peace?' I said.

Ben beckoned me close to him. Softly, he said, 'I wouldn't put it past them to hear what we say if we speak aloud. A tiny little hole in the floor, maybe. But they mustn't hear this. Listen. I think I can get out of here. Gladys can't do it and probably you couldn't either, but I think I could. It was hoping for such a chance that made me offer myself in the first place, only I'd hoped to get Gladys out as well and I don't think I can. Around dawn today, there was a shower and the roof leaked. I looked, and there's a hole in the thatch. I believe I could get through it. Well, it's a chance to get away and fetch help. I hated to leave Gladys behind, but I couldn't see what else I could do. I was planning to go tonight. Only, now that you're here . . .'

'You must try!' I said urgently. 'Things are worse than you think. At least – or have they told you?'

'Told us what?' Ben asked.

'What all this is about. Why they have seized us all and brought us here together.'

'They've said nought of that,' said Gladys. 'But it seems they've told you, mistress. So you'd best out with it. It's something wicked, I don't doubt. I smell wickedness all round us.'

'You are right,' I said. 'They mean to kill me. I don't know how and I haven't asked. They also mean to murder one of you. They want me to decide which one.'

In a horrified silence, they gaped at me. 'It's true,' I told them.

At length, Ben said, 'But . . .' and Gladys emitted a strange sound, half shriek and half cackle.

'If I refuse,' I said, 'they say they can make me. Hector

smiled when he said that.' I was using my normal tone of voice by now. There was nothing secret about this. 'I am as vulnerable to pain as any other woman,' I said. 'They plan to do it tomorrow. They want me – us – to have time to be frightened. It's a fine edge of cruelty. I could try telling them to toss a gold angel,' I added viciously, 'but when tomorrow comes, then they *can* – and they will – force me to choose and God knows what I shall say then.'

'You choose me,' said Gladys. Old, defenceless, trembling with fear, she still said it. 'I've not got long anyway, being my age,' said Gladys gallantly. 'Young Ben here has a life ahead.'

'They'll probably murder young Ben anyway,' said Ben sardonically. 'I doubt if any of us are meant to survive.'

'They intend to make me watch my chosen victim die, before they kill me too,' I said. There was a silence then, of shuddering horror; the silence of those who dare not speak in case they weep, or scream.

But then, Ben beckoned me close. 'When it's dark, I shall go,' he whispered. 'I'll be back with a rescue party by dawn. I know where this is; since I've lived here, Harry has shown me all round this district.'

'But you've no shoes!' I muttered.

'I'll go barefoot. Can't worry about shoes, not now. The only nuisance is that the hole in the thatch is at its highest point, right overhead. If only it had been where the thatch sweeps low! But I still think I can manage. Look, there.'

I stood up and went to where he was pointing. 'Can you really get through that?' I asked him, coming back. 'A cat would have trouble!'

'It's better than you think. Peer up at it and you can see glimpses of the sky.'

'There's more than one weak place. Dripped on me, one of them did, first night here,' muttered Gladys. 'I've cursed them by the four elements, by fire, earth, air and water – specially water. They're seamen. They'll drown next time they sail, they will!'

'They're just tiny leaks,' muttered Ben. 'That one at the top is the only one I think I can get through.'

'How will you get up there in the first place?' I wanted to
know.

'I'll pile up straw bales beneath it for me to stand on,'
whispered Ben. 'It won't be so difficult. You can dismantle
my straw staircase after I've gone. Now, come dusk, they'll
feed us, so Gladys here says. We'll eat. Then we'll arrange
the bales; they're good and firm, fastened with cord. After
dark, when they think we'll be trying to sleep, all despairing
and miserable, I'll go.'

The food duly arrived. It was as promised. Andrew and
Stephen brought it: flat unleavened bread, omelettes, small
ale. I noticed that Stephen was still wearing his sword. Even
if we had tried to rush them, we wouldn't have stood much
chance, and no doubt Hector too was ready with his sword
at the foot of the steps.

As they were setting their trays down, using a couple of
straw bales as a table, there was a sudden dimming of the
light through the little windows, and a rustle in the air. It made
me jump and Andrew laughed at me.

'It's the starlings, lady. They perch on our roof of a night.
They're just coming in to roost.'

'You encourage them,' said Stephen. 'You've spent a good
few nights with us here, pretending to Miller that you're
off visiting your poor widowed mother who's got eleven of
her brood still at home and needs a few pennies off your
wages, and every time you stay here, you donate bits of
your breakfast to the birds. Starlings aren't fools. They've
taken to roosting where there's a chance of an easy
breakfast. I think they're a nuisance. They drop their mutes
on the thatch and squabble among themselves now and then
and wake us up, flapping their wings. Oh, yes, talking of
the mutes reminds me. Mistress Stannard, in case you
hadn't noticed, there is a bucket there in the corner for natural
uses. It will be removed in the morning and a fresh one put
there instead.'

'I'd of told her,' muttered Gladys. 'No need for you to
embarrass a noble gentlewoman like her.'

'And as you see,' said Stephen, ignoring her, 'there is

bedding. We would prefer you to sleep well. We would like you to be comfortable for your last night on earth. Also, in the morning, you will need a clear head. You have a serious decision to make, after all. We shall ask for your decision at noon tomorrow.'

'There won't be a decision,' I said, trying to sound resolute. 'I will never make such a choice.'

'We'll see,' said Stephen, smiling. And left, without bandying further words.

Ben reached out and put a hand over one of mine. 'Tomorrow, you won't be here anyway,' he whispered. 'Best eat.'

Eating was difficult. I had no appetite. Ben seemed able to manage and so did Gladys. 'That boy Lomax can cook,' she informed me. 'They give me fried bacon at midday yesterday, very tasty, and buttery rice with it, and sausages for supper with them new potato things you've bought now and again, cut up and fried with a touch of cinnamon and salt.'

'They come from the New World,' I said. 'Merchants are bringing them in these days.'

'I heard the lad learned to cook aboard one of their ships,' said Gladys. 'Why didn't he leave them once he was back on land, and hire himself out to someone's kitchens, instead of hanging round them two bloodstained villains? There's daft if ever I heard it. He could have had an honest life and got to be a chief chef some day.'

'Piracy pays better,' said Ben dryly.

'It's more dangerous,' I said.

Lomax was very young. Seventeen at the most, I thought. If Ben escaped and brought help, then Lomax would soon be dead. He was a junior pirate but still a pirate. The Mercers preyed on English shipping, not just Spanish. And he had been involved in a plot to torment and kill the queen's half-sister. He would die at the end of a rope. I was angry with him but I knew that he had been duped by the Mercers. They had found him useful and offered him rewards for serving them. He would pay a bitter price and I could pity him.

But I didn't pity the Mercers. No, I did not.

Hector came to collect our used dishes, aided by Lomax. I was aware that Stephen was on the steps, listening to make sure that we didn't try anything. Hector passed the tray to Lomax, who went down ahead of him, and then Hector, having wished us goodnight, went down, backwards.

Ben put his finger to his lips. Gladys and I nodded.

I had a look at the straw bales. There were plenty of them; probably the Mercers needed the straw as bedding for their horses. Ben wouldn't actually need all that many for his makeshift staircase; even the topmost thatch wasn't that far above us. I whispered to Ben: 'Can you possibly get out on to the roof and not make any noise?'

'I don't know, but I must try. We must wait until they're asleep. The starlings might cover me. I expect they now and then get disturbed during the night.'

After what seemed a very long time, the light began to fade. Ben's plan was to make steps out of straw bales so that he could climb up to where the thatch was weak. A nearby beam would give him something to grip with one hand, while he opened the thatch with the other. I threw off my cloak, and we set to work.

The bales were fairly stout. One made a first step. Beside it, we piled up two. Another step. Beside that, with Ben using the first steps in order to manage the next, we piled up three, handing the last one up to Ben who was ready to receive it, balancing on the pile of two.

We had made a mistake. 'We're in the wrong place,' I whispered. 'The third pile will be too far away from the weak bit of thatch. We have to move it all backwards.'

'The head of the stone steps is in the way,' Ben muttered back.

'Turn it all sideways,' I whispered. 'So that it's sideways on to the head of the stairs, not pointing from them.'

This was tricky. In absolute silence, we must dismantle our efforts and reconstruct them, and Gladys, whose senses had retained their acuteness despite her age, muttered that she could hear something downstairs. 'They're awake. They're moving! Someone's heard something.'

Fast, silently (we hoped), we took down our straw bale steps, arranged them on the floor . . . hurry, hurry, Gladys was crouched at the top of the staircase, listening and making frantic gestures at us. We somehow put the bales back as part of the makeshift bed, pulled the sheeting over it, got on to it, pulled the fleeces over us and pretended sleep.

A light shimmered up through the staircase opening and then a head appeared, followed by a torso and a hand holding a lantern. We closed our eyes. At least, I did, and I think so did Ben, but Gladys sat up and said, 'Whassamatter? Can'cho even let's sleep in peace?' and then slumped back as if to fall into slumber once again.

I half opened my eyes and noticed that some of the bales had shed a little straw on to the floor near the staircase opening. I could see it in the light of the lantern. I shut my eyes again and prayed that no one would notice it, or think it important if – by chance – he did.

Apparently he didn't, because whoever it was grunted: 'Sorry. Goodnight,' at us and retreated downstairs.

Ben whispered, 'Can't move yet. Lie still.'

We lay still, for so long that I wondered if the dawn wouldn't break before Ben had a chance to try again. Though the darkness was a worry. I wondered how on earth we would now see to work with the bales.

Then light of a sort appeared, for the moon was nearing the full and it shone in at the dormer window. We didn't know what time it was, but I thought it must be well past midnight. The moon wouldn't be framed in the window for long, of course. It was now or never.

'Come on,' murmured Ben, and stood up. So did Gladys and I. Once more, with great care, trying not to let the bales rustle, we began to rebuild the staircase. This time we had to get it right.

We did get it right. We knew now what to do and we went about it as swiftly as the need for silence allowed. Three piles of bales were all that we needed. The moon was already passing away from the window; the patch of light it had given us had elongated and was moving away across the floor.

But for the moment, it was enough. Ben climbed up on the stairs of straw, grasped the beam to keep himself steady and thrust at the gap in the thatch.

His position was awkward, for he was so close under the thatch that he had to work hunched. We had perhaps built our staircase a little too high. The thatch resisted him but he thrust again, and then again, and it widened. Just enough. By pushing his head and then his shoulders and hands through the aperture, he was able to straighten up. Then he clutched at the thatch, heaved himself up, and was gone.

He said afterwards that he was in dread that our jailers would hear him sliding down the roof. He feared (and we learned later that he was right) that one of them would be awake, on guard. However, his hopes that the starlings would cover him were realized. The very moment he emerged through the aperture, the birds on the roof tree took fright and flew up. The whirr of their wings hid his movements as he spreadeagled himself on the thatch and slid, down to a few feet above the ground, and then straight off the roof on to grass, where his bare feet landed silently. He stood still for a while, pressed against the wall, listening.

There was nothing. He heard the starlings settle back. No one had come out to investigate them. He moved softly round the cottage and then, to his joy, the moonlight showed him the outline of another building, and his nose told him that it was a stable. He crept towards it and found the door. There was movement inside; the gleam of an eye as a horse turned its head. He went in. He felt along the wall in hopes and yes, there was tack hanging there. His groping hand discovered a bridle.

There was just enough light to show him that there were three horses here. He took down the bridle, went into the nearest stall, murmuring reassurance to the horse, took off the headstall and, more or less by feel, put the bridle on. It was a task he was used to; even in near darkness he managed it smoothly.

He didn't want to waste time finding a saddle. He led the horse outside, used one hand to close the door behind him, and vaulted astride. He hadn't done much, if any, bareback riding, and hoped he wouldn't fall off, but it was a hundred times better than trudging two miles barefoot. He walked the horse quietly away from the cottage, along the track. When he felt they had gone far enough to be out of earshot, he put his mount into a canter. In twenty minutes, God willing, he would be at Hawkswood.

EIGHTEEN
Barefoot by Moonlight

When Ben had gone, Gladys and I were left to endure the rest of the night as best we could. I looked yearningly at the hole he had left, through which I could see a patch of stars, and wished I could have gone with him. With his help, I might have managed it but Gladys couldn't and, like Ben, I hated the thought of leaving her. Anyway, I would probably have made a noise while slithering down the roof to the ground. I wondered how Ben had done it so quietly.

I did dismantle the straw steps. In any case, we needed some of them for our bed. Gladys and I arranged our bedding, using my rolled cloak as a sort of pillow and spreading the sheeting neatly over the straw. Then we lay down, pulled the fleeces over us and tried to rest.

Whether Gladys slept or not, I don't know. I only know that I didn't. I lay as still as I could so as not to disturb her, but I barely closed my eyes. I kept wondering where Ben was. Had he reached Hawkswood? Would help come? It had better come soon, for Gladys and I were both in terrible danger. The Mercers intended to kill me; if help didn't come quickly then my life was finished. Very likely, they would kill Gladys first, and make me watch. We were the living dead, unless Ben brought a rescue party in time.

Meanwhile, had I known it (what a blessing that I did not), Ben was in trouble. He was not skilled in bareback riding and the horse, which was evidently well groomed, felt as slippery as a fish. 'Slippery and knobbly,' Ben told me afterwards. 'I never knew that horses had such noticeable spines.'

He gripped his mount's sides as hard as he could, and wished the moonlight showed the way more clearly. The moon was slipping westward and distorting the shadows it

cast. The steady canter he had hoped would get him to
Hawkswood within twenty minutes or so felt perilous, and
in that uncertain light, he soon felt obliged to slow down.
Well, a walk would still get him there before daybreak,
and it was considerably safer. He drew rein and steadied his
mount to a quiet pace. He began to feel more confident, and
all would probably have been well, except that suddenly, a
small animal, either a stoat or a weasel, darted on to the
path ahead and paused to look at him, its eyes glinting green
in the moonlight.

What the little rodent thought of the horseman who was
invading its territory in the dead of the night, Ben couldn't
know, but he knew immediately what his horse thought of it.
The horse shied. It half reared and sprang sideways, throwing
him off. The rodent scuttled into the undergrowth and, as he
landed, Ben heard the faint rustle of its departure. He lay for
a moment, winded, and then discovered that he had failed to
hold on to the reins. As he recovered his breath, he sat up and
saw that the horse had dropped its nose to a patch of grass
and that the reins were trailing. He sat up and slid a cautious
hand out towards them.

The horse was too canny for him. Its head came up, and
for a moment the tricky moonlight showed him its left eye,
ringed with white, watching him and aware of his hand. Then
it veered away and was gone, cantering back the way they
had come. He could only hope that it wouldn't trip itself up
in the reins and come to harm. He got to his feet. He would
have to do the rest of his journey on foot after all.

He set off, longing for shoes. Every pebble in the track
made itself felt. The path narrowed, and the branches of the
trees on either side arched over it. The moonlight had all but
vanished. Gritting his teeth, Ben continued to plod and,
five minutes later, he came to a place where the track divided
into three. He halted, bewildered. He did not know this area
quite as well as he had claimed and here, in near darkness,
with his feet hurting, he was confounded. He couldn't
remember this place at all and he had no idea which way led
to Hawkswood.

He couldn't stand there all night, wondering. Someone had

once said that the middle way was safest. All right, he would take the central track. He did so. He was getting used to having bare feet and went on steadily until, after a furlong or so, the track veered suddenly to the left. That was wrong. There was no such abrupt turn on the correct track; he was sure about that. There was nothing for it but to turn round and go back to where the three ways met.

A few minutes later, he came to another worried halt. This damned wood must be crisscrossed with little tracks. This one forked and, earlier, he had passed the fork without knowing it. Now he didn't know which one to take. Both led back in the direction from which he had come . . .

He must think, think hard. He leant against a tree as a way of getting some rest, while he worked things out. If he could once find the way back to the place where the original track broke up into three, then he should . . . yes, surely, he should take the right-hand one. The sudden bend that he hadn't recognized curved steeply off to the left, and in all probability the left-hand track of the three cut across it at some point. He was sure that he couldn't recollect such a crossing of paths on the right track to the cottage. Therefore, once he got back to where the three paths met, then the correct choice would surely be the right-hand way. If only, if only, he could *see.*

And which fork should he choose *now*? He must decide. Finally, he picked the one that seemed the straightest, which was the right-hand fork, and plodded off again. If he had chosen well, then he would reach the meeting of the three ways within a short time, even on foot.

He didn't. After a quarter of an hour, he once more turned round and started back, peering down to the left for a glimpse of the place where the fork was.

He found it easily and realized that this was because the darkness was no longer so intense. This was a relief in one way and alarming in another. If the darkness was thinning then dawn must be near and, in that case, the time must be not far from six o'clock in the morning. He had been wandering round this accursed forest all night. Never once had he guessed right about anything, and he no longer cared whether that beastly horse caught its feet in its trailing reins and hurt itself. Why were horses as they were? They would – usually – cooperate with you if you were on their backs, or at least holding their bridles or halters, but once they were loose they behaved as though you were an entire pack of starving wolves. His feet had begun to hurt badly again.

Never mind that. Take the other fork, get back to the three-way meeting, then take the right-hand path and pray.

NINETEEN
Unwelcome Dawn

The night seemed long, but I wished it could be longer. I wanted it to stretch and stretch, to give Ben time to reach Hawkswood and raise the alarm and then give the rescuers time to get here. I also wanted it to stretch and stretch because tomorrow, if the Mercers had their way, would be my last day on earth.

It would be Gladys's last day, too. I could not now be told to choose between her and Ben, for which I was thankful, but that wouldn't help Gladys. I would plead for her, I thought. Perhaps, since I hadn't made a choice and they hadn't even had to toss a coin, they might not think it worthwhile to kill her, but they were wicked creatures and I feared otherwise.

So did Gladys. In the night, as we lay side by side, dreading the dawn, she suddenly spoke. She said, 'I can't sleep. Been thinking. It'll be the end for me, won't it? Same as for you?'

'We can't be sure of that,' I said. I recalled hearing that when the Mercers were committing acts of piracy, they had a reputation for not slaughtering the crew of the ships they robbed. They just took the treasure. But they had not shown similar mercy where my aunt Tabitha or poor Eleanor Blake were concerned, or Ursula Mary either.

'We must hope for the best,' I said. 'And hope that Ben brings help.'

'I wish I could sleep but I can't. Don't think I'll ever sleep in peace again.'

'I can't sleep either. I shall pray.'

'Think anyone's listening, do you?'

'No, not really. Don't ever tell anyone that. It's heresy.'

'Think either of us is ever going to have the chance to tell anyone anything, do you, then?'

'Maybe. If Ben is in time. Try to sleep, Gladys. Just close your eyes and try.'

After time, she did sleep, for I heard her snoring a little and then muttering in Welsh. I remained awake, as though I were on guard, looking into the darkness, which was only relieved by the stars beyond the window. The moon had gone. There was no patch of light now on the floor below the break in the thatch. The moon must now be sinking towards the west. Which meant that dawn was not far off.

Day, don't come. Sun, stay below the eastern horizon. Give Ben a chance. Give Gladys and me a chance! Darkness, endure, please, please.

I think that towards dawn, I did doze briefly, but it didn't last. Suddenly I came awake and alert and saw that the darkness was thinning. I could hear the birds above me chirping sleepily. Soon they would break into the full dawn chorus. Nothing would hold back the light.

How brave would I be when it came to the point? I had witnessed the executions of both the Duke of Norfolk and Mary of Scotland and, whatever they had done, it could not be denied that they had died with the utmost courage. I didn't feel as though I were going to match them.

Where was Ben and what was he doing? Please, please, let him bring help in time!

Then, perversely, the full dawn took an eternity to arrive. Gladys woke up and we lay there in the half-light, wondering if it would ever strengthen. The dawn chorus broke out, echoing through the world as cheerfully as though this were a normal, happy day, as though no one's life could possibly be in peril. Eventually, we got up. Bits of straw had somehow penetrated the sheeting and we had to shake them from our skirts. There was no means of washing. We used the bucket. Both of us had our hair confined in woollen nets and there it had stayed all night. I had had no Dale to take the net off and comb my hair out. I supposed that I now looked reasonably tidy and wondered why it mattered.

Hector had said that I would be asked for my decision at noon. Now that there could be no decision, would he keep to that? Probably not. He and Stephen would know that help was coming – might come – at any moment. They might want to act more quickly. Probably would! Was there a chance that they might decide to cut their losses, take Lomax and flee at once? Or would they all flee, but leave our bodies to greet the rescue party when it arrived. I greatly feared the latter.

And now there were sounds of stirring, of voices down below. Then came a smell of cooking, the homely, normal sound of breakfast in preparation. Lomax was busy at the charcoal brazier outside. It was a clear morning. I supposed they would bring the brazier inside if it rained but wouldn't have its fumes indoors unless they had to.

Gladys was sniffing. 'There's flatbread, for sure. And now there's frying, indeed there is. Eggs, I'd say. Wonder if we'll get any? Well, let's put some of the bales out for a breakfast table and hope, shall we?'

There were feet on the stairs. I stood looking down them, and Lomax came into sight. He was carrying a tray containing covered dishes but Hector was close behind him, with a drawn sword. Stephen came last, also with a tray, loaded in his case with ale jugs and goblets.

I stepped back and waited for them all to emerge into the attic and see what was to be seen. Lomax stepped off the stairs with a slight grunt, tilting the tray to keep the dishes from sliding, looked round, his mouth half-open as if to speak, and then the light through the torn thatch caught his attention. He looked up. Behind him, Hector had come to a halt on the last step of the stairs, because Lomax was blocking his way. Now Lomax was looking round, searching for Ben and not finding him. Gladys and I stood where we were, awaiting reactions.

Lomax stepped into the attic and the others followed. 'Sssso,' said Hector, with a hiss like an angry snake. But he didn't stop Lomax from going to our makeshift breakfast table and setting his tray down, and he beckoned Stephen on to do the same thing. To begin with, no one spoke, although Lomax's eyes were two big round Os, and Stephen's mouth had shut like a trap.

Then Hector turned to face us. 'So one of you has escaped. Stephen was on guard last night. He said something disturbed the starlings. But they get disturbed so often. There are owls about. You're lucky it wasn't you on the first guard duty, Andrew, my lad. If you had been, I'd half kill you for this. I'll spare my young brother.'

'There's a tawny owl lives in the stable loft and the starlings don't like it at all when he's on the move,' said Lomax. 'I've heard them go up in the night more than once.' He paused, cocking his head. 'What's that? The horses are whinnying.'

He went over to the window and peered out. 'Blaze is loose! He's outside . . . lord above, he's got a bridle on and trailing reins. Looks like Master Atbrigge got away riding bareback, only Blaze threw him. Well, maybe he's lying in the woods with a broken leg,' said Lomax cheerfully. 'Or a broken neck. That'd be useful.'

I felt Gladys reach for my hand and grip it. These horrid suggestions were perfectly possible.

Though it was also possible that Ben hadn't been hurt and had marched on, afoot.

If only we knew what had happened.

Unknown to us, a good deal was happening.

Ben Atbrigge got to Hawkswood about six of the clock. By then he felt almost too tired to stand and indeed, as he was barefoot, he could scarcely walk either. His feet were blistered and bleeding. He fairly tottered into the courtyard, but he got a good, noisy welcome from Caesar and Cleo, and there were grooms about, giving the horses their early morning feed. He all but fell into Arthur Watts's arms.

He got his tale out in a hasty babble, and the other grooms came gathering round, and then it was as though Hawkswood House was a wasps' nest and Ben had stuck a stick into it.

Harry appeared, gave him an arm into the hall, pushed him on to a settle and shouted for Phoebe. Phoebe came running, took one look at his feet, uttered a shriek of horror and fled to the kitchen. She reappeared a few moments later with a bowl of hot water and a cloth, and proceeded to bathe his injuries. The right foot was worse than the left, bleeding badly because of a thorn in the sole. Tutting in horror, Phoebe removed the thorn and staunched the bleeding. Then Bess arrived in haste, with a sizeable beaker of ale. Brockley arrived next, still trying to fasten his doublet, and hard behind him came Captain Julien, doing up his belt and already provided with sword and dagger. Ben gasped out his story a second time. Captain Julien, as shocked by the state of his feet as Phoebe was, recommended goose grease, and when Phoebe said that there was some in the stillroom, sent her brusquely to fetch it. Meanwhile, Harry and Brockley were thinking at speed and issuing orders.

Harry was counting on his fingers to see what kind of force we could muster. 'Ben Flood, take Ginger, go to the village. Gallop! Collect all the men you can. Shout in the street, shout out that all the men who work for us, our farmhands and our gardeners must come here at once, and come armed and that's an order. See that they come! Haul them out of bed if you have to.'

Most of our farmhands lived in the village, as did the three gardeners who looked after our rose and formal gardens. None of them were yet due on duty; Flood would find them at home.

'I must get Miller,' said Brockley. 'I'll saddle Firefly and go on horseback; it's a long walk through the gardens and the archery field. If I'm not back in an hour, Harry, start without me. You know the old charcoal burner's cottage?'

'Yes, of course!' Brockley hastened away and Harry once more began to count on his fingers. 'Me, six grooms – Arthur's too old—'

'Count me in, you young whippersnapper! I'm not ready yet to be dumped on a midden!' shouted Arthur, who had stepped in at the door just in time to hear what he clearly considered an insult.

'All right, just look after yourself! Six grooms from here then – probably Jem Higgs and the three other grooms from the stud – me, Hawthorn, Flood when he gets back and Edson, gardeners, farmhands . . . That will be a force to reckon with.'

By this time, Phoebe had cleaned Ben's feet and smeared them with goose grease and was bandaging them. 'Get my slippers!' he barked at her. 'I can't get my feet into boots but I can ride in slippers. Someone saddle Windfall for me . . .!'

'You mustn't come; you're exhausted!' Harry protested.

'I'm better now!' Ben snapped. The simple fact of reaching Hawkswood and the relief when the pain in his feet was stopped had made his weariness drop from him. 'Another beaker of ale and I'll be as good a man as you, as long as I'm on a horse and not on my feet!'

Harry snorted in irritation and went out to the courtyard. Ben demanded his slippers again and Phoebe reluctantly brought them. He forced his feet into them and hobbled outside to find Harry assembling the grooms. He said afterwards that he wondered if Mistress Stannard really had any idea of the weaponry her employees could assemble. Many of them, of course, had had fathers who had served in the army. Among them all, there were four swords, three businesslike daggers and a most alarming mace and chain. All their proprietors insisted that they could handle their weaponry. They could certainly handle swords and daggers, Ben thought. Brockley had seen to that.

Sooner than anyone expected, reinforcements arrived. Jem Higgs and his three under-grooms from the stud came first. Then Ben Flood returned, with the three gardeners and a dozen or so other village men, not just our own farmhands. None of them came on horseback but they would march behind the mounted contingent and either join them or avenge them. With them came Dr Joynings, not to join the march but to give it his blessing. Then, sooner than anyone expected, Brockley was back.

'Miller's ridden off to report all this to Sir Edward Heron. Heron's place is five miles off but Miller will get there in less than an hour and, if Heron's at home, he must be informed. He's the county sheriff, after all, and the mistress is sister to the queen. Miller will try to persuade him to send some men, or even come himself. They'll go straight to the cottage. Meanwhile, Captain Banks and Sergeant Wooller are on my heels. They were patrolling round the stud stables. They'll be here very shortly.'

When they arrived, Captain Banks at once pointed out something that until then, no one had considered.

'What if all this is a trap? What if they've now thought: oh, so a rescue party will be mounted from Hawkswood; well, splendid, it should be easy to get in there and do something terrible to the house or the land or the stud? I think that Wooller and I should remain on guard and have some men to help us.'

Harry at once saw the point and made rearrangements. There were only two Mercer brothers and, as far as we knew, Andrew Lomax, to contend with. Simon Adler and Joseph Henty from the Hawkswood stables, along with Sergeant Wooller, should be enough to guard the house, with Caesar and Cleo to help them. Someone should fetch Foggy; he could be useful. The Hawkswood weapon store could provide all the men with longbows. 'Shoot on sight,' said Harry. 'And shoot to kill.'

And with that, they were ready.

Captain Julien had been hovering, doing this and that, showing one of the villagers how to draw a sword quickly, helping another who was having trouble shouldering his lethal but awkward billhook. Now he looked round and said, 'I think it best if I don't come.'

'Why not?' Harry demanded.

'The Mercers were once my shipmates. I would not now come to them as part of an enemy force. What if I had to put a former friend and partner to the sword? As for them, they will see me as a betrayer, never mind that you and I are brothers. They'll care nothing for that. You have men enough. It is best that I remain here.'

'Up to you. I can hardly drag you by force,' said Harry shortly. 'What if they attack the house, with you in it?'

'I won't be. I'll slip away outside. For the moment, until that happens, I'll be in my room.' Captain Julien turned his back and went into the house.

Bess had produced some more ale for Ben and it had given

him strength. He was a young man, he told himself, not a
young wench. If he missed a night's sleep it would do him
no harm, and yes, he damn well could and would ride in slippers. Eddie Hale had saddled the chestnut gelding Sovereign,
and gave Ben a leg up so that he wouldn't have to spring off
his sore right foot. He settled his feet gingerly in the stirrups.
It was all right as long as he just pressed downwards and
didn't try to slide his feet about.

Harry gave a sharp order. They were on the move. The
Mercer brothers would have no chance against them.

If only they could get there in time.

TWENTY
The Desperate Deed

I f only help could reach us in time. The words hammered in my mind, almost drowning out Hector Mercer's gracious remark that those under sentence of death were often given one last good meal before they were sped away on their last journey.

'You may eat your breakfasts,' he said, gesturing towards the tray and the covered dishes. 'But make haste. I fear that we must bring your last moments forward. We can't wait for midday now. You won't have any grim choice to make after all, Mistress Stannard. But you shall watch your servant die before you go yourself.'

'Just who're you calling a servant?' Gladys demanded, showing a sudden spirit, even though, because she was sitting close against me, I could feel her trembling. 'I been Mistress Stannard's friend, living with her this many years, indeed I have!'

'Friend or servant, it's all the same to us,' said Hector. 'Eat. And drink. It's small ale and we haven't given you enough to make you drunk. We want you in your right minds when we hang you. Not blurred in any way. We want you to *know* what is happening to you. Eat the food as well. We would like you to have your strength. Those we are avenging lasted a good ten minutes before they died. Come, Stephen. Come, Lomax.'

They all departed. The boy glanced at us as he followed Hector on to the staircase, and he had grace enough to look upset, in fact pitying, and his eyes did not meet ours.

Then he was gone and we listened to their feet as they went down the stairs. 'So now we know,' I said. 'I was . . . wondering.'

'So was I,' said Gladys. 'And I can't eat. I can sip the ale, naught more.'

I felt much the same but I made myself eat a little. Courage, including pretended courage, required energy. The breakfast was actually very good. The unleavened bread was spread with honey; there were beaten eggs cooked in butter and spoons to eat them with, slices of fried ham, a mutton chop each. I forced myself to eat half a round of bread and a spoonful of the eggs and urged Gladys to try as well. She nibbled a piece of bread and honey and a single slice of ham. The chops went uneaten. Neither of us could face those.

And all the time, I was listening, and I think Gladys was listening too, for the sound of hoofbeats and shouts and the arrival of the force that Ben was surely bringing, that would save our lives if only it came in time.

Very soon, much too soon, we were summoned. Hector came to fetch us and ordered us to precede him down the steps. 'I wouldn't go ahead of you,' he told us, smiling broadly. 'You might think it would create a diversion if you pushed me down the stairs.'

'Yes, we would!' said Gladys pugnaciously. I prodded her, fearing that she might provoke the Mercers into adding some extra horror to whatever they were proposing for us, but Hector merely laughed.

We went down the stairs. Gladys, being lame, had to go sideways. We were pushed across the floor of the downstairs room and out of the door, emerging into a warm and sunlit morning. In the surrounding woods, birds were still singing. How could the birds sing so merrily and indifferently, how could the woods be so uncaring, echo with their music, when two human creatures were about to lose their lives, here in their midst?

As if she had read my mind, Gladys said, 'They'll stop singing when there's murder done so close to them. They'll fly up, scared. It'll disturb them. Oh, Christ Almighty . . .!'

She had come out of the doorway, limping, catching at the doorpost because there was a step down, and at first she had been half turned away from the awful thing that I had seen at once. My knees seemed to be faltering, as though whatever they were made of had turned to water. There was a tree – there were several trees – with long lower branches. The Mercers had chosen one and over it had flung two long ropes. Each had one end secured to a neighbouring tree, while the other end was a noose. Lomax was standing close to it, ready, it seemed, to help when this dreadful equipment was put to use. His head was turned away from us. Stephen was standing quite near us. He was smiling.

This was it, then. This was the machinery of death. This was what they were avenging. Two people, a man and a woman, who had shared in their crimes and had committed grave crimes of their own, had died that way. But they had died by order of the law and they had done things from which all decent folk should recoil. Here there was neither guilt nor law.

If only Ben would bring help! Where are you, Ben? What happened to you last night? Did you take the horse that came back on its own? Did it throw you? Are you lying injured somewhere, or did you get up and go on? And if you went on and got to Hawkswood, then where is the help you must have summoned?

Gladys and I were standing in front of the cottage door. She was clutching my arm. Among our captors, there was a businesslike air. All three were in shirtsleeves, with sleeveless jerkins on top, for the early morning was cool, but both Hector and Stephen were carrying swords.

'We need to get on,' said Hector. 'But we still want to extract the maximum of distress from Mistress Stannard here.' He paused, head cocked. 'Stephen, Lomax, can you hear anything? Any sound of danger approaching?'

For one crazy moment, I thought that Hector himself had heard something, but I was wrong. The forest was undisturbed. No birds were flying up, no distant hoofbeats were shaking the ground.

'Then we proceed,' said Hector, almost jovially. He turned to me. 'I believe, madam, that you have some affection for the old witch who is standing beside you. Watch her die, then!'

Stephen strode forward and seized Gladys. She cried out and kicked at him, but he spun her round and with swiftly practised movements (as a pirate he had probably done this sort of thing quite often), he bound her wrists behind her. Then he ran her forward and handed her to Hector, who pulled her under one of those terrifying loops. At the same moment Lomax had released the other end of it, and the noose came down, ready for Hector to seize it and put it over Gladys's head. There was no birdsong round the clearing now. The birds had gone up at once, in a frightened flock, because Gladys was screaming.

The screams changed to choking gulps because Hector had put the noose round her neck and tightened it, though not to the point of cutting off her breath entirely. Then he was behind her. He was a powerful man and he had begun to haul on the loose end of the rope. Gladys's feet left the ground. I saw her huge, terrified eyes and her distended mouth. I saw that she had lost control of her bladder and that water was streaming from beneath her skirts.

I am at a loss to explain what happened next. I never intended it. I thought I would have to stand there, helpless, paralysed, full of horror, of love and despair for Gladys and myself, full of hatred for the Mercers and especially for Hector, who was the creator of all this misery, Hector who was pulling at that horrible rope . . . but instead . . .

I don't remember running across the few yards of grass between me and Hector. I don't remember how my right hand must have thrust and fidgeted under my open skirt to find the pouch, to find the dagger inside it, to pull it free of its sheath. I do remember that I was thinking of the day I had joined Brockley's class in the tack room at Hawkswood, and been shown the diagram of a human body on which the heart was so clearly marked.

I reached Hector. I shrieked, 'Let go, you damned savage!' Hector laughed at me and dropped his right hand from the rope in order to fend me off. I swept his hand aside with my left arm. I succeeded in this because he wasn't expecting so strong a resistance. I wasn't expecting it, either; rage and hate had apparently given me strength I never thought was possible.

I was close to him, almost touching him. His jerkin had swung open. There was nothing between him and my dagger but a linen shirt. I had always dreaded the idea that one day I might have to use my dagger in earnest; that one day I might have to take the life of another human being. Now I did it without a second thought. On that day in the tack room Brockley had shown his audience just where to strike. *Exactly there and remember to strike upwards; never strike downwards in case you miss your target and plunge a blade into yourself.*

Hector was taller than I was anyway; to strike upwards was natural. I remembered the lesson in every detail and, as though there was a chalk circle indicating Hector's heart, I drove the dagger home.

It was sharp. I always kept it sharp. It went through the shirt, the skin, the flesh, the pulsing organ within. Hector's eyes widened. He gave a gasp of astonishment. He let go of the rope and Gladys fell, choking, to the ground. Then he was sagging, dragging at the dagger, dragging me down. There wasn't much blood; I thought distractedly that I had expected more. I let him go down, stooping after him. His eyes were rolling and then they became still, staring. I put my foot on him and held his body down while I dragged the dagger free.

Lomax had come running but he hadn't tried to intervene; he was merely standing there and gaping. I crouched beside Gladys, struggling with the noose. I tore my fingernails, trying to loosen it. Gladys lay on the ground, gulping for air. I got my fingers inside the loop; it began to ease. It had all happened so fast that I think Stephen had not at first realized what was happening. But then he did, and he too came running. He crouched beside Hector, calling his name, seeing the blood and the slit in Hector's shirt, grasping that his brother was dead, by my hand. He swore and said he would have my head. The noose was free now; Gladys could breathe. I stood up. Stephen stood up. We were face to face. He glared at me and his hand went to his sword-hilt. My dagger would be no use against that; wildly, I stooped and dragged Hector's sword from its sheath. And promptly dropped it because it was unbelievably heavy.

Stephen grinned. But at long last, birds in the deep forest were flying up, and I could hear the longed-for sound of hoofbeats. But Stephen had drawn his sword and he would have used it to avenge his brother, whatever should happen to him afterwards, except that Andrew Lomax, astoundingly, ran at him, clutching him and shouting, 'No!' Stephen hurled him aside, distracted, swearing, but by then the riders were in the clearing; Brockley was throwing himself out of his saddle, springing between me and Stephen, and he too was flourishing a sword.

Horses wheeled, what seemed like a dozen men were shouting. Blades clashed as Stephen and Brockley began to fight. Lomax had run away as if to hide in the forest, except that someone – Abel Parsons, surely – had spurred after him, then leapt out of his saddle and seized hold of him. His horse and Brockley's were loose and plunging but Jack Parsons was there, grabbing their reins to keep them from escaping. Ben – yes, surely, it was Ben – had also sprung from his saddle but he had hitched his reins round a bush and come at a limping run, to crouch beside Gladys, freeing her hands, letting her cry into his shoulder. Jack Parsons was stooping over Hector, picking up one of his wrists, feeling for a pulse.

I wanted to faint and I slid down against the cottage wall until I was sitting against it. And then didn't faint, for in front of my eyes was the remarkable spectacle of Arthur Watts throwing himself off Smoke's solid back, lunging forward and grabbing Stephen from behind, whereupon Brockley neatly disarmed him. Stephen shouted that he shouldn't interfere with a duel, and Arthur shouted back that this here wasn't a bloody tennis match and to hell with the rules of duelling. Brockley was nursing a strained wrist and looking frankly relieved. He came over to me.

'I've killed a man,' I said weakly. 'I never thought I would, but I did. I killed Hector. My little dagger came in so useful.'

There was no time for more. Our foot soldiers, with their

curious array of weapons, were marching in and, half a minute later, Laurence Miller, Sir Edward Heron and a dozen armed men arrived from a different direction.

It was over.

Well, nearly.

TWENTY-ONE
Polished Hooves

It was all confusion in the clearing. The enormity of what I had done suddenly overcame me and I sobbed absurdly on Brockley's chest until he took hold of my arms, put me back from him and said, 'A lot of men feel like that in war, when they kill for the first time. One fellow told me that it was probably the way women felt after losing their virginity. I wouldn't know about that, but I can't say I felt anything much the first time I killed someone. I just did it because I had to. The fellow was doing his best to kill *me*. I didn't have time to brood about it afterwards either because we were in the middle of a scrap and, by the end of that, I'd killed half a dozen more. I had blood all over my armour. In the evening, when it was all over, I washed the blood off in a stream and never gave another thought to the men who'd shed it.'

'He was standing there in front of me,' I said. 'Still quite a young man, tall, strong, alive . . . only I had to do it; he was hanging Gladys . . . The blade went in so smoothly, he might have been made of butter . . .'

'I'm delighted to hear it. You were wise to keep your dagger so sharp. You saved Gladys's life and you may even have saved Hector from a nastier death. I don't like to think what Stephen will have to face. Now, let's find Gladys . . . there she is, sitting on the ground under that tree. Come along.'

We went to her. Ben had settled her with her back against a tree. She looked up as our shadows fell across her. She had stopped crying but her eyes were piteous. 'I can't get up. My old legs won't do it. I ought to be swinging by now. Swinging and kicking and choking . . .'

Brockley lifted her to her feet and I put my arms about her, and then she began to cry all over again, wailing bitterly, still a prey to terror. Brockley said to me, 'Here's Sir Edward. You'll have to answer some questions.'

Sir Edward was indeed striding towards us. Two of his men were with him and so was Harry, who ran ahead of them, exclaiming: 'Mother! I was afraid, we were all afraid, that we'd never see you again! What has happened here? Are you hurt?' Then he caught sight of the pile of rope that had once been meant for Gladys, and the second rope and noose that had been meant for me and still hung over their branch. He blanched and pointed. 'Was that . . .? Did they intend . . .?'

'Yes, they did,' I said grimly. 'Me and Gladys alike. They wanted me to watch Gladys die while I waited my turn. They thought it might upset me! Well, it did. I killed Hector when he was putting a rope round Gladys's neck.'

'Christ Almighty!'

One of Sir Edward's men stepped over to examine Hector's body and now came back to say: 'There's certainly a dead man under that tree, sir.' At that, Gladys suddenly sagged at the knees again and I couldn't hold her up. Sir Edward's other man, who had a flask at his belt, very sensibly gave her a mouthful of the contents. Her eyes widened and she said, 'Wine!'

'It'll put more heart into you, old woman, than a thousand soothing words. Who is she?' He looked at me. 'What's it all about?'

Sir Edward Heron was asking me the same thing. He was a tall, bony man with a long nose which did actually have a yellow tinge. If ever a man resembled his surname, he did. He and I did not like each other. He had once interrogated me under the delusion that I was a witch, and I knew quite well that he believed that Gladys was. I answered his questions as best I could, explaining the ugly scheme that the Mercers had mounted against me, and how it had come to this final and appalling end. I told him that yes, in defence of Gladys, I had killed Hector Mercer. And now, as I spoke of Gladys, I ceased to feel guilty and maintained my right to protect those who looked to me for protection.

It didn't quite convince Heron. 'Nevertheless, madam, if

you have killed the man here, stabbed him with a dagger, that is a very serious matter. It has the look of murder, and the argument that you did it to defend Gladys Morgan is a poor one, since the Morgan woman is a known witch, to whom you have long insisted on giving protection, an undesirable state of affairs . . .'

'If you harm either Mistress Morgan or my mother,' said Harry, 'Her Majesty the Queen, my mother's royal sister, will hear of it and you may very well find yourself being removed from office.'

I looked at him, startled. I had grown used to realizing that my son was now a man, but I had never before thought of him as a formidable man. Now I saw that he was precisely that.

'I can't think what else Mistress Stannard could have done.' Brockley joined in. 'Her servant was in danger of her life!' This time, Gladys didn't object to being called a servant. Also, the two men who had come with him were looking at me with approval, and the one who had given Gladys his wine flask said, 'I would call her a brave lady, sir. What else *could* she have done, with an aged servant in such peril? I don't see where witchcraft comes into it.'

'Nor do I,' said his companion, also joining in on my side. 'It looks like self-defence and bravery to me, too.'

I didn't feel brave. Just grateful for such championship. I could only wait helplessly for the outcome.

Heron turned to his men and snapped that he was the one who was giving the orders here, but then turned back to us and found himself being confronted and stared down by this new, formidable Harry. Finally, he snorted and said, 'Very well.' It seemed that the questioning was over. While it was going on, Stephen and Lomax had been seized. They were brought to Heron, who considered them distastefully and said, 'We'll take them with us. I'll send them to my lock-up for the time being; later they'll go under escort to Lewes prison.'

'Poor buggers,' muttered Brockley, who had once been inside it.

Sir Edward was announcing that everyone must

adjourn to Hawkswood. Brockley said, 'Gladys can go up behind Ben.'

'Better in front of him. I doubt she has the strength to hold on,' I said.

Heron was giving further orders. The horses in the stable had been brought out and Hector's body was being slung across one of them. I was invited to take the other, if I didn't mind the cross saddle.

I didn't. I kilted my skirts, mounted, and we set off. Some of us went cantering ahead and it didn't take us long to reach home. Those who were on foot, which included Stephen and Lomax who were being led on leashes, and the horse carrying Hector, followed more slowly. Because of a rise in the track through the oak woods, the chimneys of Hawkswood always came in sight before the rest of it. The sight of them nearly wrenched new tears out of me. I had risen that morning thinking that I would never see my home again. Presently we were riding through the gate arch. Caesar and Cleo came bounding towards us, baying joyfully. Dr Joynings hurried out of the hall door, and hard behind him came the maids. Dale pushed through them, running ahead, calling our names as I slid down from my saddle.

Soon, everyone had dismounted. The grooms were resuming their duties, leading the horses to the trough and then into the stable. Phoebe went straight to Ben, and was shocked to see him flinch when his slippered foot came into contact with the ground. Leaning on an exclaiming and masterful Phoebe, he was taken into the house.

While we were all still exclaiming and explaining, most of us still in the courtyard, the foot contingent arrived. John Hawthorn, who because of his weight had marched with them instead of riding, strode into his kitchen at once and created a kind of normality at the top of his powerful voice, as he began to ask questions and issue orders, shouting some of them out of the kitchen door, at subordinates who were lingering in the courtyard.

Has the bread been made or was it just forgotten in all the uproar? Just because the mistress is in danger and there's a few extra people milling around doesn't mean the usual work

*comes to a stop! There's a whole horde of folk wanting food;
do hens stop laying because there's a crisis? Where's Jennet?
Jennet! Come in here, girl, and stop gawping; there's work
to do. I want a dozen eggs cracked into that bowl there and
look quick about it. I'll go into the cold room and see about
cutting chops; see that there's a good fire under the grill when
I get back and someone . . . Flood, come here and* stop
pretending to be tired! *If I'm not, why are you? Fetch a new
cask of ale into the kitchen . . .!*

In the midst of all the hubbub, the prisoners were locked
into an outhouse and left under guard. Then Harry, who had
looked after his horse himself, taking Prince to the trough and
then leading him into his stall and unsaddling him, came back
into the courtyard to find Brockley and me still talking to
Heron. Heron was still not happy about the slaying of Hector
Mercer, and Brockley was trying hard to intimidate him as
Harry had done. Harry now burst upon us, demanding,
'Where's Captain Julien? Where's my brother?'

Whereupon, Dr Joynings, who had been hovering in the
courtyard and was clearly looking for Harry, came hurriedly
to us and said, 'Please excuse us, Sir Edward. I have something
to tell Master Harry and his mother as well, and it's urgent.
Please let them come with me.'

Heron gave a chilly nod and let us go. We followed
Joynings inside. He took us through the hall and into the
little parlour, where he shut the door sharply behind him and
said, 'Captain Julien has gone. Before he went, he insisted
that I should hear his confession.'

We all stared at him blankly. Harry said, 'What do you
mean, he's gone? Gone where?'

Brockley simultaneously snapped, 'What do you mean, he
wanted you to hear his confession?'

'When I say that he has gone, I mean that he has left
Hawkswood,' said Joynings, somewhat impatiently. 'And yes,
as I have just told you, perfectly clearly, he wanted me to hear
his confession. You probably think that it sounds Popish, but
here in Protestant England it is sometimes done, all the same.
I don't think there's much time to waste. Listen.'

*   *   *

Dr Joynings himself hadn't wanted to hear Julien's confession, or anyone else's. He had studied for the priesthood and, in the course of those studies, he had learned how a confession should be heard, but he had also been told that in Elizabeth's England, it was neither necessary nor popular. Never before had he been asked to hear one. If he had been, he would have expected this embarrassing ritual to take place in his church. As it was, Julien de la Roche – a Papist, no doubt, not that Joynings had ever asked him – was here in the hall at Hawkswood, standing over him, looking urgent, insistent and intimidating, and demanding that his confession should be heard, here and now, no nonsense, *this minute.*

'I am not a brave man,' said Dr Joynings ruefully. 'He was wearing his sword and he had a hand on the hilt. I took him into that little study that you don't use very much, Mistress Stannard, and he knelt before me and confessed.'

At which point, our vicar's voice died away and I have rarely seen a man look so miserable. Brockley, irritably, said, 'Well? What did he tell you?'

'Terrible things,' said Joynings in a hushed voice. 'Dreadful. Dreadful!'

'Well? Come on!' snapped Harry.

Joynings looked at him in a pained manner and said, 'Do you not know that the confessional is utterly secret? I can no more repeat what I heard in that little room, with Captain Julien kneeling at my feet, than I can grow wings and fly to the moon.'

'Then what was the point of bringing us in here and telling us half a story?' Harry enquired, reasonably enough.

And now Dr Joynings smiled. 'I had to tell you what I could. But there's more, and I really am in haste. All this happened shortly after you all left to rescue Mistress Stannard. Captain Julien said he had made up his mind to confess, and then to leave Hawkswood. He apparently kept his saddlebags in his room, but he hadn't packed them. He said that now he had seen me, he would pack and leave at once. I said very well. He went upstairs. And I ran to the stillroom here!'

Joynings was now beaming at us, as pleased with himself

as a child who has successfully conned a difficult lesson. 'I have enjoyed Phoebe's aniseed-flavoured wine,' he said. 'And I have seen what aniseed can do to a pair of otherwise placid dogs. I ran to the stillroom, I seized a bottle of the wine – I opened it and sniffed it to make sure it was one with aniseed in it; Phoebe doesn't flavour all her wine that way – and then I snatched up a drying cloth from the kitchen and ran. Believe me, I don't go in for running; there's too much flesh on me and I'm not young. But this time, run I did, and I went to the stables and to the captain's horse – that big dark bay – and I anointed its feet, all four hooves and all four horseshoes. I picked all its feet up, one after another, and I poured wine over the cloth and wiped its horseshoes and then I polished its hooves. It's well behaved in the stable, that horse. I was nervous of it but it gave me no trouble. What lovely polished hooves they were when I'd finished. I was just in time to get back to the hall before the captain came through it with his bags. He got his horse out and rode off at once and I'm as sure as I can be that he never noticed any smell. It's not so very strong from a few feet away, not for a man. But the dogs will know it. Master Harry, take our mastiffs and chase him down. Even if he has ridden fast, and got a good few miles by now, I think the aniseed trail will still be there . . .'

He said no more, for Harry and Brockley were already halfway out of the door, dragging him with them.

I followed. They made for the hall, where we found Sir Edward waiting, still wanting to talk to us. They stopped to speak to him. He seemed puzzled at first and asked them to repeat things and I could see Harry seething with impatience and all but stamping a foot. But at last, Heron understood what they were saying and then there was movement, fast enough to please even Harry. Here was something that Heron could deal with without encountering resistance. Some of his men were in the kitchen, supping ale and consuming a bread and honey breakfast. He called them to him. They came, wiping honey off their mouths. He gave orders. In minutes they were in the stables, saddling their horses again, and Harry was with them. I shouted for Eddie, who in a general way had charge of the dogs, and Eddie loosed them and saddled Ruby for himself. She was fast and also fresh, for she hadn't been used in the dash to find me.

The dogs were shown the cloth that Joynings had used to polish the hooves of Julien's horse and they instantly became excitable. Taken to the gatehouse, they picked up the scent at once. They sped off, baying. The hunt was on its way.

'I don't like it,' said Dale. 'Hunting men as if they were deer. I liked Captain Julien. He's Master Harry's brother! And yet Master Harry is all for running him down like a hart!'

'I think Master Harry has guessed things,' I told her. 'I have half guessed at them myself. Dr Joynings wouldn't tell us the truth, but it seems to speak for itself. Come. I think we should look after Gladys.'

I seemed to be dealing with so many things at once that I hadn't noticed what had become of Gladys. However, it didn't take long to find her. Gladys slept on a truckle bed in a small attic. Long ago I had offered her a proper bedchamber, but she laughed at me and said that when I had fine folk to stay, with all their servants, I would just throw her out of it to make room for one or other of them and she'd rather have a little attic space that was all hers because I wouldn't put any of *them* in there.

There was a good deal of truth in that, unfortunately. But I made sure that her mattress was comfortable and that she had sheets and warm blankets. Dale and I found her huddled under them, and shivering. Not with cold, but with shock and exhaustion. I knelt down to cuddle her. I noticed her smell but I ignored it. I had been at close quarters with it all night, and not just that. I had shared terror and despair with her as well. Now I held her as though she were an injured child. She felt frighteningly small and fragile. I told Dale to fetch wine and some good soup. Hawthorn always made sure that there was a stockpot in the kitchen, either bubbling on the fire or keeping warm beside it, and from a good stockpot, a soup could quickly be created. Egg yolks, a little chopped bacon, some peas . . .

Gladys revived enough to say, 'Not that-there aniseed wine

that Phoebe makes. Awful stuff, indeed to goodness, makes me puke.'

The wine and soup were brought, along with a piece of bread and honey, but she couldn't take much, though we did get a few spoonfuls of soup into her, and one or two nibbles of the bread and honey. She drank a cup of wine, which I was glad to see her take, for it would both warm and soothe her. I hoped that now she would begin to revive. She had been so near death. Right to the very edge of it. For a few hideous moments, she had known what it was to hang.

Eventually, leaving another cup of wine and the rest of the bread and honey beside her, we wrapped her more tidily in her blankets, and left her to sleep. I promised that I would soon return, and held her for another few moments, saying: 'You are safe now. No harm will come to you here.'

Then Dale and I went back downstairs to the hall and sat there, wondering how long it would take the hunt to catch up with Captain Julien and how long it would take to bring him back.

I never was any good at passive waiting. I said to Dale that we must find something to do. 'Everyone's feeling like that,' said Dale. 'But I don't think I can settle to embroidery. Phoebe's out in the garden with a basket, looking for dande-lions. She wants to start another batch of wine. She says that Dr Joynings used the last bottle but one, polishing a horse's hooves! He took a whole bottle over it, seemingly. There's another batch in the cellar that's about matured by now, and it's time to get a new batch going, she says. It takes a good two years to be ready.'

'All right,' I said. 'We'll take a basket as well and see if we can find any dandelions in the archery field.'

It was something to do, something to occupy hands and feet and eyes. We filled our basket all too quickly and then walked back through the garden, where we found Phoebe collecting dandelions and weeding the flowerbeds at the same time. The three of us went together to the little stone room which at other times was used as a room for baths and washing days. Today it was where Phoebe had set out her requirements:

the largest basin we possessed, now full of well water, a jar of honey, a pot of yeast, and two lemons.

'Enough here for half a dozen bottles,' she said briskly. 'Only I've got to use honey because that man Hawthorn won't let me have any sugar. Sugar's better.'

'I expect I can talk at least some sugar out of him,' I said. I went to the kitchen and did so. Hawthorn was busy and also irritable. Flood, he said, was preparing a marchpane fantasy; dinner was to be a celebration, because of my safe return. The marchpane would need sugar! In fact, we were quite well supplied with sugar, as I pointed out. I said that whoever went to Woking market next, could put it on their list. I think that he had turned Phoebe's request down out of sheer awkwardness. He grumbled but he gave me what she needed. And then, as I carried my booty back to Phoebe, I suddenly felt so overcome with tiredness that I could hardly put one foot in front of the other. Over my right eye, thuds of dull pain had begun, the harbingers of a migraine. I told Dale to go to the stillroom and collect a phial of the remedy that Gladys brewed for my headaches (I had never dared to ask what was in it) and then went to ask Hawthorn to squeeze a lemon for me.

'I feared all this would get you a bad head,' said Dale, returning from the stillroom. 'Time you had a lay-down in your chamber, ma'am.'

When the hunt returned, therefore, I was on my bed, with the curtains closed round me. Shortly after that, however, encouraged by a good dose of Gladys's ill-tasting but effective remedy, and a cup of lemon juice, diluted in a little water and with the edge taken off it by a sprinkle of salt, the malady reached its usual end in a bout of nausea. Half an hour later, I was able to rise and go to the hall, and hear what the hunters had to say.

Sir Edward and his men were not there. 'They've gone straight on to put Captain Julien in Sir Edward's lockup before he's taken on to somewhere else,' Harry told me. 'Not Lewes for him, I think. He repeated his confession for us – Sir Edward stood over him with a dagger and made him! And after we'd got that out of him, I fancy he'll find himself in the Tower. I rather think that Stephen will too, now that we know it all.

We caught Julien only a few miles away. The dogs ran as though they were on a clear, paved road; that aniseed seems to put a spell on them. He couldn't believe it when he heard us coming. He said as much. He said he heard the dogs baying, but he was slow to look round because he didn't believe it was anything to do with him. Then the noise got louder and he drew rein and turned to see. He'd just gone across a common and up to the top of that little rise where we always canter when we go that way, and he could see down it to the track across the common, and there were our mastiffs, and we were behind them and then he knew. He swung his horse round and put spurs to it, but it was too late. The horse could gallop but those dogs can run! They held to the line until the horse started to flag and then it was all over with him.'

'I could pity him,' I said. 'So must you, surely. He is your brother.'

'And a fine brother he is too!' said Harry bitterly. 'We caught him in a little wood. The dogs were baying round his horse and the horse was plunging, scared. We hauled the dogs away, heaved him out of the saddle and roped his hands, tied the horse to a tree. Then Sir Edward pushed him on to his knees, pulled a dagger on him, as I said, and made him repeat the confession he had made to Dr Joynings. Sir Edward said that if he didn't tell it to us now, he'd tell it to Richard Topcliffe in the Tower of London. He'd put the life of the queen's sister in danger . . .'

'I'm the queen's sister now, am I?' I enquired with interest. 'Someone to be protected, even if I did kill Hector, defending Gladys Morgan?'

'Apparently,' said Harry, grinning. 'He tried to deny that there had ever been such a confession, but Sir Edward pointed out that – if necessary – Dr Joynings might be forced to reveal what he had heard. Joynings isn't the stuff of martyrs and there are many who say that confessions are Popery and should not be respected. So, in the end, it all came out.'

'What did?' I asked. 'I haven't been told yet what this confession amounted to.'

Harry looked at me gravely. 'He didn't come to warn you, Mother. He came to frighten you. He was in league with the

Mercers. It was his business, among other things, to keep them informed of all your movements, and to see that you were kept in a state of constant fear. They wanted you to realize as soon as possible that the tragedies among your acquaintances weren't just coincidences. He put on a great show of innocence, warning you against this and that but all the time, trying to terrify you. From inside our household, he could learn things that he could secretly pass to his confederates. Captain Julien made sure that the Mercers knew where my sister Meg was living and all about her children and where they were likely to run away to. They found out all that from him! And worse. Much worse. I hardly know how to tell you . . .'

'Yes, Harry? What is it? Please don't stop there.'

'He murdered Eleanor!' Harry hardly knew how to get the words out. 'He was the one who did it! He stopped her in the wood, grabbed her horse's bridle, yanked her out of the saddle and knocked her head against that tree and then, when she was stunned, did it again, harder, and made sure the job was finished by using his dagger. It was *my half-brother* who killed my future wife, the girl I loved so much. What had she ever done to him? All that talk of abandoning the Mercers because I was his brother! It makes me retch to remember it! And it was my delightful half-brother who got word to the Mercers when you sent to warn Meg and her family that they were in danger. All that business about *oh no, don't tell me where they're going, I don't want to know!* He didn't need to know. Hector and Stephen were already watching the family. They expected us to warn them; Julien was going to encourage that. They were going to let my sister's family start to run away and then they would strike. Cat and mouse, you see. Once the family were on their way to Devon, *then* they kidnapped poor little Ursula Mary. We all know what happened to her. Oh, and earlier on, it was dear Julien who had the idea of borrowing Hector's cabin boy, Andrew Lomax, so as to deposit another spy in your employment, *and* it was Julien who thought of seizing you and Ben and Gladys and making you decide between them before you were killed yourself. He had told the Mercers that the long-drawn-out business they had planned was becoming too dangerous, and this was his charming, intelligent suggestion about an alternative, a way of cutting it short but still making you, and all of us, suffer most exquisitely.'

Harry was furious and he was also hardened, so that although I longed to put my arms round my stricken son, I could not, because he would only have put me back from him. What he had learned from Julien that day had done something dreadful to him. He was stiff, remote, frozen in his rage against the man he had welcomed as a brother, only to be betrayed. There was no consolation at all that I could give him.

TWENTY-TWO
Two Young Things

Sir Edward did not return to Hawkswood after the capture of Julien. He ordered Hector's body to be deposited in an unimportant church whose vicar didn't dare to argue with him, and later, it was buried quietly in the churchyard there. Only the vicar attended, along with four of Sir Edward's men, who acted as coffin bearers, and the gravedigger. The decencies had been maintained, we were told. There was no more to be said about Hector.

After hearing that, I hoped that this would be the end of the whole wretched business, but of course it was not, however much we all wanted to close our doors against the world and let our wounds heal. I had another migraine attack and had repeated nightmares; Gladys remained in her bed, needing to have her food brought to her, having to be coaxed to eat it, and also needing someone within call at night, for she too had nightmares. The other maids had never liked her, but pretty, lively Bess was a kind girl and took the task on without complaint.

Harry seemed to be encased in ice. He was infallibly courteous to whomever addressed him, from me down to Tommy Reed the spitboy, but such careful courtesy was in itself a form of intimidation.

But we could not shut ourselves off from the world for ever. Lomax and Julien had been marched off on foot, which meant that we were left in possession of the two horses that had been in the stable at the cottage, and Julien's dark bay gelding. After a time, however, Sir Edward sent for them. They would be kept at the country's expense until either their masters should be vindicated and able to claim them, or condemned, in which case they would be sold and the money paid into the Treasury. We were glad to see them go, for their presence in our stable was a constant reminder of unpleasant things.

We had, of course, to tell the Blakes what had happened. Eleanor Blake had been one of the Mercers' victims. They had a right to be told that justice was going to be done.

We rode over on a Saturday afternoon, near the end of September. It was a mild, slightly misty day, but as we trotted on to the Blakes' land, we noticed that they had had a successful harvest, just as Hawkswood had. The weather had been fair; the wheat had ripened early, been reaped early, and the sheaves had been carted away from the fields to be built into stacks. Ours were being thatched that day, but the Blakes' corn was ahead of us; the thatching was already finished.

'That's how it should be,' Brockley said. 'Whatever happens, the land mustn't go into mourning.'

There were five of us: me, Harry, Ben and the Brockleys. I think we all felt uncomfortable about our errand, but we knew it had to be done. On arrival, we were greeted pleasantly by the butler, grooms came to take our horses, and we were shown into their parlour. It at once felt congested, for Cobbold Hall was not a spacious property. Like Hawkswood, it had an old-fashioned hall, but it was half the size of ours, and its one parlour was only a little bigger than my little parlour and nowhere near the size of my East Room.

We were invited to seat ourselves and then the family came to welcome us, which crowded the room still more. Master and Mistress Blake were there, and so were the sons, John and Richard, and the two young daughters, Margaret and Susannah. Mistress Blake and her daughters were still in black, although the sons and their father Reginald seemed to have abandoned it in favour of ordinary garments. The usual tray of refreshments was brought. There was small talk. Until I cleared my throat and said, 'We actually came with a purpose. We have news for you. The man who murdered your daughter has been found and seized, and so have two others who were concerned in what we now know was a very wicked plot. One other offender is dead.'

'We had heard something,' Master Blake said. In normal circumstances he was a quietly cheerful man with a few grey hairs in his shoulder-length brown hair and his short beard. Now, he was grave and sad, which didn't suit him. As I studied him, I hoped that it wouldn't congeal into a permanency. Mistress Blake, who had cried so much when Eleanor was killed, looked as though she still cried, often. Her brown eyes were tired and there was a pinkness round them.

'Our servants and yours meet sometimes,' she said now. 'One of our maids is the younger sister of your Phoebe. But we don't know details; only that you were in danger, Mistress Stannard, but were rescued and the miscreants were taken away. We want to know everything that happened.'

Between us, with Ben, Brockley and me telling our own parts of the story, we filled the gaps in for them. Mistress Blake's eyes and mouth opened wide when I admitted to stabbing Hector Mercer.

'I don't know now how I did it,' I said. 'I didn't want to; I always hoped I would never have to do such a thing. Even though I carry a dagger, I only do so in case I need it for self-defence. But in the end I did it for Gladys.'

'What, for that smelly old woman?' John Blake said, somewhat crudely. His father shook a reproving head at him and I said, 'She is old and frail. She is still keeping her bed, still shaken with frightful memories. She nearly died. The rope was round her neck and Hector had already pulled her feet off the ground when I ran at him. She was choking, and weeping with terror, and she is my responsibility. I am glad I saved her.'

Ben took over then, describing how he had arrived at Hawkswood on bloodstained feet and how the rescue party had been assembled. Then I told of the moment when it arrived. Finally, I told them how Julien de la Roche had made his terrible confession, what Dr Joynings had done to the hooves of the dark bay horse, and how Julien had been hunted down and caught and what he had said when he repeated that confession.

I also told them how Andrew Lomax had saved my life at the last moment, by hindering Stephen's attempt to put me to the sword. Master Blake nodded and said, 'Will you plead for clemency for him?'

I nodded, and he said, 'Young things are easily led astray.'

While we had been talking, the mistiness had dispersed and a shaft of sunshine had found its way into the cramped parlour. Now, little Margaret – who was nearly sixteen and no longer so little – said, 'It's going to be a fine day, after all. May this young thing suggest that Master Harry might like to visit Eleanor's grave and lay some flowers on it? I can show him the way. He wasn't at the funeral.'

Mistress Blake protested. 'They can't just go off together; St Peter's church is in Woking, two miles off. Some older person should go with them – what will people think?'

'What people?' said her husband, suddenly showing a spark of liveliness. 'What does it matter? Nothing seems to matter these days,' he added wearily. 'If Eleanor had lived, they would be lawfully brother and sister by now. Don't fuss, Anna, let them go. There are still plenty of flowers in the garden. Take a vase or two, Margaret. Harry can carry a water bottle. You can fill the vases with water and put the flowers into it. It will keep them alive for a while. Just laid on the grave, they simply die and that's sad. Everything's sad these days; no need to add to it.'

Therefore, Margaret and Harry cut flowers in the garden and set off, on foot, for Woking. The rest of us were invited to dine. 'It will be salad and hot mutton pies,' said Mistress Blake, 'and then some almond cakes. Those two can have a cold pie each when they get back. Oh, I hope that no one recognizes them and starts to talk. Margaret is still in mourning.'

'They have a sorrow to share. They'll be good for each other. It's time that Margaret was out of mourning, a young wench like her,' said Reginald Blake. 'You too, Susannah. You and your mother should go out into the garden until we dine. Go and do some weeding and let the sun put some colour into your cheeks. You're both too pale.' Mistress Blake murmured something about doing things like weeding would look heartless, after the news we had brought, but her husband said firmly, 'You as well, my dear,' and she gave in.

I joined the gardening party and Dale came with me, leaving the men together, until we were called to dine. As promised, it was a simple meal; it looked as though the Blakes had extended their mourning into the kitchen. Now that we had said what we came to say, I began to wish we could go home.

We couldn't go until Harry and Margaret returned, but they came back not long after we had finished dinner and were able to partake of half-hot mutton pies, slightly wilted salad and the last two almond cakes.

'I know we are not supposed to pray for the dead,' said Margaret, a little defiantly. 'But Eleanor was my sister, and if I want to pray for her soul, I don't see why I shouldn't. Anyway, I did. We stayed for a while beside the grave, and we prayed for Eleanor.'

'We both did,' said Harry. The expedition had done him good. He no longer looked or sounded quite as much as though he were encased in ice. 'It was a good day for walking,' he added. 'The sun is still warm and we found the grave very tidy. The verger is conscientious.'

'What did you talk about, on that long walk, to and fro?' Mistress Blake wanted to know.

'Eleanor, partly,' said Margaret. 'But then, what a good thing it was to get the wheat crop in so promptly, and we talked about our horses. Harry was telling me about Captain Julien's horse that Sir Edward Heron has taken away, and wondering if he'll keep it; it's a well-bred animal. And we talked about the Michaelmas Fair in Woking. Mother, I'd so like to go. It wouldn't be disrespectful to Eleanor's memory, would it? We could visit the grave at the same time. But the fair might help us to feel better. We've got to, one day, and I'm sure that Eleanor would want us to. She'd know that we would never forget her.'

'I don't think—' began Mistress Blake, but Reginald interrupted her.

'I think the wench is right. Eleanor would not have wished to impose all this sorrow and deprivation on us. That wasn't much of a dinner today, my dear. Dinner never does amount to much these days. The cook must be finding life dull. It's time to put the past away. We will keep Eleanor in our memories but continue with our lives and have ordinary enjoyments. We will all go to the fair,' declared Master Blake.

And added to me, 'Perhaps, Mistress Stannard, you will join us. We can make up a party.'

'Yes, of course,' I said. 'Harry?'

'I agree. It could be most enjoyable – provided the weather is all right,' said Harry, and as I looked at him I realized that the old Harry was back. Somewhere in between Cobbold Hall and St Peter's in Woking, Margaret had melted the ice.

We did as Reginald Blake and Harry had suggested and made up a party to go to the fair. It wasn't altogether a success because the weather had changed by then. There was a chill wind and a heavy grey sky. However, when we had all assembled at Cobbold House, we agreed that we all still wanted to go, because by then we had all decided what we wanted to buy.

Mistress Blake and Dale alike wanted silk thread in several colours; Margaret wanted a length of warm woollen cloth to make a new winter gown. 'In any pretty colour; Susannah and I are weary of black. Nothing will bring Eleanor back. We'll remember her always but we're *girls*. Girls want pretty things. And we would like some earrings too.'

Anna Blake protested that they had their gold keepers which kept the ear piercings from closing up; they were pretty but not obtrusive, why not be content with those for a few months longer? This resulted in an argument that lasted most of the way to Woking, until Reginald Blake finally said, 'For God's sake, Anna, let the girls have their way,' and Anna finally gave in.

Overcast though it was, it wasn't actually raining, and the fair was well attended and lively, not to say raucous, with stallholders promoting their wares at the tops of their voices, apparently in competition with each other, and the racket of livestock as it was carried or led to the place appointed for selling it.

A mule plodded through the crowd, pulling a cart in which a very angry pig was squealing and thrusting an indignant muzzle against the net that held it in place. A pony went past us, pulling a similar cart in which coops of geese and poultry squawked and clucked loudly enough to drown the shouts of the stallholders they happened to pass. A man carrying a coop of chickens collided with a woman clutching a basket in which eggs nestled in a bed of straw, and upset the basket. We edged round them as the woman bawled that her eggs were all spoiled and the man with the chicken coop owed her their worth and she'd call the constable if he didn't pay up. The two local constables were on duty and they had sharp ears for altercations. One of them appeared at that moment. We never knew what the outcome was because we were tired of all things connected either with wrongdoers or the law, and pressed on to where a fire-eater was demonstrating his alarming skill to an admiring, and in some cases nervous, audience.

We split up to go shopping, the women going in one direction and the men in another. Margaret was pleased to find a stall offering lengths of good-quality light green woollen cloth with little silver flowers embroidered on it. Dale wanted material too, but being Dale, preferred something plainer. She let me buy her a length of velvet but it was brown, and had no embroidery.

The men were more concerned with leather and metal. When we met again, by arrangement, at a stall selling ginger cakes and pies (all hot, because their vendor had a charcoal cooking fire on a wheeled trolley), we found that the Blake boys had bought spurs and belts with ornate buckles while their father had purchased a new waterproof leather cloak. Brockley was holding an awkwardly shaped bundle that contained an earthenware mixing bowl, which he said John Hawthorn needed, because Tommy Reed, the spitboy, who still had an urchin tendency to wild and excitable movements, had unfortunately broken one.

We were consuming hot meat pies and ginger cakes, along with cider, which their proprietor also had for sale, when a new disturbance suddenly arose all round us. A thin, ragged man had been looking enviously at the wares on the stall. We didn't see him try to filch a ginger cake, but the stall proprietor did, and was after him in an instant. The would-be thief fled and our stallholder went after him, shouting *stop thief* and people in the crowd joined in. We heard the hunt fade in the distance and then grow louder again as the quarry lost his sense of direction and doubled back. He came in sight, his ragged cloak flying and his eyes wild and terrified. As he came level with us, a man who had been buying gloves from a stall nearby turned, put out a casual foot, and tripped him up. The mob was on him instantly, and we saw that a constable was in its midst. The constable seized on his prey and dragged him away. The proprietor of ginger cakes and meat pies resumed his place, fed some more charcoal into his fire and said with satisfaction, 'He'll likely be flogged at the cart's tail. He won't thieve a second time.'

But thief or not, he had looked desperate. Those ragged clothes and thin body cried out *hunger*. He was probably too poor to buy food. And suddenly, I was reminded of – and concerned for – Andrew Lomax, who at the end had intervened to stop Stephen from killing me.

The trial was still to come.

TWENTY-THREE
The Fate of Traitors

The trial was held at the end of October, beginning on All Souls' Day, which seemed to be in some way appropriate. It took three days and was altogether a much bigger affair than I expected. We went to London and took lodgings while it was on.

It took place in Westminster Hall. I was surprised at that, and said as much to Sir William Cecil, who attended, though his goutiness was getting worse, and he was limping and leaning heavily on his stick. He came over to me as soon as he saw me and, when I mentioned my surprise, said, 'You are Her Majesty's sister, and that is now widely known. If you become the object of conspiracies, then the queen will take the matter seriously. If your person can be threatened, some may think, so can hers. And when such a conspiracy does arise, and one as thoroughly evil as this, then it must be clearly shown what the queen and her council think of it.'

I was not there alone, of course, for Harry was there and Brockley and Dale were with me too. I was only present because I would have to testify. I dreaded that, because to give evidence that may condemn a man to death is a heavy task. I felt its weight, even though I had once faced death at Stephen's hands and had every right to want the world purged of his rage and his hate. When he was brought in, manacled, between two guards, he caught my eye and I saw that the rage and hate were still very much there, probably increased now that, as well as all the other things he could hold against me, I had killed his brother in front of his eyes.

To be the target of such passions is frightening, even when you are safe from them. Stephen Mercer's fierce eyes made me shiver. Harry was beside me and I suspected that he felt much the same, although I didn't ask him. Then Julien de la

Roche was brought in, similarly manacled and guarded. Harry had learned to see him as a friend and to love him as a brother. He had been hurt and enraged by Julien's betrayal, but he didn't relish having to give evidence against him, all the same. The third prisoner was Andrew Lomax, of course. The others were bearing themselves haughtily and, in Stephen's case, angrily, but Andrew Lomax was visibly so frightened that the guard at his side was almost holding him up.

The death of Hector, brought about by me, had not been pursued. It had been accepted as defence of a dependent servant. I looked round at this solemn and powerful court and was thankful.

A little too soon, as it turned out.

There was a considerable crowd and a ripple of sound when the prisoners were led in, but otherwise, there was a hush in the courtroom. I thought it was probably because our surroundings were so impressive, the hall so long and high, its curving timber roof beams drawing the eye and inspiring wonder. How were such beams made and installed? It looked like the work of magicians, or angels. It didn't by any means encourage trivial gossip about the weather.

The proceedings began. Details of the case, the names and crimes of the prisoners, the name of the judge and the presence of the jury were all read out by a clerk. A priest then recited a prayer. After that, Harry and I and a number of others were taken away into an anteroom. Witnesses were not supposed to hear each other's testimony before giving their own.

There were stools and benches to sit on while we waited. We were ourselves under guard, and under the watchful eyes of our guardians, I think we all felt as though we were on trial as well. The other witnesses included Sir Edward Heron, Dr Joynings, Laurence Miller, Phoebe, Ben Atbrigge, Captain Banks and Sergeant Wooller. Also among us was a former acquaintance of mine, Captain Tyler, who had once presented evidence, before the queen, that English pirates were attacking English shipping. Wisely, someone had decided that Gladys should not be called. She had recovered her health and was back to her old self and she grumbled much at being excluded. She scowled horribly on the morning when we set off for London, leaving her behind.

Since I was in the anteroom for a long time, I missed a good deal of the trial. I believe that there were speeches from lawyers before any witnesses were called at all. Sir Edward was summoned first, and then Laurence Miller, followed by Captain Tyler and then Captain Banks. Wooller was never actually called at all. Only after the others had testified was I sent for. I followed an usher out into the court, where I climbed two steps up to a small, railed platform. I took an oath before God to speak the truth and a lawyer ordered me to describe the events at Evergreens the previous year, when, acting under orders from Cecil, I had done the things that had so incensed the Mercers.

I did as I was bidden, which took some time, and was then led on to describe the arrival at Hawkswood of Julien de la Roche and the frightening things he had told me. I explained that the danger had been reported to the authorities, and that Captain Banks and Sergeant Wooller had then become part of my household and done their best to protect me. And then I told the court how, at last, their efforts had been circumvented; I had been kidnapped and held captive by Hector and Stephen Mercer, and my near death at their hands.

At this point I had to admit to killing Hector, and it seemed that, after all, this matter was not going to be buried, because a lawyer who had apparently been hired by the Mercers got to his feet and demanded that I should be arrested for Hector Mercer's murder. I listened to this awful distortion of the truth, cold with fright and trying not to let my teeth chatter. I was asked what I had to say about this, and I tried to explain that I was attempting to save the lives of Gladys and of myself.

Here there came an interruption to the main proceedings. The judge didn't wish to enquire into Hector's death, at least not then and there. It was not what the court was there for; if it had to be dealt with, this would be done at another time and in another place. Whereupon, the jury foreman stood up. He was a stout man, past middle age and with an air of authority. He asked permission to address the judge and, when this was granted, he said that his jury wished to give their opinion of the matter here and now. The judge, sounding annoyed, said *very well but waste no time*, whereupon the foreman said that he and his fellow jurors believed, to a man, that I had acted in defence of myself and another.

One juror wanted to know why the woman Gladys Morgan was not present, and I had to explain that she was very old and too ill to travel. Her experience at the hands of the Mercers had come near to killing her, with fear, I said. At that point, to everyone's astonishment, Andrew Lomax called out that he wanted to testify on my behalf.

The judge said that as far as he knew, there was no precedent for letting an accused man testify on behalf of the witnesses against him, but then sat back and observed that sometimes new precedents had to be created and old ones overthrown, and he would permit the prisoner Lomax to speak.

Lomax did. He said he had seen me rush forward to save the woman Gladys from the rope and yes, he thought I must have done something to Hector Mercer but, if I had, it was for the woman Gladys's sake. He had been sorry for the old woman when Hector tried to hang her, and he thought Mistress Stannard had acted rightly. He added that when Stephen Mercer ran at me with his sword, then he, Andrew Lomax, had wanted to stop him and had tried. That was all.

One of the lawyers, a man with a round, pleasant face which I thought was quite at odds with the words that came out of the shapely mouth, got up and tried to pretend that Lomax and I had conspired together to give testimonies that would put each other in a good light. This, however, was rapidly, heartily and unexpectedly refuted by Sir Edward Heron. He now spoke up boldly and out of turn, making it clear that Lomax and I had never had the opportunity to conspire about anything. We could not have foreseen Stephen's attempt to attack me, and therefore couldn't have in any way planned Lomax's attempt to stop him, and after that we had never had the slightest chance to confer together.

The judge looked exasperated by this interruption to the proper business of the day, but he also allowed it. I was permitted to finish my testimony and I upheld Lomax's assertion that he had attempted to save my life by interfering with Stephen's attempt to kill me. My guilt or innocence were referred to the jury and I found myself being officially vindicated.

After all that, I was allowed to sit once more with Brockley and Dale, and so was able to listen to the witnesses who followed me. In between witnesses, Laurence Miller, who was sitting just behind me, leant forward and in a whisper told me how he had made the court laugh with his account of how he tried to lay an aniseed trail on Ben's shoes. Bit by bit the whole story was emerging. Sir Edward Heron had explained how he had been fetched by Laurence Miller to join the rescue party and how, once he had fully understood what had struck him as a garbled story to begin with, had been persuaded to join in and was glad that he had done so.

Ben was called next, and related how he had escaped through the thatch of the cottage and stolen a horse, only the animal had thrown him. At this moment, there were grim smiles from Julien and Stephen, who tried to nudge each other and were jerked back by their guards. Ben ignored them, and described how he had got up, gone on, missed the track and got lost in the darkness and the forest, but found his way in the end and came to Hawkswood on feet that bled. Phoebe was called and spoke of Ben's arrival and her efforts to tend his feet.

Then Dr Joynings was brought in and was required to reveal Julien's confession. Although he had already, once, been forced to reveal it, he still balked and begged not to be asked to do such a thing again. Especially, he said, as Julien de la Roche had in fact repeated it to Sir Edward Heron, which was not under the seal of the confessional. Could Sir Edward not be asked to tell it instead of himself?

There was a pause, while the judge consulted with the lawyers. Finally, Sir Edward Heron was recalled, although, as the judge said, very sternly, there were those who did not feel that such Papistical practices as confessions should be encouraged or held sacred.

Sir Edward calmly repeated the dreadful things that Julien had said to him. Harry was summoned, to describe how he had realized that Eleanor Blake's wound was no accident, and how he had taken charge of the rescue party, after Ben had arrived at Hawkswood to summon help. I was recalled to tell the court about the death of Aunt Tabitha and the visit of the mysterious man who said his name was Nicholas Trent.

All this had not gone on without a break. On the first day, there was a dinner break, and when the autumn dusk began to fall, the session was declared at an end. It reconvened the following morning. The last testimonies were heard that afternoon. Not until the third day did the trial reach the point of verdicts.

As a group, I think that the witnesses did their work well. One and all, we had told the truth. The accused were invited to testify, and Captain Julien tried to maintain that he had indeed come to Hawkswood to meet his brother and to warn me of the steel net that was closing round me, and he also tried to maintain that his so-called confession, as he put it, was a fabrication. However, when it was staunchly confirmed by Dr Joynings, Captain Julien backed down and admitted that he had made it because guilt had driven him to it; he had grown to like his half-brother Harry and become ashamed of his part in the Mercers' scheme. I remembered how, when Gladys was seized, he had looked at me with pity in his eyes and said that he wanted to leave my household. *It has been a happy thing for me to meet you; I had no idea what a joy it can be to have a brother. Before, I had only the brotherhood of – well, you know.* Clearly, he had been planted on me by the Mercers to be their man under my roof, to tell them what I was doing, to tell them about my family and friends and what they were doing, as well. The Mercers would have found it all too easy to track Meg and her family as they set out for Devon! Captain Julien was obligingly telling them just where to find the family, all about Riverside and probably all about Ladymead as well.

They had let Meg and her family get halfway and then, yes! Cat and mouse. I thought angrily. Let them think they were escaping, and then – *pounce*. Bartholomew and Thomasina had had a narrow escape. The Mercers had decided – as I had surmised – to bring their campaign back to Hawkswood and to me.

On that day when he looked at me with pity, had he then almost repented of his part in the Mercers' deadly scheme? I rather thought he had. But he had not repented quite enough. He had gone on, racked by guilt, but still, gone on, until at last the guilt compelled him into confession. I didn't think it would help him much.

The trial was ending. The judge made a speech, trying to make the whole complicated story as lucid as possible. The jury consulted together and the verdicts were declared.

They had never of course been in doubt. There never had been the slightest possibility that they would be anything other than 'guilty', in all cases. The jury did recognize that Andrew Lomax had been very young when he fell into the hands of the Mercers, and at the end had apparently had a change of heart, but they were not unanimous, and one of them interrupted the foreman by shouting that seventeen was old enough to know right from wrong and that he ought to have had his change of heart a damned sight sooner. I looked at the boy as he stood there in his chains, and saw that he was white as a ghost and trembling.

I watched the prisoners as they listened to their fate. For Julien de la Roche and Stephen Mercer, it was the fate of traitors. They would be hanged, drawn and quartered. I had done Hector a favour. They heard their doom in apparent calm, though God alone knew what they were thinking. Lomax, however, would not die. His belated change of heart had saved his life. But he would be flogged through London at the cart's tail first. I saw his knees give way, and the guards stoop to hold him up.

I turned to Brockley. 'I want to get a message to Lomax. When he is free, I wish to take charge of him. I don't know what will happen to him after that flogging, but he will hardly be able to stand. I want him brought to Hawkswood. As far as I am concerned, I am still his employer.'

Dale gasped and Brockley said, 'Madam, you intend to take him back? He's sailed with pirates, he's been the catspaw of murderers. He could contaminate our household.'

I turned my head to Miller, who had been sitting in silence just behind me. 'What do you think? Would you have him back?'

'He's good with horses and you can't contaminate a horse,' said Miller coolly. 'And if we don't take him in, who will? He'll be homeless, without work, and as the mistress says, hardly able to stand. Or not able to stand at all. If he survives, he'll end up sleeping in fields, stealing so as to eat, maybe getting into the hands of a gang of pickpockets. Then it'll be prison and a beating again, round and round in a circle until he dies. To take him in would be an act of Christian charity. We can make it our business to see that he never gets into trouble again. The Mercers won't be there to claim him back.'

'We take him in,' I said.

Brockley, cynically, said, 'How many wards have you had now, madam?'

'He won't be a ward. And that, Brockley, was impertinent.'

'I beg your pardon, madam,' said Brockley, who wasn't, of course, begging my pardon at all, merely going through the motions.

I inclined my head, also going through the motions, and then Brockley said, 'I will go and find out how to get word to him. I will join you at our lodgings later on, madam. I will do as you ask, whatever my private opinions.'

It was one of those special moments between us, when shared memories occupied both of our minds. I turned to Dale and said, 'Your husband is a reliable man.'

Dale replied, 'Yes, ma'am,' in a small, polite voice, and I knew that this was one of the special moments which we hadn't been able to hide from her. I was sorry for it.

Brockley, competent as ever, was able to find out when the sentences were to be carried out. Banks and Wooller were no longer part of my entourage, of course, but Brockley caught hold of them as they were leaving the court and explained what he was about. He not only received useful advice from them, but also arranged to get in touch with them, if necessary, to get Lomax into my hands. They were apparently on leave and were free to help us. 'You'll pay, madam?' he asked anxiously when he arrived back at our lodgings.

'Yes. Don't tell the landlord here who Lomax is!' I said.

'I don't think he'll like to house a condemned criminal. We don't want to be thrown into the street! As it is, as soon as we have Lomax with us, we should leave at once for Hawkswood and get there the same day.'

On the day when the sentences were carried out, I stayed in the lodgings. I never heard the details of how Julien and Stephen died, nor did I wish to do so. I had a vivid memory of the day I had first seen the Mercer brothers. They were just home from a voyage, two handsome, sunburned, smiling young men. Beautiful young men, bringing gifts to their mother and sister. An emerald. A roll of soft, pale green velvet. A jaguar skin rug. And I remembered my first glimpse of Captain Julien, and how he had reminded me not just of Harry, but of Matthew de la Roche, who had fathered them both. The beautiful bodies of Stephen and Julien were now to be torn apart, in front of a baying crowd. I did not wish to be a witness, even by hearsay.

Brockley, Banks and Wooller waited at the endpoint of Lomax's ordeal. His guards had orders to release him, but also to deposit him in someone's care – a minister of the church, if no one else presented themselves. As it was, Brockley presented himself, acting on my behalf. He had my carriage ready. A guard captain handed him the document of release, and Brockley, together with Banks and Wooller, put him into the carriage, where a seat was padded with blankets and there was a sheet to put over his back, and brought him to me.

I got into the carriage and looked at him. He was semi-conscious, but moaning, and no wonder for his back was a horror of blood and welts. He would be scarred for life . . . if he lived. The landlord of our rooms came out to see what the to-do was about, looked into the carriage and said, 'Who's he? Not that young miscreant that was tried for being in the Mercer plot? If he is, you can't bring him in here. This is a respectable house.'

'We're already packed to leave,' I said coldly, feeling thankful that I had prepared for this. 'What do we owe? May we purchase some food from you, to eat on the way home? Brockley, will you see to it, and settle up, please?'

We set off for home at once, but it was already past noon
and we couldn't hurry because I didn't want the carriage to
jolt. I travelled inside, where I could keep an eye on our
passenger. My horse Jaunty was tied behind. The roads were
muddy through recent rain; even in good conditions, it would
have taken about four hours to reach Hawkswood. As things
were, it was late evening before we eventually rattled through
the gate arch and into the courtyard. Eddie, who was driving,
got down, and between them he and Brockley carried Lomax
indoors. With some extra help from Abel Parsons, he was
borne upstairs and into a spare bedchamber.

He was in a bad way.

For the next few days, I thought of little else but taking care
of Andrew Lomax. During that time, Gladys was the greatest
help to me. She had witnessed Lomax's attempt to defend me
and she was willing to do what she could for him. The fact
was that Gladys, with her knowledge of herbs, which embraced
almost everything that grew in the English countryside, could
do wonders.

We called a physician, of course, but although he recommended some sensible enough herbal washes, he also wanted
to bleed the patient, and the boy had lost blood enough. I
preferred to let Gladys be in charge. I don't know half the
things that she used. Burdock and camomile were two of them
but there were others. In my turn, I made sure that his back
was washed twice a day and the welts, where the skin had not
been broken, were salved. He was feverish for a long time
and hardly able to eat. I spooned broth and wine into him, but
there was infection in places and that was dangerous. It was
here that Gladys's knowledge was so valuable. She worked
over Lomax as though she were paying a debt. And gradually,
the pus dried up and scabbed, his fever went down and his
pain grew less and at last he was able to take solid food, and
finally, to rise and dress.

Meanwhile, of course, I had thankfully resumed contact
with various friends, who were no longer in danger because
of our friendship. Christopher Spelton and Mildred returned
to West Leys and visited me; I wrote to tell the Ferrises that

they were safe, and later on dined at White Towers and told them the whole story, across white napery, gleaming pewter and silver, polished glassware and excellent food. And, of course, I called on the Blakes. Harry and I dined there too, to celebrate Margaret's sixteenth birthday, and later on, Harry went there on his own to go hawking with Richard and John.

Gladys remained on duty in the sickroom until she was sure that she was no longer needed. A few days later, shortly after dinner, evidently feeling that he was able to face whatever the future might hold for him, Lomax asked to see me. I went to his room. He looked at me warily and said, 'I want to thank you.' Then, nervously, he said, 'What now, Mistress Stannard? You have restored my health. I shall soon be able to go back into the world. I am wondering . . . I mean . . .'

'You are wondering where you go from here. You can stay, if you wish, and resume your work at the trotter stud. Master Miller is agreeable. Whatever your past, the horses won't know about it. The Mercers have no more hold over you. They are both dead.'

He was still essentially a boy, and a boy who had been cast out into the world at fourteen and had had to make his way ever since, and be grateful to anyone who would give him work and provide him with a roof above his head and enough food to eat. He was sitting on his bed, and now he turned for a moment and buried his face in his pillow. Then he sat up and brushed a hand across his eyes and I saw that he was trying to hide tears of relief.

I pretended not to see them. 'Laurence Miller is your master henceforth. Obey him, do your work well, and you will have a place at Hawkswood for as long as you want it. The Mercers are gone; you can forget them. You can start next week.'

We went downstairs together. Lomax said he would go out and help my grooms with whatever needed to be done. I had already told the household that Lomax would be staying and that, as I owed him my life, I expected them to treat him amiably. Brockley said he would go out to the stables for a while, and would make sure my orders were obeyed.

Harry had gone hawking with the Blakes again. Dale was upstairs, busy with sprucing up my ruffs. I went to the little parlour, where there was always a fire, and settled down to read. It was there that Harry found me. I looked at his face and came to my feet at once. He was white and stricken. I said, 'What is it?' I had an awful feeling that history was somehow about to repeat itself, that I was going to hear of another accidental death that was no accident. But Harry read my face and produced a shaky laugh.

'Oh no, Mother, no one is dead. But . . .'

TWENTY-FOUR
Parental Duties

'Harry, what is it?'

He had stopped in mid-sentence and didn't seem able to go on. He was staring at me as though he wanted to bore a hole into my head.

'Harry?'

'The trouble concerns you, Mother. Oh, dear God, I'm so sorry. It's so awful. I don't know how to tell you.'

'Tell me what?' The most appalling ideas were streaming through my brain. Was the Mercers' plot somehow not dead? Had someone else snatched it and was running onwards with it?

I remembered a fair in Guildford that had ended with some sporting contests. There had been a wrestling match, with people loudly laying bets on whether Mighty Thews, the champion wrestler who had represented Surrey in various contests, or Big Bold Butcher, his young challenger, would win (Mighty Thews did). There had also been a donkey race that caused great hilarity. Some of the donkeys failed to get into the spirit of the thing and either balked or ran backwards. And there had also been some running races. One was a race against teams instead of individuals. Team member number one, holding a baton, would go round the course once and, without slowing down, hand over his baton to team member number two, who would run the next circuit, and so on. Had the Mercers arranged for their baton to be passed on to someone else if their attempt failed?

I said, 'I thought you were hawking with the Blakes. It's kind of them to lend you a goshawk. I really must set up a mews for you here. You were going to dine with the Blakes as well.'

'So I did. We went after pigeons and, when we came back,

we handed our kill over to the cook and then we had ale in the parlour until dinner was ready and, during dinner, I decided to do something that had been going round and round in my mind for some while. The thing is . . . Mother, it's Margaret. She is delightful. In the last year or so . . . she's changed. She was a little girl before; now she's a young lady. It happened . . . so suddenly.'

'It does,' I said. 'It can happen within a single month, like a berry ripening.' I had witnessed it myself, with Meg. She was married at fifteen and I was worried about it, felt it was too soon, and then looked at her, really looked at her, in the way you hardly ever look at those close to you, and realized that – literally within a matter of weeks – she had made the journey from childhood into womanhood. She and George were in love, and it was real. I let them marry and time had proved me right.

Margaret Blake had probably gone through the same sudden ripening. 'And so?' I said to Harry, and I smiled as I said it.

'It's somehow awful to say it, but in some ways I like Margaret even better than I liked Eleanor. She has such a sparkle. She can play the lute and sing just as well as Eleanor and she rides even better, and she is just as well trained as Eleanor was in the womanly arts; she can embroider so well and she can cook – when we came back from hawking, her mother was busy in her stillroom and it was Margaret who told the cook to make pigeon pie for dinner and just how to prepare it . . .'

'Harry.'

'Yes, Mother. I'm sorry.'

'Just what is it that you decided to do?' I was guessing already but I wanted to hear it from Harry.

'I loved Eleanor, but she is dead and gone. She can't come back. I still want to marry. It can't now be Eleanor. And Margaret, dear Margaret . . . I went to find Master Blake. He was reading in his study. I asked him for Margaret's hand and he said no.'

'He said *no*?' I was very surprised, and somewhat hurt, on both Harry's behalf and my own. How could any father, I thought, *not* want a handsome, well-found lad like Harry as a son-in-law? 'Did he say why?' I asked.

'Yes. Oh, yes.' Harry fell to his knees and buried his face in my lap. I took his head between my hands and raised it so that I could see his face. 'Come along, Harry. Out with it. What did Master Blake say that has so overset you?'

'He said . . . he said . . . I can't repeat it.'

'Yes, you can. You must, Harry. If Master Blake has in some way spoken against me, I must know what he has said, if only so that I can refute it. *Out with it!*'

Harry stood up. 'He said that ours wasn't a safe family for a daughter of his to marry into. He said that if he had known then what he knows now, he would never have let Eleanor be betrothed to me, and Margaret must not be, either. He said that you . . . that you were a dangerous woman, that you had enemies who might at any moment appear and threaten not only you but your family. And that wasn't all.'

'All right, Harry, let me hear the rest of it.'

'He said that on the one hand – and this had disturbed him even when I was betrothed to Eleanor – you were the sister of the queen and therefore, as your son, I was too far above plain folk such as the Blakes. And on the other hand – something that he has only slowly realized, because when I was betrothed to Eleanor, he knew little about you – he doesn't now feel that you are . . . are . . .'

'That I'm what?'

'Womanly enough,' said Harry miserably. 'He feels that you aren't a good example for a young girl like Margaret, that it shouldn't be for women to involve themselves in matters of state, in . . . in plots and counterplots . . . that you were a *questionable* woman. He doesn't mind me going hawking with his sons; young men are a different matter. But where Margaret is concerned, you and your family are at once too noble for her and not noble enough.'

I was silent. In Harry's voice, and also in his eyes, as well as misery, there was accusation. I said, 'It is true that I am the queen's half-sister, though I am not legitimate. It is also true that I have served Her Majesty as loyally as I can, for nearly all my life. My late husband, Hugh Stannard, approved of this and encouraged it. My work has sometimes brought me into danger, yes. The queen herself knows what danger is. There is no shame in that! How can there be? I have been rewarded for my work, yes. As a result, I have substance enough to make this a household in which Margaret would have a pleasant life. And as far as I know, now that the Mercers are gone, I have no other secret enemies who are planning to attack me or mine. I take it that Margaret herself is aware of your suit, and is willing to marry you?'

'Yes, Mother, of course! I would never have approached her father unless she wished it.'

'Very well. Harry, don't be angry with me. Please don't be ashamed of the work I have done for the queen my sister, and for England. I will try to put this right. I will go now, at once, and see if Master Blake will let me talk to him. Ask the grooms to saddle Jaunty for me. I will go without delay.'

I spent the ride to Cobbold House wondering what in the world I was going to say to Master Blake. Part of the trouble was that he was right in some respects. I did sometimes draw danger towards me; it was the natural result of the duties I carried out for Queen Elizabeth, and I couldn't be sure that it wouldn't occur again, nor could I guarantee that it wouldn't bring danger on others. It was also true that in the eyes of many – Walsingham had been one of them – in performing those duties, I was not behaving as women are supposed to behave. Not that such considerations had ever stopped either Walsingham or Cecil from using me whenever it seemed convenient.

It was a fact, then, that in the eyes of many, not just Master Blake, the son of such a woman as me was not the ideal catch he seemed to be at first sight.

But nevertheless, here I was, riding towards Cobbold House, and I had no inclination to turn back. For the sake of these two young people, this must be dealt with.

I arrived at the gatehouse and the porter greeted me with a smile; whatever Master Blake's opinion of me, he hadn't yet banned me from his home. The porter's boy ran to announce me, the butler was at the door to admit me and a groom was ready to take my horse. So far, so good. I went inside.

Then came the first hitch. Hesitantly, the butler said, 'Madam, the house is in some disarray. But if you will wait in the parlour, someone will come to you and I will send in some refreshments. I feel sure—'

He flinched. I flinched. Somewhere in the house, a girl was crying. She was not hysterical; what we were hearing was the sound of grief, of sorrow. The butler tried to ignore it and continue leading me towards the parlour, but I stopped short, biting my lips. Master Blake's voice broke in, loud and angry, and then we could hear Mistress Blake apparently remonstrating, and then more crying and the sound of a slap, at which the crying ceased, but, quite clearly, we both heard Margaret's voice saying something in protest or anger – the words were not intelligible – and there was a slammed door and running feet.

'The parlour is this way,' said the butler, flustered. I followed him, knowing perfectly well where it was but letting him keep to the conventions. Once there, I took a seat as he suggested. I was glad enough to sit down in one of the handsome chairs and draw a few quiet breaths. This wasn't going to be easy.

The parlour looked as it always did. It faced south-east and the sun was shining through its square-leaded casement. It was strewn with fresh rushes, the cushions on its settle and its four chairs were plumped, showing off their beautifully embroidered covers. The chairs were elegantly carved, a sign that their owner was well to do. The three small tables were polished, and so was the shelving on the wall and the glassware that it held. There was a small fire in the hearth and on the mantelshelf above there were two bronze candlesticks and a little rearing horse in silver.

It was all new since the days of the Blakes' predecessor, but I had never taken much notice of it before. I did so now because the Blakes were a long time in coming. The refreshments arrived – slices of apple tart and small cakes with raisins in them, and a glass of wine. I didn't want anything to eat but I gulped the wine down gratefully, feeling that I needed courage.

I felt it even more when, at long last, the door was flung open and there was Master Blake, flushed with wrath, and using even conventional courtesy as some kind of weapon. He was no longer in mourning for Eleanor, but his grey velvet doublet, the matching puffed breeches and stockings, the black silk slashings, with only his white ruff for relief, told their own tale of mourning barely past. *Eleanor is hardly cold in her grave and now this!* He had probably taken so long over greeting me because he first had to damp down his temper and decide how to address me.

Even so, the temper was only just under the surface.

'Mistress Stannard!' He paused in the doorway. 'I take it that you are here on behalf of your son.' I could see the effort with which he kept his tone neutral. 'I see that you have been looked after.' He looked over his shoulder, snapped at someone to fetch him a glass of wine, at once, and then came right into the room and threw himself into a corner of the settle. 'If I am right, I have to say that you have had a wasted errand. I meant what I said to Harry. I presume that he has repeated it to you.'

A manservant appeared with the glass of wine on a tray, set it in front of his master and removed himself with an air of getting out of the way of cannon-fire. I wasn't surprised. There was aggression in every inch of Master Blake. He picked up his wine, drank half of it in one gulp and stared at me, inimically.

While riding from Hawkswood, and again as I waited in the Blakes' parlour, I had had time to think. I had planned a strategy of a sort. If Master Blake met me with anger, as I feared he might, I would do well not to respond in kind. Let him be as angry as he liked; I would be gentle. Let him be like a swordsman trying to fight a feather bed.

It certainly wasn't going to be easy; in fact, it looked likely to be very difficult indeed. I could only do my best.

'Your doubts concerning me and my household are very understandable, Master Blake,' I said mildly. He didn't reply, but went on staring at me. I ploughed on. 'But you may not be quite right about everything. Could we not talk? Perhaps with Mistress Blake too?'

'I told my wife that I would see you alone. There was no need for her to be present.' He drank the rest of his wine, in another single swig.

'Very well. But it's a fine morning,' I said, still in my mildest voice. 'And your garden is well cared for. Perhaps we could walk there?'

'If you are trying to convince me that your son is after all a suitable match for Margaret . . .'

'I only want to convince you of true facts, Master Blake. We are neighbours, and neighbours should be on good terms with each other. Let us talk together and therefore not have misunderstandings. And it *is* a fine morning.'

Grumpily, and with an air of, *I am only doing this to be polite to a neighbour/lady of standing/sister of the queen/ confounded woman who is so persistent that it's easier to say yes than no*, Master Blake consented to walk with me in the garden.

It was autumn now and there were few flowers, but the garden was well kept and evergreen shrubs had been skilfully used. A good gardener could do much with variations of leaf shapes and colours and here, somebody had. I had not been in the garden of Cobbold House in October for years, and the admiration that I now expressed to Master Blake was genuine. He became gruffly appreciative.

'I can't say that I had anything to do with the way the garden is planned. Our predecessors did that. But my gardeners are skilled and have added to the variety of evergreen shrubs. I am thinking to have some topiary work done. A few cockerels or something similar to mark the boundary of the garden, perhaps. I shall have to plant some yew hedges first, though. Well, Mistress Stannard.' He stopped short and swung round to face me. 'What is it that you wish to say to me, to correct something that I have apparently made a mistake about?'

I smiled at him and began to walk forward again. Perforce, he came with me. 'I only wanted to tell you that the appalling series of events that has so harmed your family and has also harmed mine, has never happened before and is not likely to happen again. The perpetrators are dead. In the past, it is true,

I have carried out various tasks for Her Majesty the queen, but they have not hitherto rebounded on to those around me. I have protected my privacy and theirs.'

This was not entirely true. The earlier incidents had not been as ghastly as the efforts of the Mercer brothers, but once, in France, I had nearly managed to get Dale convicted of heresy. However, I had no intention of letting any of my people suffer such risks again.

'Not only that,' I said, taking courage from his continued silence, 'it was Sir Francis Walsingham who usually insisted that I took on this or that task, and he too is gone. I can say this: that although I have worked in the interests of the queen since I was a girl in my twenties, I have never led anyone into danger unless they were willing to come.'

I supposed that this was true, more or less. Brockley and Dale need not have come to France with me, though it was a fact that none of us had foreseen the peril we were all running into. I went on: 'My good friends Brockley and Dale have shared danger with me at times, but not because they had to. The same applies to some of my wards. I have sometimes run risks in order to get *them* out of danger! One of them,' I said, half humorously, as I thought back over the years, 'was a young lady with a gift for falling in love with disastrously unsuitable men. I am quite sure that Margaret isn't like that. And nor, of course,' I said, now pitching my voice to the softest tone possible, 'is my son an unsuitable man for her. Far from it.'

I stopped speaking but went on quietly walking. After what seemed like a long pause, Master Blake said, 'My daughter is in her room, crying. I have told her she cannot marry Harry Stannard, and I find that he has stolen her heart without asking me first whether I wished him to do so. It doesn't make me happy to hear my girl cry so bitterly. If your son had waited and spoken to me first, Margaret's grief could have been avoided. Was that a proper way for Master Harry to behave?'

'I am tender to young lovers,' I said. I looked back over the years, to when I and the young man who had just become betrothed to my cousin Mary, suddenly and unexpectedly fell in love with each other instead, with the result that deep in one night I climbed out of the window, slid down the sloping roof of a one-storey room below, slithered down an ivied wall and into Gerald's arms. I had no regrets. Until the smallpox took him, we were happy, and I still had my daughter Meg to remind me of him.

As we paced along a pathway between parterre gardens, I remembered Gerald and our runaway marriage. However, it also occurred to me that it might be unwise to tell Master Blake about it. It wasn't likely to improve his opinion of me. My own romantic history was assuredly something he shouldn't find out about until Harry and Margaret were wedded and bedded.

'Young lovers aren't always in the wrong,' I said, and instead of mentioning Gerald, I told him about Meg and George instead. At the end, I said, 'I like Margaret just as much as I liked Eleanor, and I am not surprised that Harry has taken to her as well. He is a healthy young man and Eleanor, alas, is gone. That he should mourn and then find a new love seems to me natural and right, and I am happy with his choice. I am so sorry that you have found my – er – unusual career to be such an obstacle. Does it really need to be? Tell me, have you any objection to Harry himself? For instance, how would you feel if he belonged to a different, more conventional family than mine?'

'In that case, I would welcome him.' I think Master Blake found this difficult to admit but he was honest enough to do so. 'He is a fine lad in many ways. But your family isn't so fine. As I said, it doesn't seem to me to be a safe one for my daughter to enter.'

I heard that answer with a sinking heart. But then, refusing to admit defeat, I took up my errand again.

I said, 'Is there really no means at all by which I can persuade you to change your mind? Harry is heartbroken, you know, and Margaret – well, you have said it yourself. When I came into this house, was it Margaret crying that I heard?'

'Yes, it was. She is distressed; you are right. But she is young. She will get over it and we will find her someone else.' There was a depressing obstinacy in Master Blake's voice.

I said, 'When I saw them together the day they went to lay flowers for Eleanor . . . well, it moved my heart. They seemed so right together. Margaret did Harry good, you know. He had been brooding over the business of the brother he had found and lost. She cured him of that. Dear Master Blake, they belong together.'

'Do they indeed?' The man was implacable. 'You evidently heard what was happening just as you arrived. Margaret had just been told, very plainly, that she cannot marry Harry Stannard. Yes, it does make my heart ache to hear her cry like that, but it will pass.'

'And is that really the end of it? Margaret is distressed and Harry . . . he has been heartbroken twice already, once over Eleanor and once over the brother who failed him. Must he endure a third such sorrow? Is there truly no way out of this impasse? No way at all? If there is, please tell me.'

There was a long pause. Master Blake was considering his answer, which made me hope that there was something to consider. We walked round the edge of a vegetable garden and strolled back towards the house, between flowerbeds, none of them in bloom. There would be no colour here until the spring, when the primroses and the crocuses would come out.

The pause went on and on. We left the empty flowerbeds behind and passed under the boughs of some fruit trees: plum and apple and cherry. They were still in leaf though not for long. At last, Master Blake said, 'There is one. The only one.'

'And that is?'

'And that is . . . if Master Harry's household were completely separated from yours. If he had a house of his own. As though he were not connected to you.'

'If he were the master of Hawkswood, and I lived elsewhere, in another county? Would that do?'

'We . . . ell . . .'

'I have two houses in Sussex,' I said. 'One, the smaller one, I sometimes use while Hawkswood has a thorough cleaning out. The other, I have just inherited, and for the moment I have taken no decisions about it. It is, in fact, the house where I grew up. I would be happy enough to remove myself there. I have been thinking about it already.'

'You would have to move before I would give my consent to this marriage.'

'I will leave Hawkswood the morning after the wedding.'

We came to a halt under the boughs of an apple tree. It came into my mind that there was a small orchard at Faldene, on a shelf in the hillside that ran down below the house. In spring, the blossom would be visible from the windows on the south side of the house. I could choose a bedchamber on that side. The Hawkswood orchard couldn't be seen from any of the windows.

Would I be happy at Faldene? I had certainly considered moving there but I hadn't expected the moment to come so soon. Would I be able to keep from making visits back to Hawkswood and – worse still – giving Margaret advice that perhaps she neither needed nor wanted? Well, I would have to, and that was that. It was fortunate that I did have alternative homes; that moving out of Hawkswood would be so simple.

Furthermore, I knew my Harry. If he was forbidden to marry Margaret, he was capable of asking her to elope with him! I wouldn't like that any more than the Blakes would. But I *would* like the two of them to marry. In Margaret, I thought, Harry would regain much that he had loved in Eleanor and perhaps find more. Eleanor's smile had been lovely, but she was essentially a serious girl. In Margaret – Harry himself had seen it – there was a sparkle that Eleanor had not had. In Margaret, there was laughter. On no account must I put up barriers against this marriage. I would withdraw to Faldene with good grace.

Master Blake was looking at me. I realized that I did not know him well and indeed had never thought much about him before. Now, studying him, it occurred to me that he was a man of business. A man who liked to drive hard bargains.

I smiled gently at him and said, 'I have an idea. Though I don't wish to offend you and you must just say if the notion doesn't appeal to you. But I suggest that I lift the expense of the wedding away from you. On the wedding morning, would you like to bring Margaret and your marriage party to Hawkswood – and allow her to be married at St Mary's in Hawkswood village? I will provide the feast afterwards, and host it. Then, next morning, you shall with your own eyes see me depart.'

I leant against the apple tree and waited quietly for his answer. It was some time in coming but finally he actually grinned. 'A bargain! I agree to the match; you leave Hawkswood and pay the expenses too. Well, you are a woman of honourable reputation. I will grant that much. The Ferrises at White Towers speak well of you.'

God bless Christina and Thomas.

'And yours is the better house for a big feast,' he added. 'You will bear *all* the cost?'

'Yes. Apart from Margaret's wedding gown. I fancy your wife will want to attend to that.'

'Then I agree. It must be put in writing. We could do that now. And when I arrive on the wedding day, unless I see signs of imminent departure, the wedding's off.'

'I would never let such a thing happen to Harry and Margaret,' I said, still gently, but with steel behind it. 'I shall send much of my baggage ahead. But some of it will go with me on the day after the wedding. You shall find it in the vestibule of my home. There for you to see.'

'So be it.' From the gleam in his eyes, I gathered that he had heard the steel and respected it. 'On these terms, I will consent. That is . . .'

To my alarm, I realized that another obstacle had arisen. 'Tell me,' he said, 'are there no dangers of a different kind in your royal connection? I am well aware that royal blood can be the high road to the block. It isn't just your extraordinary profession that makes me fear for Margaret.'

'Harry knows that,' I said sharply. 'I long since warned him against using his royal connection as a means to further any ambitions he might nurture. My son is no fool. He knows that the life of a country gentleman is best for him and any family he may one day have. He may occasionally be sought out by people hoping that he will use his influence on their behalf, but he has no such influence. It happens to me at times and I have none, either. That kind of thing soon fades away, if it ever happens at all. Harry has never been to court. He joined me for Walsingham's funeral, that's all.'

'Will you have to ask the queen's consent? I believe you did so when your son became betrothed to Eleanor.'

'Yes, I did. Harry is her nephew, after all, even though it is through an illegitimate line. Yes, I shall seek it. I am sure she won't refuse. I shall be at court for a few weeks in the new year and I will ask her then. What month would you like for the wedding?'

'Late April. When the apple blossom is out. It smells so sweet,' said Master Blake, becoming unexpectedly poetic.

TWENTY-FIVE
Apple Blossom

'So,' said Queen Elizabeth, 'my nephew is after all to marry, and into the same family. Is Margaret pretty?'

'Yes, ma'am, she is. She is a sprightly lass – I think a brighter spirit than her elder sister was. She will suit Harry even better, I am sure of it.'

'It is gracious of you to seek my consent. I am very happy that my nephew should have found a new bride. Eleanor's death, in such a dreadful way, must have borne hard on him.'

'Yes, ma'am. It did.'

'And you are to resign Hawkswood to him? You feel that he is ready?'

'Yes, I do. Besides, his former tutor Peter Dickson is still with us – becoming aged but still in good health. He is a music master for the boys now. He knows all the ways of the house and he is there to guide both Harry and my ward Ben Atbrigge, who is settling in as the new steward. I need not disturb the household by my move. Faldene has a full complement of servants and so I can leave the Hawkswood staff as it is, and just take Brockley and Dale with me. And perhaps Eddie. Hawkswood has plenty of grooms. I'm taking the carriage; Dale can make the journey in it. She undertook some long rides during my recent troubles, but they made her so exhausted and so sore that I must never ask such a thing of her again.'

'When will you move?'

'Much of my baggage has already gone, ma'am, but I shall depart from Hawkswood the morning after the marriage. I have promised Master Blake that I will do so.'

'So, because you are one of my most trusted agents, you have had to leave your home. That is the price of Harry's bride?'

'I don't think of it like that, ma'am.'

'No. I see that you don't. You are generous to your young people.'

It was early in 1591. We were at Richmond, always one of her favourite Thameside residences. It was a regular feature of my twice-yearly attendances on her that every time, at least once, she would summon me to talk with her in private. These occasions usually took place in one of her inner rooms, sometimes the anteroom to her bedchamber, sometimes whichever room she was using as her study. She had one in every palace; they were all halfway between a study and a private parlour. The Richmond study was where we were now. It overlooked the Thames, where a pair of swans and some coots were nesting on the banks. There would soon be cygnets and ducklings on the water, little fluffy balls swimming solemnly behind their mothers.

The room itself held the queen's desk and chair and her bookshelves, but it also had seats on either side of a hearth, where an applewood fire was now burning. We were sitting there now. Elizabeth sat opposite me. She was not in full dress, but in a loose robe over a long brocade gown. She had neither ruff nor farthingale and she had kicked her shoes off. And her face was that of a woman aged fifty-seven, with years of turmoil behind her.

I had known her as a spirited princess, who wore gowns with trains that she could whisk like the tail of an angry cat whenever anything displeased her. She no longer did that, at least, not often. The old, fiery Elizabeth did occasionally re-appear. But now, she just looked tired, and no more regal than any lady of her years and sorrows. In the course of her lifetime, she had had to sign death warrants for relatives, had been in mortal peril from the incessant plots against her, had had to hold her own in an all-male council and force them to respect their female sovereign. Such things drain strength, sap energy.

'I believe,' she said now, 'that this place Faldene is close to Withysham, which I ceded to you many years ago?'

'Yes, ma'am. I remove to Withysham regularly when Hawks-wood needs sweetening. I shall do the same when Faldene does. Faldene was my childhood home.'

'That I understand. Oh! Let me remind you! You may call me sister, as long as we are alone. It is a comfort to me. Now that you mean to retire to Faldene, are you assuming that you will also retire from your work as my agent?'

'I would like to be just a country lady,' I said. 'I am fifty-six, after all.'

'Cecil and I will try to respect that,' said Elizabeth. There was a pause. Then she added, 'But I make no promises.'

'I hope not to fail you, my sister,' I said, though with a degree of effort. I could see myself at the age of eighty, still carrying out secret tasks for the throne. They would have to be secret from Harry's father-in-law, anyway!

Elizabeth smiled, that delightful, slightly triangular smile that had such a power of bewitchment. Someone, once – an archbishop, I thought, or was it a French ambassador? – had said that she had a spirit full of incantation. She was young then but she had it still.

'One thing I can promise,' she said, 'is a really splendid wedding gift for your Harry and his Margaret.'

Apple blossom. When I think of Harry's wedding day, the first picture that leaps into my mind isn't the pretty bride and her family, arriving from Cobbold House so early in the morning, or the breathtaking handsomeness of the young bridegroom, my son. It is the blossom on the apple trees at Hawkswood and in the garden next to St Mary's Church in Hawkswood village. There were apple trees close to the fence beside the track, and they had cast their petals on to it. There was birdsong in the air about us and the scent of apple blossom as we all rode to church.

And then the pictures change. The day was sunlit, as we had all hoped it would be. Margaret was in blue brocade, which changed from blue to silver as the sunlight played on it. It was an expensive material, but it suited her; I think that Mistress Blake, who when not abandoned to grief was really a very capable woman, had chosen it on purpose to enhance her daughter's looks. Master Blake had probably had to deplete his coffers to pay for it.

Otherwise, there was little extravagance. Margaret was still

very young and some of the latest fashions were not suited to
young girls. Not for Margaret a ruff like a starched wagon
wheel, or a farthingale that forced her to go through doorways
sideways. She would have looked absurd in such things. Her
ruff was neat and small, and she had no farthingale at all. Her
shoes were of white satin but of a simple design. The one and
only touch of extravagance was in her jewellery. Queen
Elizabeth's gift to the bride was a long rope of deep-sea
pearls and a pair of pearl and diamond drop earrings to go
with it. Mistress Blake had arranged the pearls in a neat double
row. The earrings swung and glittered in the sunshine. None
of it looked especially spectacular; everything was suitable
for wear by a bride but, in fact, Margaret was wearing a
queen's ransom. The queen had said to me, when she placed
the pearls in my keeping for me to present on her behalf,
that if ever Margaret had desperate need of funds, then the
pearl rope could be shortened and a few pearls sold. Even
singly, they were valuable. Master Blake, that natural-born
businessman, was delighted when I told him that.

Now, adorning Margaret on her wedding day, they made
her look enchanting.

As for Harry, he was in a crimson doublet, slashed with
silver, with puffed breeches to match and grey stockings,
with a sword at his side. He had bought a set of crimson
saddlery for his white horse, Prince. When we set out for the
church, his party, which included Brockley, Ben and Dickson,
went ahead; I followed in Margaret's train, with her parents
and her family's guests. At the church, she and her father
dismounted and handed their horses to grooms and waited
outside while the rest of us went in and found our seats.

Once we were settled, there came the entrance of the
bride on her father's arm. He led her to the altar. While
the vows were exchanged, Mistress Blake, to whom tears
came so easily, wept in silence. I wept too, but not just out
of sentimentality.

Every garden has its serpent.

I was well aware that at the very moment when Dr
Joynings, in a pristine surplice, beaming with pleasure at this
happy occasion, pronounced the couple man and wife, I

ceased to be the lady of Hawkswood. Oh yes, I had organized the feast that would follow. On my orders, John Hawthorn and Ben Flood between them had striven mightily and created wonders. Also, later on, when the feast was over, I would still be in command, and would make sure that the couple were bedded in decent privacy, with none of the raucous encouragement that occurred at many weddings. There would be dancing after the feast. I would tell them to trip a measure or two and then slip away, and to bar their bedchamber door.

But it would be the door of the bedchamber that had once been mine. I would sleep that night in a guest room.

And so it was. On the morrow, by mid-morning, everyone was up and breakfasted. It was plain from their smiles that Harry and Margaret were pleased with themselves, and from that I guessed the wedding night had gone well. It was time for me to take my leave. The Blakes had been very alert for signs of baggage, and I made sure that, although much of my gear had gone on ahead, down in the Hawkswood vestibule there were several hampers and boxes. Now I watched as these last items of baggage were carried outside to the courtyard and loaded into the carriage. Dale, after bidding goodbye to the maids, went out and she too got into the carriage. Brockley and I would ride our own horses alongside, Dale's Blue Gentle would be tethered behind, and Eddie would drive us home. Home was Faldene now.

Margaret would be all right. She knew very well how to run a household; her mother had taught her that. She would not be lonely. She had so far shared a maid with her mother but, now that she was leaving home, her mother had found a personal maid for her, good-humoured Katherine FitzJohn, aged in her forties, who would not only care for Margaret's wardrobe, but would also be a companion for her, and an adviser, the experienced older woman that such a young chatelaine would need for a time.

Katherine had been married and had married daughters, but her husband's death had left her penniless. She told us drily that he had been a man who liked gambling, to a calamitous extent. But he and her parents had all been minor landowners.

She was Margaret's social equal. They could make friends as equals and already had.

I had noticed that they both seemed to take Gladys in their stride. Gladys was not to come to Faldene with me. She had wanted to but I was firm that she must not. Harry was fond of her and would see that she was cared for and the household at Hawkswood was used to her. The household at Faldene would probably look askance. No, Gladys must stay where she was. As for me, much as I loved Hawkswood, I belonged to it no longer.

There was one extra passenger in the carriage, and that was my bright young maid Bess. This was because Eddie was not only driving the carriage, he was coming to live at Faldene too. He had been unwilling at first, and under questioning had finally admitted that he and Bess were genuinely courting. Bess had chosen Eddie instead of Ben, in the end. I hoped that she wouldn't regret it. Eddie already had two children in Hawkswood village.

He hadn't wished to marry their mothers and neither of them had wished to marry him. Both were young and, fortunately, were remaining with their parents and bringing up their offspring just as extra members of their families. He was going to marry Bess, however. I had virtually ordered it. It would be within the month, at the church in Faldene. Bess would be an extra maid there.

The problem of Laurence Miller, who was not only my senior stud groom but also watched over me on behalf of the queen and Cecil, had been solved. Another senior stud groom had been found and Miller had moved to Withysham, my other Sussex house, three miles from Faldene, along the same hilltop ridge. He would be my tenant there and he would ride over once a week, ostensibly to report to me on events at Withysham; in truth to find out about any events of interest at Faldene.

He had brought Foggy to Withysham with him, but he wouldn't be bringing him to Faldene. Faldene had three dogs already: a spaniel, a lurcher and a terrier. They and the big tabby tom who looked after the Faldene mice, were a companionable group. On winter nights, when a low fire was kept going all night in the hall hearth, they slept in front of it in a furry heap. But when, on his first visit to Faldene, Miller tried to introduce Foggy to them, it was fortunate that Eddie had had the forethought to put a pail of water handy. Otherwise the snarling, snapping pile of enraged canines would have been very hard to disentangle and one of them might well have been badly hurt.

As it was, Miller got Foggy safely back on his leash and secured to a gatepost while the others were locked indoors until Miller's visit should be over. We could laugh about it then. It passed into the history of Faldene.

Faldene as the home of Mistress Stannard. My time at Hawkswood had ended. It was tearing me to pieces.

But, here I was. I had left Hawkswood in the hands of Harry and Margaret and travelled to Sussex. I arrived late, took a light supper and retired to my chamber, where I slept uneasily, waking now and then, not sure where I was. Now, dressed for my first day at Faldene, I stood at my bedchamber window, looking out over the valley and across it to the downs.

Faldene's fields lay like a patterned coverlet over the hillside below and across the valley floor; on the further side, sheep and cattle, the property of myself and also of some of the villagers, were grazing. Hearth-smoke rose from the village in the valley below, and I could trace the long chalky track that led down to it and then continued beyond it, over the hill and down into the village of Little Dene in the next valley. I could also see the Faldene orchard, where some of the trees were still in bloom.

It was all familiar to me. After all, I had been born here, and for the first twenty years of my life I had lived here. My youth had been overshadowed by the severity and disapproval of Uncle Herbert and Aunt Tabitha, who didn't consider that I had any right to exist. If they had known who my father was, things might have been different, but my mother would not tell them. I think that before she left the court, someone, quite possibly Queen Anne Boleyn, had exacted a promise from her that she would never tell the truth. Had possibly arranged some money for my maintenance as long as she held

her tongue. If my uncle and aunt had known the name of her
lover, my girlhood might have been happier, and Faldene was
a place where I could have been very happy indeed.

As for whether I would be happy there in the years to come,
I didn't know. I wasn't the same person now as the Ursula
who had run away with Gerald. I was Ursula Stannard, sister
of the queen, experienced agent, and I had killed a man.
Though I didn't brood on that, not now. In view of the way
Stephen had died, I had done Hector a kindness.

Still, it did seem perverse that now, when I was the lady of
Faldene, free to enjoy it to the full, I wished I could be back
at Hawkswood instead.

Well, I wasn't. Harry was its master now and Margaret its
mistress. They were young and capable; the future was theirs
and so was Hawkswood, and Katherine FitzJohn would watch
over Margaret and give her the feminine company that she
would need when Harry was otherwise engaged. Harry in
turn would need the friendship of Ben, now the official
steward, and advice from Peter Dickson, from Arthur Watts,
the senior groom, and from Jerome Billington, the chief
forester and an unofficial bailiff, watching over my
farmhands.

The household at Hawkswood was complete without me
and it hurt.

But I must not give way to this. I considered the sky. It was
a clear day, cloudy, but the clouds were high and thin and
didn't seem to threaten rain. I turned to where Dale, having
made the bed, was folding my nightwear away into a drawer.

'I shall break my fast now,' I said. 'And talk to the cook
about dinner and supper and examine our stores. There may
be things to be bought in now that there are extra mouths to
feed. Then I shall take Eddie for company and ride for an
hour or two.' There was an exhilarating track westward along
the top of the ridge above the house.

Dale said, 'Roger will be busy today. He thinks that now
we've brought our horses to fill up the spare stalls, we probably need to order more supplies of hay and bran. He is going
to ride into Petersfield – our nearest town – to buy what's
wanted. Perhaps you could look at the stores and ask him to

buy anything that's running short in that line as well; there's a market there today. Roger says that he can arrange for things to be delivered as well – that's always been done here. Petersfield is a good distance away; he may not be back until supper time.'

'When I come back from my ride,' I said, 'you and I can have a quiet time with our books and embroideries, until dinner. Or I might practise some music. There's a virginal in the parlour and I brought my lute. Tomorrow I will examine the stillroom and, the day after that, we'll go through all the linen. We shall soon settle into a routine. I also have some letters to write.'

One of them would be to Meg and George, congratulating them on the birth of their twins. Their letter, announcing this happy event, and telling me that they had returned to Riverside after an easy journey, had reached me two weeks ago, but in all the business of preparing for the wedding and the move to Faldene, I had not yet had a moment to reply. Both of the babies, Meg's new daughter and the son who had been born to Ursula Mary, were said to be healthy. They had been christened as Julius and Juliet, thus bonding them firmly together. No one outside the family must ever *ever* know that one of them was Ursula Mary's child and that Julius had been fathered by one of the Mercer brothers, though heaven alone knew which.

Better not brood about that. Meg and George were both honest and determined; they would manage. Aloud, I remarked, 'It will all be much the same as the routine at Hawkswood.'

No, it won't. No Harry, no Ben. I never realized before how much I enjoyed male company. At Hawkswood I often talked, easily, with Hawthorn or Flood or Billington. Here, it will be Laurence Miller – and I have never really liked him – riding over once a week, and my dear Brockley. And with him I must always be careful, for Dale's sake. It won't be like Hawkswood. Nothing will ever be like Hawkswood.

Cheerfully, I remarked, 'Soon we shall have to think about getting to know people in the locality. I know that my uncle and aunt had friends in Little Dene; I must introduce myself to them, unless they introduce themselves to me first, which is quite likely . . . Well, well, I can see a couple of riders coming over the hill from that direction. Perhaps we are going to have visitors this first day!'

It would be all right in time. I would become the lady of Faldene, seeing friends, riding out, working in my garden, helping in the kitchen, reading, embroidering, playing the virginal or lute, doing the household accounts and checking the stores, attending the church in the village.

As long as the queen didn't decide that she needed my services again. I hoped she wouldn't.

Don't lie to yourself, Mistress Ursula Stannard. You know quite well that you hope she will.